ABIGAIL'S DREAM

ABIGAIL'S DREAM

KAY D. RIZZO

Pacific Press® Publishing Association
Nampa, Idaho
Oshawa, Ontario, Canada
www.pacificpress.com

Cover design by Gerald Lee Monks
Cover design resources from iStockphoto.com
Inside design by Aaron Troia

You can obtain additional copies of this book by calling toll-free
1-800-765-6955 or by visiting http://www.adventistbookcenter.com.

Author assumes full responsibility for the accuracy of all facts and
quotations as cited in this book.

Library of Congress Cataloging-in-Publication Data:

Rizzo, Kay D., 1943-
  Abigail's dream / Kay D. Rizzo.
      p. cm. — (The Serenity Inn; bk. 5)
  ISBN 13: 978-0-8163-2422-4 (pbk.)
  ISBN 10: 0-8163-2422-0 (pbk.)
  1. Women pioneers. I. Title.
  PS3568.I836A64 2010
  813'.54—dc22
                                            2010026544

10 11 12 13 14 • 5 4 3 2 1

Contents

CHAPTER ONE

SLIP OF THE TONGUE

MELTED BUTTER, EGGS, MILK, FLOUR . . . Abigail Sherwood whipped the ingredients for the mouthwatering Dutch babies with a fury that equaled the force of the miserably cold and wet summer storm forming outside the kitchen window.

Sleet whistled through the pines behind the three-story garrison house on Babbington Boulevard in Chelsea, Massachusetts. Overhead, angry clouds swirled in a frenzy that only a New England nor'easter could generate.

Seething from the previous night's altercation with Ralph, her sister's husband, Abigail sputtered angry invectives as she poured the batter into a heated baking dish and placed it in the hot oven. She slammed the oven door with more force than necessary and straightened to her full five feet eight inch height. (Abigail carried herself like a general reviewing his troops, intimidating to men of diminutive proportions.)

She brushed the flour from her hands with satisfaction. In twenty to twenty-five minutes, the puffy and nicely browned Dutch babies would be ready to serve, when topped with powdered sugar and genuine Vermont maple syrup. She considered sautéing apple slices with cinnamon and sugar—Ralph's favorite.

"*Pshaw!* I should sauté prunes in blackstrap molasses for his topping!" The popular formula for laxatives brought a chuckle to her lips, only to be replaced by an intense scowl. The idea of tolerating Ralph's narrow-minded and ignorant opinions for the next forty years of her life set her teeth on edge, which would be her fate, since she knew it was too late to find a man to marry. She had no other option than to be a nanny to her sister's children.

Ralph's rampage at the dinner table last night regarding women's rights to vote had infuriated Abigail to the point of rage. When the discussion began, Abigail wasn't sure what her opinion was on the sensitive suffrage issue. She had attended several meetings with her mother before they left England, but, for the most part, she had not bothered to take a position on the flammable topic—at least until Ralph blustered her into one over the previous night's New England pot roast and dandelion greens with hollandaise sauce.

She knew she owed her sister's husband a lot for bringing her and her mother to America, and she truly tried to like the man. "Lord, please help me to be generous and gracious," she prayed in the early morning silence. The words had come automatically to her lips, since she prayed them so often. "What I should be praying is for the Lord to get me out of here!" Her words echoed off the high, tiled walls of the New England kitchen. "If I never had to see or speak to him again, I'd rejoice!"

The recipient of her ire was Ralph Oakley Porter. Ralph had emigrated from England to Revere, Massachusetts, with his bride and a slight knowledge of fabric manufacturing. A short, round, and balding man with a loud voice and a salty attitude, Ralph used his six months of experience working in a cotton mill in Birmingham, England, to buffalo and hoodwink his way into New England's flourishing fabric industry. In ten short years, with the help of his wife, he'd fathered four sons and one daughter, and he'd grown rich off the sweat of immigrants like himself.

After the first baby arrived and Rebecca was pregnant with the second, she begged her mother, Pamela, to immigrate to America. "We have a big house, large enough for you and Abigail to have your very own rooms. If you don't like it here, Ralph promises to pay for your return ticket to England as well."

For years, eighteen-year-old Abigail had dreamed of seeing the New World. When her father, a small-town pastor, died of consumption, she and her mother were forced from the parsonage into a cramped and dingy room in a boardinghouse outside London. After

Rebecca left England, Abigail watched her mother grow gaunt and sallow, receding into a crumpled shell of a woman.

When her sister's invitation arrived, Abigail accepted it immediately without consulting her mother. She determined she would drag her mother to America in a rowboat, if necessary, to save her life. Surprisingly, Abigail's mother, Pamela Sherwood, had reacted positively, even becoming enthusiastic about their travel plans.

The sea voyage, which Abigail feared would be difficult for her mother, perked the woman up enough to attract the amorous interest of the ship's captain, a bulky, jocular man whose deep brown eyes twinkled as if they held a delicious secret.

Moving into her sister's household was a trial at best for Abigail. If a young woman hadn't snagged a husband by her eighteenth birthday, what could she do other than become a nanny to a relative's offspring? Being the daughter of a rural parish minister, she hadn't had the money or the sponsorship into British society's marriage market. And caring for her ailing mother had kept her from any chance meeting she might have had with a less-moneyed eligible man. So Abigail accepted the role of spinster which nature had given her.

As the babies continued arriving at Rebecca and Ralph's home, both Abigail and her mother were kept busy caring for the energetic little boys. Between pregnancies, Rebecca played hostess to her friends, members of the burgeoning newly moneyed social class of New England's era of prosperity. This venture involved Abigail's talents as well.

Cooking had been one of Abigail's greatest pleasures while growing up—cooking and sketching. With her mother and older sister being the social butterflies of the community, the young Abigail often found herself alone, except for the friendship of the family's plump and jovial cook, Bessy.

A widow, the gray-haired peasant woman was a culinary genius, or so Abigail believed. Bessy's second talent was sketching. The woman used any extra money she received to buy paper, pencils, and charcoal sticks.

As the young Abigail watched Bessy make her mouthwatering dill pickles or draw a humorous sketch of a stable hand being thrown from his saddle, the girl pretended Bessy was her mother.

It was obvious to everyone, including her own parents, that Abigail lacked the polish and congeniality of her mother and older sister. Nor did she inherit their sparkling effervescence and soft, English rose loveliness. Her hair was too brown and too straight; her nose was too narrow; her figure, too angular. Only her flashing green eyes betrayed the fiery nature and rapier wit she held tightly in check.

To be fair, Pamela Sherwood had tried to interest Abigail in developing the necessary skills of a cultured English lady. Pamela had been born to royalty before she married a member of the common clergy, one not of the Church of England. Abigail's grandfather had been seventy-fifth in line for the British throne, or so Abigail had been told many times.

While their mother instructed the two girls in the necessary social skills, their father insisted they both learn to read and to figure. Abigail had taken to reading much faster than her sister, since book learning was not a desirable skill for proper British ladies of the day. When Abigail's mathematical skills surpassed her father's, she began keeping the church's finances.

On cold, rainy days, Abigail would disappear to her room with a classic narrative while her sister sat by the fire with her mother and her mother's friends, nibbling on Bessy's bonbons and the latest tidbits of gossip. Abigail's intuition told her that the women didn't really want her company.

Abigail shook the painful memories from her mind and set her jaw, as her mama would say, to the problem at hand—breakfast. One, two, three, four, five, six—she cracked the eggs against the side of the stoneware mixing bowl. Scrambling the half dozen eggs in a bowl, she added salt and cream and poured the mixture into a grease-spitting frying pan.

She glanced toward the ceiling at the sound of bed ropes groaning above her head, followed by the scramble of several feet thudding on hard oak floors. The family would be down any minute, hungry as bears. The family—though not her family. The truth be known, Abigail would prefer spinsterhood if her only choice of husbands was a man like Ralph Oakley Porter.

It had been ten years since she and her mother arrived in Massachusetts and seven years since Abigail's mother announced that she and her sea captain were getting married and moving to Tortola, an island in the Caribbean.

With her mother's departure, Abigail picked up the slack in the Porter household staff. She'd become nanny, nursemaid, chief cook, and bread maker. But she was lonely. Elsa, the chambermaid; Rachel, the laundress; and Chester, the family butler and all-around handyman, thought of Abigail as a member of the Porter family, while her brother-in-law treated her like a servant. She didn't belong with either, or so it seemed to her.

Abigail's only joy was slipping off to her room to work on her pet project. Years previous, she'd purchased a fine, brown, leather-bound journal. In it, she'd recorded all of Bessy's favorite recipes, along with helpful hints the woman had shared with her over the years. By accident more than design, the doodles she drew in the margins grew into sketches depicting the good times she and Bessy had shared.

In the evening, after Abigail tucked the youngest child into bed and kissed him good night, and after she'd scrubbed the last copper-bottomed pot and returned it to the iron rack above the stove, she would slip away to her tiny attic room beneath the eaves of her sister's three-story home to continue working on her project of love.

Abigail seldom dwelt on the bleakness of her future. When she contemplated the possibility of living countless years under Ralph's roof, like she had after retiring to her room the previous night, she prayed for the strength to deal with him. "And Lord, if You can't change him, change me, or my situation."

* * * * *

The thought of leaving her sister's employ, of branching out on her own never entered the young woman's mind until two days later during the garden luncheon her sister hosted for a young missionary returning from the Oregon Territory. As she replenished the hors d'oeuvre tray with sweet potato balls and cod cakes, she paused to listen to the intense young man tell of the land of tall trees, rushing rivers, and rich farmland available for the asking. He told of Indian tribes who'd never heard the name of God.

"We Christians must spread God's Word from sea to sea. To do that, we must populate the Willamette Valley before more British come in or the Russians sweep down from the Far North and take it over. Your contributions will help me put together a wagon train, a caravan of Americans seeking their destiny and the glorious destiny of our beloved country."

His challenge captured her imagination. She restacked the ladyfingers on her sister's imported crystal platter and wondered what it would be like to be a part of such a magnificent event.

When the presentation ended, the guests swarmed the young missionary. As Abigail watched, she decided that she had to meet him; she had to hear more about his exotic adventures in the incredible Northwest.

Picking up a silver tray of cut vegetables, she angled toward the gazebo where the man stood talking to his eager listeners. As she passed, several women helped themselves to the food on the tray. Abigail had almost penetrated the crowd of women when Mrs. Clarissa Darlington announced, "I'd surely go with you to Oregon, Mr. Farnsworth, if I had a lady's companion to care for my needs." She fluttered her hands and coyly tipped her head, shamelessly batting her eyelashes at the lean young man. Recently widowed, she had to be ten years Mr. Farnsworth's senior.

The gracious young man grinned and tipped his head toward the middle-aged dowager. "And you would be most welcome, ma'am."

Abigail didn't know what came over her, but without warning she said, "Mrs. Darlington, I would be willing to go with you to Oregon as your traveling companion."

Mr. Farnsworth's eyebrows shot into his hairline. Mrs. Darlington's mouth dropped open in surprise. Someone had called her bluff. Rebecca Porter stared in disbelief at her suddenly impulsive younger sister.

"Abigail!" Rebecca hissed. "What are you saying?"

The missionary picked up the on the dynamics of the moment. He took Abigail's free hand in his. "What a brave gesture, miss, er, have I met you yet?"

"No, sir, I'm Abigail Sherwood. My sister, Rebecca Porter, is your hostess this afternoon."

He turned to the astonished women. "It's this kind of brave and patriotic woman who will make a difference in Oregon. Well, Mrs. Darlington?" The missionary's smile broadened slowly.

Not to be outdone by a servant girl, even if she was her hostess's sister, Mrs. Darlington slipped her arm into the missionary's. "My, my, this is an interesting turn of events. I would have preferred to give this endeavor more thought, but a Darlington woman always keeps her word. Perhaps, Mr. Farnsworth, you and I can slip away for a few minutes where you can give me more details on the journey it seems I am about to make."

The man released Abigail's hand and turned his attention to the woman at his other side. Abigail and her sister's guests watched the couple stroll across the lawn to a wooden glider swing beneath the branches of a mighty elm tree. With the enigmatic Mr. Farnsworth trapped in the clutches of Clarissa Darlington, Rebecca's other guests prepared to leave the party.

After the final guests departed, including the giggly and blushing Mrs. Darlington and the suave, silver-tongued missionary, Rebecca snapped, "What were you thinking? To say you'd move to Oregon! How ridiculous! How could you even consider leaving me and the children?"

Abigail brushed the last crumbs off a white linen tablecloth and gathered it into her arms. "Don't worry, Rebecca. I'm not going anywhere. You know Mrs. Darlington. She'll never leave Boston. Can you see her battling flies and mosquitoes in a covered wagon on the prairie?"

Rebecca chuckled aloud and then saddened. "You're right, of course. But why would you even suggest that you might want to leave? Are you so unhappy with us?"

"Becky, I love you dearly and I love your children, but if I had a chance to do something exciting like Mr. Farnsworth talked about, I'd seriously consider doing it. Raising your children and catering your parties is not the life I would choose for myself. Would you?" She took a deep breath. "But alas, it's neither here nor there. Mrs. Darlington will lose interest in her big adventure in a day or two. But Rebecca, you should know that sooner or later, I hope to strike out on my own."

Rebecca looked stricken. "I don't understand. Ralph and I adore you."

"I know you love me, Rebecca dear," Abigail smiled and shook her head. "But you must admit that I am a thorn in your husband's side, a burr under his saddle."

"What will Mama say when she learns of your folly?" Rebecca's lower lip extended into a practiced pout.

"First of all, I'm not going anywhere right away. As to Mama, I think she'd be delighted for me—she and her sea captain." The more Abigail thought about her brash remarks to the young missionary, the more the idea appealed to her.

Rebecca dabbed at her eyes with her lace-edged handkerchief. "But the children, they love you. What would they do without their auntie Abigail?"

"Sooner or later, they'll grow up and no longer need an auntie for a governess. Then where will I be? A tottering old aunt shaping crab cakes in the kitchen? Living off your husband's largess?" The thought of Ralph being generous to anyone, family included, made her chuckle.

"Abigail! Stop being so impudent. What's gotten into you?" Rebecca threw her hands in the air and strode into the house. "I don't understand. You try to do something nice for someone and what do you get in return? You are being very selfish, Abigail Sherwood!"

"Maybe so." Abigail followed her sister into the kitchen. "But I will keep my word, Rebecca. I will go to Oregon with Mrs. Darlington if she goes."

Rebecca clicked her tongue in anger. "And if she doesn't?"

Abigail frowned, "I don't know . . . yet."

She watched her sister flounce down the hallway toward the parlor. Taking advantage of the blessed reprieve, Abigail prepared the evening meal and fed the children before Ralph returned home from work.

By the glares Abigail received from both Rebecca and Ralph, she knew he had heard all about it by the time she served the appetizer and main course. Despite the icy atmosphere, Abigail maintained her calm demeanor.

After collecting the dinner plates and serving the Norwegian lace cookies left over from the garden party, she excused herself. "I'm not very hungry tonight. I think I'll go right up to settle the children for sleep."

"Abigail, before you go," Ralph leaned back against the upholstered dining chair and stared down his bulbous nose at her, "please tell me that my dear wife is mistaken, that you aren't really considering traveling to Oregon with Mrs. Darlington."

Abigail dipped her head and reddened slightly. "To tell the truth, I don't know what came over me. I was caught up in the moment, I guess. Besides, can you see Mrs. Darlington leaving her comforts behind for the wilds of Oregon?"

Ralph grinned and nodded approvingly toward his wife. "See, my love, there is no cause for vapors. Your sister has a good head on her shoulder. She's too sensible for this sudden flight of fancy. She knows her place."

"My place?" She arched one eyebrow.

"Yes, of course, you are hardly the kind of woman to turn your back on your responsibility, and yes, even your calling, for some outrageous adventure."

"My responsibility? Excuse me? Just what is my responsibility and my calling, Mr. Porter?"

"Now don't get your dander up." Ralph rolled his eyes toward the ceiling. "I didn't mean anything personal, but it's not as though you have many options such as marriage and the like." He gave a low disapproving growl and sent a sidewise glance at his wife. "I should have said, the children depend on you. We, your sister and I, depend on you."

"Yes, dear, we truly do." Rebecca reached out for Abigail's hand.

Abigail snatched it away.

"Oh, don't be touchy, love."

"Touchy? I beg your pardon? My responsibility in life is to raise your children? They're your children and your responsibility." She straightened to her full five feet eight inches, "I may never have a brood of my own, but if I ever do, I hope I'll love them enough to enjoy spending time with them."

"Abigail, what do you mean? We love our children dearly!" Rebecca scolded, her eyes brimming with tears.

"I know you do, dear, but you're missing so much by not spending time with them. Do you know how much Jefferson craves his daddy's attention? He stands at his bedroom window every evening, watching for your carriage, Ralph. That's why he acts up with his tutor. He knows that when you find out, you'll give him some attention, even if it's a scolding or another punishment.

"And William, did you know he loves birds? He can name every bird in the neighborhood and tell you incredible details about each species. He's put together a sketchbook of his favorites. He's becoming quite a little artist, in fact. And little Harry has run away from home three times this month alone. He has a serious problem obeying people in authority. While he never back talks like his older brother, there's a lot going on behind those stormy blue eyes.

"Oh, and Ralph Junior. He's in love—his first crush, Miss Pringle, his piano teacher. He would swim to Cape Cod and back to please her. And Baby Lucille has an invisible friend named Jenny, who steals cookies from the kitchen and entices her to wander into the woods behind the estate, a definite no-no."

Abigail couldn't believe her candor or her passion. Seeing the stunned expression on Rebecca's face, Abigail regretted the force with which she'd spoken. Then she regretted her regret when she saw the anger on Ralph's face.

"I beg your pardon!" He shot to his feet and threw his linen napkin on the table. Rounding the table, he stared up into Abigail's face, shaking his index finger for emphasis, "I will not have you, a subordinate, talk to me in such a manner!"

"Subordinate? Is that what I am to you? You think I'm in your service?" Abigail's green eyes flashed with renewed fury. She heard Rebecca sniffle behind her, but Abigail hardened her heart against her sister's tears.

Abigail took a deep breath to regain her self-control. "Ralph, Rebecca, perhaps the best thing I could do is leave and force the two of you to stop playing high society and spend time getting to know your children."

"Why—" Ralph sputtered.

"The sad part is that our airing of the family's dirty linen has probably been in vain as far as Mrs. Darlington is concerned. I doubt she'll actually go. However, knowing how you both feel about me, the poor ugly stepsister . . ." She balled and unballed her fingers, "I do not want your pity! I will find employment elsewhere as soon as it can be arranged. If you'll excuse me." She tipped her head graciously toward Rebecca, curled her lip at Ralph, and glided from the room.

Chapter Two

Preparing for a Journey

REBECCA FOLLOWED ABIGAIL UP THE STAIRS, apologizing as she went and begging Abigail to reconsider her hasty words. "I know Ralph upsets you. I can understand. He upsets me, too, sometimes. But I'm sure if you apologize to him before turning in tonight, tell him you didn't really mean it, he will forget everything you said."

"Rebecca!" Abigail snapped around to face Rebecca. "I meant every word that I said! It would be wise for you to begin interviewing for a cook, a nanny, and a new sister!" She stormed up the stairs to the third landing. Rebecca called to her from the second landing. "You don't mean that, Abigail dear. I know you don't mean that."

At the top step, Abigail turned to see the genuine tears rolling down her sister's cheeks. Her heart broke. She hurried down the flight of stairs and gathered her sister into her arms. "No, no, don't cry. I didn't mean the part about getting a new sister. I love you, and I'll always love you."

From the base of the stairs, Ralph ordered his wife to return to the dinner table. Without a word, Rebecca wiped the tears from her eyes with the linen handkerchief she carried in her pocket. She looked longingly at her sister and then headed back down the stairs.

That evening, the children, especially Lucille, took some time to calm down after overhearing their father and their auntie quarreling. Finally, after three fairy tales and two lullabies, the little girl fell asleep, and Abigail could escape to her own bedroom.

A gentle breeze ruffled the white eyelet curtains at her leaded glass window, but it did little to cool the attic room. Abigail stared out at the starlit sky as she did every night. Tonight, her heart was heavier than usual. She picked up the heavy, black leather Bible her father had used for preparing his sermons. She opened the gilt-edged pages to Ephesians, chapter 4, and read aloud the words of verse 29: " 'Let no corrupt communication proceed out of your mouth, but that which is good to the use of edifying, that it may minister grace unto the hearers.' " Abigail fell to her knees.

"Dear Lord, my words were, indeed, bereft of grace. Please forgive me," she prayed. "I don't know what got into me tonight. I'm a terribly hateful person to say all those things." A tear slid down her cheek. "If it weren't for Ralph! No! I won't put all the blame on him. I admit I enjoyed venting my anger a little too much." She paused and sighed. "Of course I won't leave my sister's home, Lord, if that is Your wish. Rebecca's my sister even if she did marry a plug-ugly, seven-by-nine like Ralph."

Abigail cringed when she realized she'd used a slang term she'd heard the gardener use when he scolded his assistant for planting the tulip bulbs on the left side of the house instead of the right. "And I used it in a prayer! I am so sorry. Ralph isn't a cad. He's my sister's husband, and he's Your son."

Abigail slowly rose to her feet and returned to her Bible reading. " 'Let all bitterness, and wrath, and anger, and clamour, and evil speaking, be put away from you, with all malice: and be ye kind one to another, tenderhearted, forgiving one another, even as God for Christ's sake hath forgiven you.' " She shook her head and broke into tears. "That's so difficult to do, Lord, with Ralph. Forgive? I know I must forgive Ralph, but I can't," she wailed, falling face down onto her bed.

Exhausted, Abigail fell asleep. A few hours later, she awakened with a start. She'd been listening to one of her father's sermons in her dream.

" 'Love one another as I have loved you.' His command is simple to understand—love God, love one another. Ah, but the Savior's command proves to be the most complex and difficult of all commands to carry out. It was easy for the Pharisees of His day to measure out the weight limit of their bundles on the Sabbath day. All they needed was an accurate scale. And measuring the distance they traveled during the Sabbath hours was also simple to do. But love one another as Jesus loved?"

Abigail watched her father take off his wire-rimmed spectacles and walk from behind the pulpit to be closer to his parishioners. "Living God's love has never been easy. It wasn't easy for the apostles when they were being hunted like animals, then when caught, tortured, burned at the stake, or thrown to the lions. It wasn't easy for the victims of the Spanish Inquisition. Nor was it easy for the French Huguenots to love the soldiers that massacred their loved ones and to watch the blood of thousands of loyal children of God flow ankle deep through Parisian streets."

Abigail lay in her bed, recalling the bittersweet memory. If nothing else, her father knew how to love. He might not have been as ambitious as her mother would have liked, but he knew how to love. "Loving is never easy, but it is simple. Loving is not a matter of time, money, prestige, or power. All you have to do is treat your fellow man the same way you want to be treated." Abigail thought about his words returning to her so many years later and so far from the English country parish church.

"Think of all the wars that have been fought in the name of religion. Yes, even in the name of Christ. What a waste! Don't be fooled, my children. The Savior doesn't ask us to fight the infidel. He asks us to love one another. Best of all, when He was on this earth, He showed us how to do so."

Abigail could almost feel her father's eyes resting on her face. "Are you at war with a neighbor? Do you carry a grudge against a brother or sister? A mother or father? Jesus showed us how to love. With His dying breath, He cried, 'Father, forgive them.' "

In the loneliness of her attic room, Abigail fell to her knees and asked for forgiveness. "Tomorrow I will go to Ralph," she vowed, "and, Lord, I will completely surrender my dreams, my aspirations, whatever they are, to Your divine leading. I want Your blessing on my life. And whatever Your will may be, I will be content."

The next morning at the breakfast table, Ralph accepted her apology as something due him. Instead of replying in kind, he tasted his poached egg and made a face. "I really wish you'd learn to get my egg right. Look at this! It's hard-boiled, for pity's sake!"

Abigail bit her tongue. She determined not to fire back a retort.

And when no remark came, Rebecca looked at her sister in surprise.

* * * * *

No one, including Abigail, could have predicted the swift determination of the indomitable, dimpled, five feet one inch Clarissa Darlington. When she took something to mind, she wasted no time in carrying it out. Before the end of the week, a note delivered by footman to Abigail announced that the widowed Clarissa Darlington wished to call on her. "Would 4:15 P.M. be convenient?"

Abigail wasn't surprised when Rebecca sent a note to Ralph at the factory and he answered by returning home an hour earlier than usual. Abigail had put the finishing touches on supper's orange chutney chicken and placed it in the oven when the luxuriously appointed, burgundy Jenny Lind buggy pulled up in front of the house and the stylish Mrs. Darlington made her way up the brick steps to the front door.

Chester, the Porter's butler, met the woman at the door and escorted her into the parlor where Rebecca and Ralph patiently sat waiting to welcome her. Abigail paused outside the heavy mahogany parlor doors and eavesdropped as her brother-in-law strode back and forth in front of the massive pink marble fireplace, belittling the foolishness of a single woman, even if with staff, trying to cross the country without a spouse. "You are an intelligent woman, so I am sure you're here today, Mrs. Darlington, to explain to my sister-in-law, Miss Sherwood, the foolhardiness of your momentary overexuberance."

Abigail's eyes widened. "How dare he!" she mumbled, straightening to her full height. She placed her hand against the door, ready to open it.

"I am here to speak with your sister-in-law," Mrs. Darlington said, "if I may." The trill in Mrs. Darlington's voice sickened Abigail. "So if you would—"

"Mrs. Darlington." Abigail's spring green taffeta skirts rustled as she swept into the room, carrying a silver tea set. She placed the tray on a low Hepplewhite table in front of the sofa. "I hope I haven't kept you waiting. Please, make yourself comfortable." She gestured toward the mauve, silk-brocade upholstered sofa. "Do you take cream? Sugar?"

Mrs. Darlington smiled broadly and winked conspiratorially toward the young woman. "Yes to both. Two cubes of sugar, please. And did you make these delicious-looking sugar cookies? I understand that you're quite a cook."

"Why, thank you. I do enjoy cooking." Abigail beamed with pleasure. Out of the corner of her eye, she noted the stunned surprise on both Rebecca's and Ralph's faces. "And, sister dear, may I serve you? Actually, if you'd like, feel free to excuse yourselves. I can handle everything from here—"

"Now wait just a minute," Ralph interrupted. "I am Abigail's legal guardian."

Abigail's eyebrows arched into her hairline. "Legal guardian? Brother dear, that's ludicrous. I'm twenty-eight years old."

"By the by, that's the way the law reads in Massachusetts." He tucked his thumbs in his vest pockets and strutted to the fireplace.

Mrs. Darlington extended her crocheted-lace gloved hand toward the pompous little man. "Please, Mr. Porter, by all means, both you and your sister should stay to hear what I have to say."

Mollified somewhat, he planted himself in a massive wing-backed chair across from the sofa.

Mrs. Darlington turned to Abigail and took her hand. "Miss Sherwood, did you mean what you said about accompanying me to Oregon?"

"Yes, ma'am, but I'm not so—"

The diminutive widow clapped her hands in glee. "Oh, I'm so glad! I was afraid you'd only gotten caught up in the glamour of the moment, not that Mr. Farnsworth isn't a dandy specimen of a man," she giggled and blushed. Catching herself, she turned toward Ralph, "Begging your pardon, Mr. Porter. I didn't mean to get carried away."

Before he could reply, she returned her attention to Abigail. "Now, Miss Sherwood, I plan to leave Boston on March 1 of next year. That gives us—let's see, this is the last day of August—one, two, three, four, five, six months to prepare. You can be ready in that amount of time, can you not?"

Speechless, Abigail nodded.

"Wait just a minute, Mrs. Darlington," Ralph interrupted, "what Abigail hasn't told you is that she—"

"Excuse me, Mr. Porter. I'm speaking with your sister-in-law, I believe?" She waved him away. "As I was saying, dear, we will travel by rail most of the way, out of respect for my dear departed husband, Charley. He was a railroad man, you know." She giggled as if privy to a private joke. "I will, of course, send my man on ahead to make all the arrangements for every possible convenience."

Abigail stared in amazement. The woman came on like a whirlwind on a dusty road.

"Cat got your tongue, girl?"

"Excuse me," Abigail began, "what will be expected of me? I've never been a lady's companion before."

"Oh, I'm getting to that. I'm taking a staff along to care for our everyday needs. You won't be expected to do that. Nell, a little Irish lass I hired practically straight off the boat, will perform the heavier chores. My butler, Winters, will hire teamsters to help him perform the manly tasks. And you, my dear, I need you to help Nell with the cooking; she's excruciatingly bad! Your main duties will be to keep up with my correspondence and accompany me to social functions. You will do any light repair work on my clothing and, most important, you will keep me company. Heaven knows Nell can't carry on an intelligent conversation, at least one I can understand, what with that heavy brogue of hers! Do you think you are up to the challenge?"

Abigail gulped. "I think so."

Mrs. Darlington leaned forward. "Miss Sherwood, may I call you Abigail?"

Speechless, Abigail nodded.

"And you may call me Clarissa. Tell me, are you in good health? Mr. Farnsworth warns that no one should strike out for Oregon who is not in optimum health." She sent a knowing glance toward Rebecca and Ralph and then returned her attention to Abigail. "Well, are you? Healthy, that is?"

"Absolutely."

"I thought so, a strapping young woman like you. And obviously you have a level head on your shoulders. I don't want someone who is going to run off with the first eligible man she meets!" A lavender buckram rose poised on the left side of Clarissa Darlington's beehive straw bonnet bobbed freely as she emphatically nodded her head.

"Before he resumed his speaking tour of New England, Mr. Farnsworth warned me that there are five men to every woman west of the Mississippi River." A satisfied smile barely lifted the corners of her mouth.

"Mrs. Darlington, er, Clarissa, you needn't worry about me fraternizing with any gentleman along the way."

Ralph gave a loud guffaw. "That's for sure. We've introduced Abigail to several eligible men since she arrived from England and my dear sister-in-law sent every one of them running in the opposite direction!"

Mrs. Darlington leveled a disapproving stare at Ralph. "Mr. Porter, there are eligible men, and then there are eligible men. Take it from me, Abigail is to be commended for being discriminating."

Clarissa opened her pale green satin reticule and withdrew a sheaf of papers. "Here is a list of things you will need for the journey. Did I tell you that Winters will arrange with the Conestoga Wagon Company in Conestoga, Pennsylvania—I hear they are the best vehicles for westward travel—to design a Conestoga wagon to carry our necessary luggage, household goods, and food supplies. You will be allowed to bring two trunks, two large suitcases, and a hatbox, of course. Winters is also arranging to have a Clarence brougham built by the same builders, one designed especially for our traveling comfort." The woman acted pleased with her efficiency. "Of course, we'll pick up the wagons in Independence, Missouri. Winters will take care of everything."

One glance through the list of personal supplies and Abigail realized Mrs. Darlington was being generous to a fault.

"Abigail, I have no intention of traveling to Oregon looking or living like a pauper, and I expect the same from you. I know that your family will want to contribute to your needs as reimbursement for your years of service, of course. But as soon as you sign the papers agreeing to go, I will give you an envelope of cash as an advance so that you may purchase the special things you may want to bring.

"And please," the woman groaned and pressed the back of her hand dramatically against her forehead. "No calicos made out of flour sacks or drab linsey-woolsey! I abhor the way the farmwomen dress on market day in Boston. Shameful! Shameful!"

As Abigail read through the extensive list, her blood rushed with excitement. When the time came, would she actually go? Would she leave her only family and traverse the continent, knowing she might never see her sister again?

Mrs. Darlington seemed to read Abigail's thoughts because she reached into her purse once again, removed a second piece of paper, and handed it to Abigail. "Now, my dear, I have drawn up an agreement for you to look over and sign. Once you sign it, I will give you the promised sums of money. But once you sign it, you will be under contract, obligated to me, so think hard on your decision before you dip your pen in the inkwell."

As Abigail accepted the second piece of paper, Ralph snatched it from her hand. "Let me see that! Abigail Sherwood, you will not sign any agreement without my permission—"

"Oh, Ralph," his wife interrupted, snatching the paper from her husband's hand. "Do stop bullying my sister. She is an adult and can make up her own mind." She handed the contract back to Abigail. "Of course, I hope you won't sign it."

Abigail looked into her sister's soulful eyes and bit her lower lip. "I know. I know."

"If you do, you'll have to write and tell Mama."

Tears glistened in Abigail's eyes. The impact of the moment caused her heart to feel like lead in her chest. "I will. As soon as I make up my mind, I will."

Rebecca dabbed at her eyes. "Oh, you're going, all right. I know you are. I can see it in your eyes, just like Mama looked before she ran off with her sea captain."

"She didn't run off with the captain; she married him," Abigail reminded her sister.

"What will I do without you?" Rebecca fell into her sister's arms. She clung to Abigail as if she were leaving for Oregon that very day. Sniffling, Rebecca held her sister at arm's length. "I love you so much."

Mrs. Darlington rose to her feet. "This is all very tender, but our business is not yet complete. I want to be certain you have no questions. You will notice on that contract I have promised to pay you, from the moment we leave Boston, a double eagle coin each month—cash. Once we reach Oregon, you may either remain in my employ or branch out on your own. Either way, I will give you the equivalent of one year's wages to help you get started." She paused but a moment before adding, "Should you wish to leave my employ at any stage of the journey after we leave Massachusetts and prior to Oregon, I will give you a six-month severance pay. Is that understood?"

Abigail nodded. "Yes, ma'am."

Ralph gasped. His face revealed honest horror. "What pray tell, does a young woman need with so much money? My sister-in-law has no idea of how properly to care for—"

"Mr. Porter! My patience with you is growing thin. This is 1851, man, not the 1790s! Your sister-in-law has no experience with money because you have kept her penniless. Believe it or not, we ladies can manage a few dollars without a husband's wisdom. If you don't believe me, ask my solicitor. I've more than tripled my husband's estate since his death five years ago."

At the lift of one of Mrs. Darlington's disapproving eyebrows, Ralph gulped and reddened, for he suddenly remembered that the Darlington House of Finance had recently become a shareholder in Porter Mills, his company.

With Ralph quieted, Mrs. Darlington returned her attention to Abigail. "Now back to the situation at hand. Do you have any questions?"

"Not that I can think of right this minute."

"Well, make a list as the questions come to you. A month from now we will meet again, and each month thereafter until we leave for Oregon. And you, Mrs. Porter, be assured I will take care of your baby sister as I would my own. Is there anything you might like to ask me?"

Rebecca flashed a quick look toward Ralph, then back at the indomitable Mrs. Darlington. "N-N-No, just take good care of her, please?"

Mrs. Darlington smiled tenderly at the teary young woman. "I will, my dear, I promise."

* * * * *

A week later, the first Friday of September, Abigail returned the signed contract to Mrs. Darlington.

"And here, my dear," the wealthy dowager removed an envelope from the top drawer in her ladies' secretary and handed it to Abigail, "is the promised advance I've been holding for you."

"You knew I would go all along, didn't you?"

A glint of humor dancing in Mrs. Darlington's eyes and the dimples deepening at the corners of her mouth answered Abigail's question. "I'm a pretty good judge of character."

Mrs. Darlington made numerous suggestions that Abigail scribbled on her notepad as best as she could. By the time she returned home, the young woman's mind was bursting with her own ideas of what she might take along on her great adventure across the continent.

That evening she made her a list. If she was going to have to help with the cooking, she'd need to take her favorite spices and herbs. She'd need to dry mushrooms, wild grapes, peppercorns, and cranberries. She'd add in a stock of art supplies. Who knew what would be available once they left the populated cities of the East? The tall mahogany grandfather clock in the hallway gonged midnight before she stopped writing.

Before she signed the contract, Abigail had explained in cool, reasonable terms that she was going, with or without her sister's or her brother-in-law's blessing. But now her manner softened, although her resolve did not. "I would prefer your blessing, of course. But I've come to believe that God has a plan for my life beyond raising your adorable children, Rebecca dear. I don't know what it is. I will miss the children terribly. I certainly never expect to marry and have my own babies." Sadness swept across her face. "Please try to understand. Please be happy for me?"

Ralph threw down his table napkin and exited the room without comment. Rebecca looked stricken. "I haven't told you, Abigail, but I'm expecting another child."

Instead of distress, happiness filled Abigail's face. "Oh, I'm so happy for you. Then it's imperative that we find you a suitable nanny immediately. You're going to need all the help you can get."

Rebecca started to speak but changed her mind. Abigail was grateful since she knew what her sister was about to say. Since they were young children, Rebecca had always gotten around Abigail's wishes by weeping and telling how much she loved and needed Abigail's help.

This time Rebecca did an about-face. She made her sister's upcoming adventure her project. The six months before Abigail left for Oregon were the best of times for the two sisters. Recognizing defeat, Ralph agreed to foot the bill for several gowns and accessories his wife wanted Abigail to have. "You will be the best-dressed pioneer woman the Oregon Trail has ever seen," Rebecca declared.

The Christmas season proved to be one of the happiest for Abigail. The children, the gifts, the garlands of evergreen over the fireplace, a candlelit tree, the wreaths in each window, and Christmas caroling in the snow—all made idyllic memories that she would treasure for a lifetime. With the arrival of the New Year, Rebecca began interviewing candidates for the nanny and cook positions.

The cook position was the first to be filled. Bertha Culpepper, a cheery, plump, red-cheeked forty-year-old from the town of Worcester won both women's hearts immediately. It didn't take too many breakfasts before she also won Ralph's heart by preparing his morning egg to perfection.

Finding a nanny with a healthy sense of discipline as well as a relaxed sense of humor took a while, but on the first of February, they interviewed Rose Shelton, a penniless, thirty-year-old widow. As the oldest child of eight and educated privately from the Back Bay area, her credentials were impressive. When Lucille crawled up on the woman's lap uninvited and asked the gentle woman to tell her a story, Abigail's eyes glistened with tears.

It was happening. She was really uprooting herself from the only family she had and venturing into the frightening unknown where she would be nothing more than a servant to a wealthy and vain widow.

Before Rebecca told Mrs. Shelton she had the job, she asked Abigail one last time, "Are you sure you won't change your mind?"

Abigail gulped back the lump forming in her throat and whispered, "I'm sure."

Abigail still encountered difficult moments when Ralph would say something completely ridiculous or cruel, but she was learning not to fire back the first thought that entered her head. Most things she let go by; they weren't important enough to her. Occasionally, when she couldn't remain silent, Abigail would answer softly and decisively with such careful logic even Ralph could not refute it. It wasn't easy, but it was rewarding.

Alone in her attic room at night, she'd study God's Word for wisdom, pray for strength, and try to imagine what the stars looked like in Oregon's night sky. And while she couldn't put her thoughts into words, in the deep recesses of her heart, Abigail knew that if she didn't go she'd always wonder what her life would have been like if she had. She determined to follow her destiny, no matter where that might lead.

CHAPTER THREE

THE GREAT ADVENTURE BEGINS

FROM THE START, NELL O'GRADY WAS AN enigma to a serious and proper Englishwoman like Abigail Sherwood. Nell had red hair, freckles, a dimple in her chin, and the biggest, most toothy grin Abigail had ever seen. Abigail began training Nell in the fine art of cooking the week before they were to depart Boston.

Abigail watched the bubbly, pockmarked, redheaded girl in amazement. If her soufflé fell or her French rice clumped or her clam chowder scorched, Nell O'Grady would laugh and say, "Oh well, if at first you don't succeed, practice is what you really need. That's what my mum always said."

To come to America, the young Irishwoman had indentured herself for two years to a wealthy family from Peabody, Massachusetts, a light sentence that had allowed her to escape a life of drudgery and poverty in her homeland. When the two years passed, her employer informed her that his business was taking him back to England and that she was welcome to return with them. Nell, however, had no intention of leaving the great land of opportunity she now called home.

So when her employer learned of Mrs. Darlington's need for a cook, he arranged to have Nell interview for the opening. The girl's exuberant personality did more to help her land the position than did her dubious culinary skills, Abigail was sure.

Listening to Nell talk about the events of her life, Abigail speculated that there was more to the girl's story than a potato famine. And the way the girl spun yarns, Abigail was sure Nell would reveal every detail of her life before they crossed the Mississippi River. One thing was certain; there would never be a dull moment in Nell's presence.

Abigail received a reply from her mother the day before her departure from Boston. If she ever had doubts about going west, the letter removed them.

> Dearest Abigail,
> You have my blessing; follow your heart. I did, and I'm so thankful for that. As to your concern for your sister, Rebecca, she followed her heart and her man to America, remember? Why shouldn't you have the same privilege? Be happy, my dear, for me. I will always love you. And should we never meet again on this earth, I'm expecting a full report on your adventures once we're reunited with your father in God's kingdom.
> Love,
> Mama

At the train station, Rebecca and her family came to see Abigail off. After kissing each of the children goodbye, Abigail shook her brother-in-law's hand. He surprised her by becoming teary. When she turned to her sister, Abigail could no longer stop the flow of tears. Only the conductor's "All aboard" broke their embrace.

"If things don't work out, you know you can always come back home," Rebecca whispered, dropping a fist full of double eagles in Abigail's carpetbag.

Abigail frowned at her sister. "Rebecca, no. You've done enough."

A porter dressed in a bright red jacket, dark pants, and shiny boots, tapped Abigail on the shoulder. "Train's leaving, miss. Your party's on board."

Abigail climbed up the steps and rushed to the nearest window where she waved goodbye until the car in which she rode rounded the bend out of the station yard. She slumped in the seat as if weighted by a heavy sack of flour. It wasn't until Nell called to her from the back of the car that Abigail realized she was sitting in one of the all-male cars.

Mrs. Darlington and Nell were situated in the next car, the ladies' car. One of the newest innovations on America's trains, thanks to the southern railways, were the ladies' cars, designed for a woman's more delicate constitution. The seats were upholstered and cushioned with springs and horsehair. Velvet brocade window curtains could be either closed or opened, according to the passenger's desire. The ladies' cars were further back on the train to avoid having the engine's belching sparks burn holes in women's garments.

Abigail soon noted that this precaution worked only when the wind blew in the proper direction. She did, however, appreciate the ability to escape the tobacco-smoking, spitting, and flirting of the male passengers. Males traveling with females were permitted to ride in the ladies' car.

While Clarissa complained about the discomforts of train travel and Nell became fast friends with every other traveler in the car, Abigail busied herself sketching scenes and people. She found the face of the young train butch an interesting study in innocence and guile. After each stop, the butch peddled newspapers, magazines, dime novels, cigars, and sandwiches to the passengers. With each trip through the car, his offerings increased—apples, oranges, figs, peanuts, and maple sugar candy. He would throw an item onto a passenger's lap unbidden, then insist the passenger pay for it. His prices were extravagant, and Abigail noted that he was not above cheating his customer when making change.

Abigail was thankful for the large basket of goodies that Rebecca insisted she take, especially when they stopped for meals at the refreshment saloons where the food was sometimes rancid and the prices outrageous. While she avoided dining in the saloons for either lunch or dinner, she did join Clarissa and Nell for breakfast. After a long night trying to rest in a cramped sleeping car, half suffocated by the foul air, Abigail needed to stretch her legs on solid ground once again.

For the other meals, Abigail used the allotted fifteen-minute meal stop to walk the length of the train and back. She appreciated the short break from Nell's incessant chatter and Clarissa's fussing about the lack of common decencies aboard the train.

Mrs. Darlington's patience finally snapped at a station in western Massachusetts. Clarissa had been suffering all night from a frightful headache. In the morning, she complained to the conductor, asking if the passengers could have an extra ten minutes in which to eat. To persuade the conductor, she invoked her dead husband's name. The name had no effect on the railroad man.

Without blinking, he hauled out his pocket watch and shook his head. "Sorry, ma'am, but we have a schedule to keep. You wouldn't want to keep that man of yours waiting at the station, now would you?"

"Waiting at the station?" She stared at the conductor in horror. "That would be impossible! Mr. Darlington is dead!"

"Sorry, ma'am. You'd better hustle now if you're going to purchase your food before the train leaves."

"Why, I have never, in all my years, experienced such insolence!" Clarissa sputtered as Abigail led her into the crowded dining saloon. "That odious man treated me as if I were one of the common riffraff on this train!" Regardless of her headache, Clarissa and her entourage were aboard the train when it pulled out of the station.

The train rumbled across the rest of Massachusetts and into New York, where they changed onto another line and proceeded across the width of New York State, past orchards and farms, quaint little towns and noisy industrial cities.

As the train neared Buffalo, Clarissa announced, "Pack up your belongings, ladies. This is where we get off!"

Both Abigail and Nell started at the announcement. They needed to cross Ohio, Indiana, Illinois, and Missouri. The two hired helpers looked at each other in surprise.

"But I thought—" Nell began.

"Well, you thought wrong!" By the tightness of Clarissa's lips, Abigail knew the wealthy widow's mind was set. Upon what, Abigail knew not.

The train hissed and screeched to a stop at the Buffalo train station. The conductor strode through the ladies' car announcing that the Buffalo stop would be an hour long.

Clarissa called out to the conductor. "Sir, would you be kind enough to have my baggage and that of my companions removed. We are leaving the train for good!" She offered him her travel itinerary.

"Madam?" He took it from her and studied the sheet of paper for a minute or two. "Your itinerary says you'll be with this train as far as Lake Erie."

"Indeed!" She sniffed, handed Nell her giant leather hatbox, and then glanced coyly over her shoulder at the surprised man. "I have had it with hot cinders burning my gowns and my eyes. And I can take not one night longer sleeping on board this beast and eating food of questionable origin. Railway money or not—forgive me, dear husband—but we are continuing our trip west by steamboat. We may still have to battle the cinders, but we can do so in much greater comfort."

The change delighted both Nell and Abigail. Yes, they continued to battle hot cinders, but the ride itself was smooth and unhurried. The luxury of the riverboat called the *Linn* that would take them across Lake Erie to the Mississippi River was like nothing Abigail had ever seen. The living conditions on the ship that brought her and her mother from England were cramped and primitive compared to the floating palace of the riverboat.

As they boarded, Abigail lingered behind her benefactor's entourage of porters to admire the pristine white bric-a-brac that made the vessel resemble a three-story royal wedding cake. She clutched her trusty leather art portfolio to her breast and vowed to sketch the riverboat from every angle possible before she transferred to the next riverboat. Surely another boat could never compare in elegance.

Life on board the riverboat resembled one continuous party. Abigail wondered when the housekeeping crew had time to clean up the boat before the next onslaught of customers. While Nell and Clarissa were both enamored with the lighthearted atmosphere aboard the boat, each woman went her separate way, leaving Abigail to her own devices. Nell flirted with the boatswain and his crew, while Clarissa sashayed about the boat on the arm of a different gentleman dandy every evening.

As for Abigail, she could be found at all hours of the day and night with her portfolio in hand, sketching. Several passengers asked to purchase her sketches of the boat and the boat's crew. Before long, she was doing sketches of the travelers themselves, who insisted on paying her for the likenesses. When Clarissa discovered what Abigail was doing, the younger woman was fearful that her benefactor might object. Instead, the wealthy widow told her she admired her for being an entrepreneur.

"That's the way I tripled my husband's fortune, by looking for a niche and filling it," Clarissa confided.

Abigail's responsibilities aboard the riverboat were light, as Clarissa was too busy partying to need many letters written. The wealthy widow did keep in constant contact via telegram with her man who waited for them at a place called Serenity Inn in Independence, Missouri.

Being the daughter of a conservative English minister, Abigail didn't feel comfortable sitting around the gaming rooms or the theater in the evenings. Clarissa, on the other hand, was only too happy to be the center of attention with the riverboat's upper crust, without the threat of another woman nearby to distract any of her admirers. Though engaging and flamboyant, Clarissa understood the power of the subdued, serene beauty found in a woman like Abigail Sherwood. That the younger woman wasn't aware of her beauty made her even more appealing to many men.

The transfer to the Mississippi riverboat caused nary a break in the wealthy widow's social calendar. The grandeur of the Mississippi paddleboat called the *Liberty* surpassed that of the smaller *Linn*. And while the *Liberty* dazzled Abigail with its luxury, the great Mississippi River didn't live up to her expectations. The "soul of America" was muddy and sluggish. All the reading she'd done about this magnificent river didn't prepare her for the disappointment.

After unpacking Clarissa's trunks and organizing their stateroom, Abigail wandered out onto the deck. The late afternoon sun had left a lingering glow in the western sky. The taverns along the shore rang with raucous music. An aging colored man sat on a barrel on the end of a dock, strumming his guitar and singing quietly. Behind her, Abigail could hear laughter coming from the gaming saloon and music coming from a steam-powered calliope. And if the placard on the easel beside the etched glass doors was to be believed, the curtains were about to rise on the balcony scene from *Romeo and Juliet* in the paddleboat's theatre.

A cool breeze whipped about the sides and angles of the riverboat. Despite the unseasonably warm temperatures for March, evening would bring cooler temperatures. She wrapped her white woolen shawl about her shoulders, drawing one end closer to her face. A wispy strand of soft brown hair strayed from its confines in the bun at the nape of her neck, escaping the navy poke bonnet and teasing her nose and cheek. She brushed it aside, only to have it return with the next unsettling breeze.

As she stood at the brass railing, watching the shantytowns pass by, a stranger, garbed in a shirt and pants made of deerskin, stepped out of the shadows further down the deck. Enchanted with this first sign of western culture, she watched him out of the corner of her eye. The six-inch-long fringe, running the length of his sleeves, fluttered in the breeze as he leaned over the railing and stared into the brackish water. In one hand he held what appeared to be a brown suede wide-brimmed hat.

Removing a pad of paper and pencil from her leather portfolio, she began to sketch the man's strong profile. His shoulder-length hair was caught into a tail at the nape of his neck. His back was as long and strong as a New England pine tree. His shoulders and head staunchly faced the wind.

It wasn't until her fingers began to cramp from the cold that Abigail realized how long she'd been sketching. As she turned to enter the corridor leading to her stateroom, the stranger strode toward her.

"Ma'am," he said, reaching for the door handle, "may I get that for you?"

"Yes, thank you." She smiled in surprise at the man's cultured voice and deep blue eyes.

Her skirts swooshed against his pants' legs as she stepped over the threshold into the wood-paneled corridor. The flames from oil sconces lit the long corridor.

"Begging your pardon, ma'am," he gestured toward the pad of paper she clutched in her hand. "I couldn't help but notice that you're an artist. May I see what you were sketching?"

Abigail blushed uncomfortably, first, because she didn't consider herself an artist, and, second, because she'd been caught sketching his likeness without asking permission. She swallowed hard, opened the tablet of paper, and handed it to him.

Catching the corridor door with his boot, he examined the sketch of himself and flipped back the pages to other sketches she'd done of people aboard the paddleboat and of the paddleboat itself. "These are good!"

Her first instinct was to fire a sharp retort at his obvious surprise at her talent, but she bit her tongue. She found she appreciated his compliment.

"With whom did you study?" he asked.

It was her turn to be surprised. "Study? Why, er, Bessy."

"Bessy? Excuse me, but I'm not familiar with—"

Seeing his discomfort at not being able to identify a famous artist named Bessy, she chuckled. "Bessy, my family's cook, in England."

"Incredible!" He continued to examine the sketches. "These could bring big money back east. Anything western is a great moneymaker in New York and Boston, but then, you wouldn't know that, would you?"

She smirked in spite of herself. "Actually, I am traveling from Boston, sir, to Oregon."

His face brightened. "A Boston lass, originally from Great Brit." He bowed his head in greeting. "Forgive me, my name is Englebert Horatio Lassiter, esquire, and wilderness guide. My friends call me Hawk."

Her reply came out in a stilted proper English form as she took the art pad from his hands and pressed it against her breast as a medieval knight would a shield. "A pleasure, Mr. Lassiter."

Abigail found it difficult to adjust to the relaxed social code of the riverboat society. A lady and a gentleman became acquainted and exchanged their given names in proper society east of the Mississippi when a third party introduced them. She wondered if such casual etiquette was typical of western society in general. She wasn't sure she liked it.

Mr. Lassiter peered into her eyes. "And you are?"

She batted her eyelashes and smiled. Even as she did so, she groaned inwardly at herself. "And I am retiring to my cabin for the night, if you will excuse me."

He straightened as if he'd been slapped across the face. "I beg your pardon, madam. Forgive me for detaining you. If you will excuse me."

She smiled graciously, batted her eyelashes a second time, turned, and hurried toward the first-class cabin she shared with Clarissa. Once inside the room, she closed the door and pressed her back against it. She could feel the high color blazing in her cheeks. Her heart pounded in her throat.

The last visages of daylight seeped in through a small porthole. She caught a surprising glance at herself in the silver-backed mirror hanging on the wall directly across from the cabin door. The flush in her cheeks and her wide, unnerved green eyes belied the attributes of a different woman, certainly not those of the old maid sister of Rebecca Porter, high society's little darling.

What had come over her? Batting her eyelashes like she'd seen her older sister do so often before the latest lovesick swain draped himself over the family's sofa! How indecent. And to be so direct! Abigail stood eye to eye with most men, but she'd learned the skill of dipping her head in proper deference as well as the art of slipping into the background as quickly as possible.

"You can be as interesting as wallpaper when you're around an available man!" her sister had declared often in their earlier years.

Abigail lit the oil lantern on the wall between the two berths and examined her reflection once more. The heather-blue woolen traveling dress she wore, along with the modest navy-blue bonnet tied at her chin by matching grosgrain ribbons complemented her soft, translucent complexion. She studied her large, capable hands, gloved in gray kidskin, and reasoned that nothing was different about her since leaving Boston. Yet, she would never have lingered for a moment on a Boston street with a stranger, esquire or not.

Blaming her slip of good judgment on the relaxed society of the riverboat, she removed her gloves and bonnet and tossed them onto the foot of her bunk.

"I must guard against developing such habits," she announced to the empty room. "I may no longer be in Boston or London, but I certainly don't need to compromise proper standards of conduct!"

As her fingers fumbled with the bone-white buttons on her short, waist-fitting suit jacket, she regretted returning to her room. Like it or not, she was stuck until morning. She'd much rather have attended the play or wandered about the deck. But after telling Mr. Lassiter she was retiring for the night, she couldn't risk being seen by him again.

As she unpinned her watch broach from her jacket lapel, she noted it was barely past 7:00 P.M. What would she do with herself for the next several hours until bedtime? She'd never been one to retire early. Slowly, she removed her suit jacket, skirt, and crinolines. She undid the tiny pearl buttons on her white silk blouse. Gathering her discarded clothes, she put them in her trunk.

From the ruffle at the neck to the soft folds about her ankles, the warmth of her robin-egg blue flannel nightgown engulfed her. She released her waist-length hair from its confines. The silky, shimmering curtain of rich brown hair draped down over her left shoulder and one side of her bodice. Picking up the ebony-handled, boars' hair brush her father had given her for her thirteenth birthday, Abigail brushed through her hair vigorously—one hundred strokes—as she did every night before retiring. Satisfied that all the snarls were gone, she wove her heavy sheaf of hair into one braid and tied the ends with a strip of grosgrain ribbon.

With her evening chores completed, Abigail glanced about the room. She could read one of the books she'd brought along: a Jane Austin, an old Washington Irving, or a new Edgar Allan Poe. No, nothing interested her. Her gaze rested on her father's Bible. She squeezed the bridge of her nose with her forefinger and thumb to relieve the headache threatening to start.

Not able to come up with much else to occupy the next few hours before Clarissa returned for the night, Abigail grabbed her recipe book and sharpest pencils and curled up in her bunk to fine-tune some of her earlier sketches.

At dinner, the chef had served, along with several other entrées, a venison dish with sour cream and mushrooms. While she enjoyed it, it was not quite as tasty as the one Bessy used to make, a recipe Abigail had not yet included in her book.

"Let's see, I could taste garlic, basil, and onion. What was missing? Marjoram! That's what made the difference."

In a graceful scroll, Abigail printed the ingredients as she remembered them. Later she'd trace over the pencil marks with pen and ink, but for now, she'd at least have the dish recorded.

Thinking about Bessy's recipe made Abigail realize how much she missed her old friend and confidant. The young woman laughed to herself. She wondered what Bessy would think if she knew her little Abby was on a riverboat heading for Independence, Missouri, and all points west. She fell asleep while sketching from memory the mounted head of the buck Ralph shot after his one and only hunting expedition. It wasn't until Clarissa burst into the room—the woman never gracefully entered the cabin but attacked like the commander of Napoleon's shock troops—at 2:00 A.M. that Abigail realized how long she'd been asleep.

While helping the talkative Clarissa remove her many layers of crinolines and undergarments, Abigail listened as Clarissa told of her evening's adventures. "After the theater performance, a most marvelous gentleman joined our party. The man has been absolutely everywhere, London, Paris, Hamburg. He's dined with the likes of the Hapsburgs and, of course, Queen Victoria and her romantic Prince Albert. Can you imagine?"

Abigail nodded and uttered an acknowledging grunt.

"The strange thing is, to look at him, you'd think he was a country bumpkin from the wilds of Arkansas or something, all garbed in deerskin, fringe, and all."

The word *fringe* caught Abigail's attention.

"Mr. Englebert Lassiter, esquire." Clarissa giggled and blushed. "I hope we see him at breakfast tomorrow morning. I'm sure he'll ask us to join him. He told me to call him Hawk. Doesn't that sound frightfully wild and dangerous?"

Abigail looked at her benefactor with surprise. When she talked about the man, Clarissa looked a good ten years younger than her age. Which would probably make her five years younger than the man in question, so Abigail figured.

How embarrassing! How can I possibly avoid seeing him again? I suppose I could hide out here in the cabin until we change to a Missouri paddleboat. Abigail giggled to herself. The image of her skulking around the riverboat and hiding in dark alcoves at the sight of Englebert Lassiter was ludicrous. Dimming the oil lantern wall sconce, she slipped under the bedcovers once more.

Out of the darkness, she heard Clarissa say, "Mr. Lassiter is a magnificent man indeed. Wait till you meet him."

Abigail groaned. "Yes, just wait until I meet him," she mumbled into her pillow.

CHAPTER FOUR

ON TO INDEPENDENCE

THE STILLNESS OF THE MOONLIT MISSISSIPPI River was broken with sudden fury.

A woman's scream penetrated Abigail's sleep. There was a frightening urgency to the scream.

Abigail lifted her head. Anxious shouts and scuffles from a desperate struggle echoed in the passageway outside their cabin. Abigail threw her robe over her nightdress, stumbled across the small cabin, and opened the door a crack.

"What are you doing?" Clarissa whispered from her berth. "Abigail? Don't go out there!" The light from the hall lantern showed Clarissa Darlington huddled against the headboard of her bunk, clutching her quilts about her neck. "Abigail! Close that door. I forbid you to go out there. Who knows what might be happening?"

Abigail turned and pressed her finger to her lips. *"Ssh,"* she scolded. Removing Mrs. Darlington's silver tipped umbrella from the umbrella stand behind the door, Abigail cautiously stepped into the hallway. She hurried in the direction of the scuffle and on to the deck where she spied a woman, her back pressed against the brass rail, and two men looming over her. Each time they lunged at her, the woman jabbed at them with the metal point of a parasol she carried.

Abigail glanced about, hoping some man would appear out of the shadows to defend the trapped woman. When no one came to her rescue, Abigail straightened her shoulders, held her umbrella with both hands, and shouted, "What do you think you're doing? Unhand that woman!"

The larger of the two men swung his bearlike head in Abigail's direction. "Mind your own business, lady. Go back to bed!"

The second man grabbed at the trapped woman while she was distracted by Abigail's intrusion. The woman screamed and flailed a ruffled parasol in the air. The metal tip of the parasol connected with the larger man's neck. He yelped and whirled back toward her.

Not knowing what else to do, Abigail swung her umbrella at the back of the larger man's head and shouted, "I said, 'Unhand that woman!' "

At that instant, the other woman jabbed the larger man in the stomach with her parasol. He doubled over with pain. "Get her, Ben," he called to his partner. "The wench jabbed a hole in my belly!"

From the man's accent, Abigail knew he was a river rat, one of the hoodlums who hung around river towns drinking whiskey and bamboozling tourists. As Abigail raised her umbrella to deliver a blow on the second man, a shadow darted past her and slammed into the larger man. They tumbled to the wooden deck. The smaller man quickly released the victim and scurried into the darkness.

The sound of smacks and grunts filled the air as the attacker and the rescuer tumbled about the floor of the deck. When the attacker broke free, Abigail braced herself for action. But the river rat had no stomach for pressing his cause further. He leaped over the railing into the murky water. Like most bullies, he was a coward at heart.

Abigail rushed to the sobbing woman's side. Her anger at the two men changed to surprise when she discovered the identity of the woman— Nell.

Nell's rescuer slowly rose to his feet as if in pain. Seeing his face, Abigail gasped. "Why, Mr. Lassiter, it's you."

He reached for his suede hat, which had rolled under a deck chair. "Why, yes, ma'am, I guess it is." He dusted off his hat with his elbow and forearm. To Nell, he asked, "Are you all right, miss?"

Wide-eyed with admiration, the tiny redheaded woman bobbed a partial curtsy. "Yes, sir."

"Begging your pardon, ma'am, but what was it those men wanted?" Mr. Lassiter asked.

Nell blushed and grinned nervously at Abigail.

Lassiter turned his attention to Abigail. "You certainly swing a dangerous umbrella, miss. I wouldn't want to be on the receiving side of your weapon. And by the looks of you, I'd say you were not a part of the skirmish originally."

It was Abigail's turn to blush. In the excitement, she'd forgotten she was wearing her flannel peignoir set. "I heard a scream, and I . . ." She gestured toward Nell. "I know this woman. I'll just take her to my cabin where she'll be safe."

The rangy guide grinned. "You can come to my rescue any day, miss. Let me walk both of you to your cabin—"

"Oh no!" Visions of Clarissa's reaction to the unexpected arrival of the enigmatic gentleman cowboy sprang into Abigail's head. "I mean, it won't be necessary. My room is the first one on the left."

In two long strides, Mr. Lassiter walked to and opened the corridor door for them. "If you won't be needing my services further, good evening, ladies."

Abigail hurried Nell into the corridor. They paused outside the cabin door. "What was that all about? What were you doing out here at this hour? You should have been asleep in your quarters."

While Clarissa wanted Abigail to stay in her luxurious cabin, she insisted Nell be assigned to the women's servant quarters on the lower deck. "And what did those men want?" Abigail whispered.

Nell touched her hand to her forehead and took a deep breath. "I talked my way into a private poker game and had the audacity to win. Those men are thugs for a wealthy slave trader, Mr. Savage, and they," she dug into her pockets in the folds of her gown and withdrew two handfuls of gold coins, "they were sent to reclaim his money any way they could. Please don't tell Mrs. Darlington."

Abigail clicked her tongue in frustration. "Oh, Nell, how could you do such a stupid thing?"

At the creaking of their cabin door, the two women froze.

"Just what was that you didn't want Abigail to tell me?" It was Clarissa, an angry Clarissa. Abigail and Nell looked at each other in surprise. "Nell, I have half a mind to send you packing to Boston come dawn. Of all the irresponsible things to do! What were you thinking? A lady would never compromise herself in such a fashion." Clarissa gulped a lung full of air and continued, "And you, Abigail, what do you have to say for yourself, charging out of the cabin in the middle of the night with only an umbrella for protection? I would have thought better . . ."

At the mention of the umbrella, the three women eyed the weapon in Abigail's hand. Abigail looked up in time to see a muscle in Clarissa's cheek twitch and then wrinkle into a smile. The woman covered her mouth with one hand, but the twinkle in her eyes gave her away. "You two look absolutely ludicrous! Nell clutching her gold and you clutching that silly umbrella." Clarissa threw back her head and laughed.

Abigail looked at the terrified Nell and giggled. "We do look rather silly," Abigail observed.

"So, tell me. Did you fight off the demons yourselves or did someone come to your rescue?"

"A dashing stranger rescued us," Nell sounded breathless, like a teenager.

Abigail shot a disgusted look at her. "We were doing just fine without his help."

Nell giggled. "Oh, yes, one minute longer and one of us instead of our attackers would have been thrown over the railing into the river. By the way, where is my parasol? I must have lost it in the shuffle."

"And does your dashing rescuer have a name?" Clarissa led the way back into the cabin.

Nell, eager to please her mistress, didn't wait for Abigail to speak. "Abigail knows him. She called him Mr. Lassiter."

Clarissa whirled about in surprise. "Mr. Lassiter? And how, pray tell, do you know him?"

Abigail placed the umbrella in the stand behind the door, yawned, and walked to her berth. "I am certainly tired now," she started.

"Abigail? How do you know Mr. Lassiter?" Clarissa insisted.

"It was nothing really. We met after dinner on the deck. I'd been sketching him from a distance and—"

"And you let me babble on about the man without telling me you'd already met him?"

Abigail lifted her chin in defense. "I didn't officially meet the man, so I didn't feel that our short conversation counted."

Planting her hands on her hips, Clarissa flung her head to one side. "How very British of you, my dear."

Nell giggled.

Clarissa swung her head toward the young woman. "As for you, I expect to hear every lurid detail of your nefarious adventure in the morning.

But now, I need to get my beauty sleep." She turned down the flame in the oil lantern and removed her robe. "Nell, you may sleep here tonight, on the floor. Your attackers probably know where you've been staying. Abigail, there is a spare quilt on the shelf in the wardrobe. Good night."

In the darkness of the room, Abigail padded to the pine wardrobe at one end of the small cabin and located the quilt, as well as a spare pillow which she gave to Nell, before removing her own robe and hopping onto her berth.

When morning came, Abigail dressed quickly and left. She didn't want to endure the scolding Clarissa would deliver to Nell. Knowing they would be changing riverboats to head west across Missouri that afternoon, Abigail wanted to locate and thank Mr. Lassiter for coming to her aid. If he left the riverboat, she might never have another chance to do so. Wandering from one eating saloon to another, she found no sign of her brave benefactor.

The transfer to the last riverboat on their journey went smoothly and without incident. The subdued Nell hung close to Clarissa's and Abigail's sides. The lass's Irish spunk had been tamed, at least for the time being, by the Bostonian's lethal tongue.

Aboard the new vessel, Abigail searched once more for Mr. Lassiter, but again, to no avail. She had no reason to think he would transfer to the new boat, though she had to admit she was disappointed. Scolding herself for having such frivolous thoughts about a man, any man, Abigail set out to enjoy the last leg of her river voyage. If all she'd read about the convenience and comfort of covered wagon travel were true, they were in for more pain than pleasure on the rest of the journey to Oregon.

* * * * *

The midpoint of their trip was Independence. When the riverboat docked, Clarissa's man, Winters, was waiting for her at the dock. Adrian Winters had trained at the foremost school for butlers in England. He'd apprenticed with the queen's butler at Windsor Castle. His gray pin-striped trousers and black cutaway jacket seemed curiously quaint amid the buckskin-clothed Indians, rough canvas-clad cowboys, and sweaty longshoremen. Mexicans wearing brightly colored ponchos and wide-brimmed hats stared curiously at Winters as he escorted the elegantly clad

Clarissa Darlington down the gangplank to the shiny, black brougham carriage.

Before leaving Boston, Clarissa had planned what she'd wear for her arrival in Independence. She'd chosen a heather-blue, Donegal-tweed, wool suit with matching suede lapels. On the left lapel, she wore an intricately designed silver broach in the form of a dove. The dove's eyes were cut diamonds.

Beneath the jacket that nipped tightly at her tiny waist, Clarissa wore a light blue silk blouse with rows of ruffles filling the bodice from neck to waist. On her matching blue hat, three white peacock feathers were held in place by a lifelike dove.

As she descended the gangplank on the arm of her butler, Clarissa looked beyond the curious and admiring faces gazing up at her to her waiting carriage, a beauty in its own right. Shiny black, with gold scrollwork along the sides and gold velvet-tasseled curtains at the windows, the waiting brougham was drawn by four matching dapple gray sorrel mares. Tiny silver bells on the harnesses jangled as the horses shifted, impatient to be underway.

The crowd of spectators parted as Clarissa and Winters strode to the carriage. As she inspected the elegant coach, she clasped her hands and squealed with glee. "Oh, Winters, it is as lovely as I imagined. I could just kiss you!"

The ever-proper butler blushed and took a step backwards. "Oh, don't worry, Winters, dear, I won't bite! Just help me into the carriage."

While Abigail and Nell waited to be assisted into the carriage, a farm wagon pulled up behind the fancy brougham and several longshoremen loaded the women's luggage on to it. Winters helped Abigail and Nell aboard, then climbed in to the carriage, signaled the driver, and closed the door.

With the crack of a whip, the vehicle lurched forward. "Now, tell me, Winters, what is this place called Serenity Inn? Is it a spa of some kind? Please tell me everything."

"Well, madam, one might call it a retreat. The boarding establishments in Independence are hardly places where a lady such as yourself would want to be found. Serenity Inn is more, er, should I say, family oriented? And the couple who run it are quality folk."

Clarissa patted Winters's hand affectionately and smiled adoringly into his emotionless face. "You take such good care of me."

Winters cleared his throat. "I try, madam. So how was your journey?"

His question was all Clarissa needed. For the next seven miles to the inn, she reported every detail with such flourish that Abigail began to wonder if they'd been traveling on different trains and riverboats. In the midst of her descriptions, Clarissa introduced Abigail.

Before the inn came into sight, Winters explained about the building's construction being of sod.

"Mud?" Clarissa exclaimed. "You expect me to sleep in a mud hut like an African native?"

Where she'd learned about African natives and their housing, Abigail didn't know. Winters hastened to assure Clarissa that the building was both safe and clean. "The inside walls are whitewashed," he added. "All very tastefully done for a prairie establishment."

Clarissa was still muttering about sleeping in a mud hut when they rounded a bend in the road and the cluster of buildings called Serenity Inn came into view. "And this is the best you could find for me?"

Winters shrugged. "Short of renting you an entire house. We won't be here long enough for that. I've already purchased us a place on the first wagon caravan out of Independence for Oregon."

"Really?" Clarissa squealed like a schoolgirl. "Oh, what fun! And have you met Mr. Farnsworth?"

Winters nodded. "He will be a part of our caravan."

"Oh, delightful!" The driver slowed the team to a stop, climbed down from the driver's seat, and opened the door. Winters disembarked first and then helped the three women from the carriage.

Before starting for the front door of the sod inn, Clarissa spotted the farm wagon following with their luggage. "I do hope that isn't the wagon I sent you to Pennsylvania to buy for us!"

"I assure you that it isn't." Winters's voice sounded indignant. "Your Conestoga is waiting for you at the campground west of Independence, loaded and ready to roll."

"Splendid, truly splendid. And who might this be?" she asked as a tall, ruddy-faced young man with rolled-up sleeves and arm muscles the size of melons rounded the corner from the house.

"Clarissa," Winters called, "let me introduce you to Mr. Caleb Cunard, the owner of Serenity Inn. Caleb, meet Mrs. Clarissa Darlington of Boston, Massachusetts."

Caleb extended his hand to the woman. "Welcome to Serenity Inn, Mrs. Darlington."

"And this is Abigail Sherwood, Mrs. Darlington's personal traveling companion, and her lady's maid, Nell O'Grady."

"Nice to meet you, Miss Sherwood, Miss O'Grady." The innkeeper shook the women's hands. Abigail appreciated the firm handshake and the man's easy smile. He struck her as a man of integrity.

Caleb gestured toward the front door of the inn. "Come inside and meet my wife, the powerhouse who keeps the inn running. Our other guests, Mr. and Mrs. Evan Chambers and their three children, will be part of your wagon train."

"Children?" Clarissa said the word as if it were cursed.

"The Chambers children are well behaved and delightful."

From the look on her face, Abigail could tell Clarissa wasn't so sure.

Winters passed Clarissa to Caleb. "I'll oversee the men as they unload the luggage. What will you be wanting inside tonight, madam?"

Clarissa thought for a moment, her gloved hand delicately poised before her lips. "Everything, I suppose."

Winters bowed his head. "As you wish, madam."

"You're in time for supper. My wife makes a scrumptious pot of venison stew, if I say so myself," the innkeeper encouraged as he held open the heavy oak front door.

Before following Clarissa and Nell into the sod house, Abigail turned and gazed at the open prairie that stretched for miles in every direction. A golden orb of sun hovered a mere inch above the western horizon. One stark tree atop a small incline stood in silhouette against the pending sunset.

"Beautiful, isn't it?" Caleb asked, his question drawing her out of her reverie. "I never get tired of prairie sunsets."

"It's so empty," Abigail whispered.

The man smiled. "Ah, you get used to that, so much so that when you find yourself in the big city, you feel closed in."

By the big city, Abigail assumed he was talking about St. Louis, not Independence.

CHAPTER FIVE

AT THE INN

A BIGAIL WAS PLEASED BY HER FIRST SIGHT OF the inn's interior. A feeling of warmth and cheeriness permeated the simple great room. The artful use of reds, yellows, and browns produced a casual, homey feeling. Serenity, the woman who appeared to be the proprietress, dropped her dish towel onto the large oak dining table and crossed the room to welcome Clarissa and the other guests.

From the minute Abigail was introduced to the comely young woman, she knew she liked her. Abigail considered herself a good judge of character, and she could see no trace of guile in Serenity's face or that of her husband's.

"I'm Serenity. Come right on in and make yourselves at home," the innkeeper urged. "You're just in time for supper." She turned and gathered a slight, cheerless woman into the circle. "Let me introduce my guest, Mrs. Chambers."

"Sara, please call me Sara." The woman shyly extended her hand toward Abigail. Uninterested in the paltry exchanges between commoners, Clarissa had already glided across the room to the open fireplace.

Abigail smiled broadly as she shook the other woman's limp, moist hand. "Nice to meet you, Sara. I understand your family will be part of our wagon train."

A shadow crossed the young woman's face. By the calluses on her hands, Abigail could see that Sara's life had not been easy. Sara maintained an attitude of resignation. She appeared to be a woman who did not expect to find much happiness in life. *A farmer's wife*, Abigail suspected. Such was the lot of most women living in rural communities. Abigail also guessed that it had been her husband's dream, not Sara's, to sell everything and move west.

"Come, let me introduce you to Mr. Chambers and to the children." Serenity guided Abigail and Nell across the room to the cluster of men hovering about the laughing Clarissa. Clarissa's charm came alive in the presence of new males to conquer, married or otherwise. The three children, two boys and a girl, were equally enamored with the elegantly dressed woman with the sparkling rings on her fingers and diamond droplets suspended from her earlobes.

When introduced to Mr. Evan Chambers, Abigail's reaction was cold and curt. She'd seen too many men who charted their own courses regardless of their wives' opinions. As a result, the mild-mannered man appeared miffed. "Miss Sherwood, it's nice to meet you too."

Abigail cast him a fleeting smile and turned her attention toward the children. "Now let's see, I heard someone call you Chip, right?"

The older boy nodded and grinned at her. "Does that mean your full name is Evan Chambers Junior?"

"That's right, ma'am," the twelve-year-old boy replied, pleased to be the center of attention.

"And this is your little brother, Tyler, right?"

"Yes, ma'am, Tyler's four come April."

"Four? You're a mighty big boy for only four." Abigail gently squeezed the child's biceps, nodding solemnly. "And who's this?"

"Aw, that's my dumb sister, Amy," Chip snarled. "She's a terrible pain."

"I am not!" The eight-year-old with brown pigtails and freckles stomped her foot in protest, and then smiled sweetly at Abigail. "I am pleased to meet you, Miss Sherwood."

"And I am pleased to meet you, too, Miss Chambers." A wave of emotion flooded Abigail as she shook the child's hand. She hadn't realized how much she missed her sister's children.

After allowing the children their moment of glory, Clarissa wrested the attention back to herself. "Our trip from Boston seemed interminable. I thought we'd never get here. I am totally exhausted!"

"You came by riverboat?" Serenity asked. "Your arrival was all Mr. Winters could speak about these last few days." She smiled at the sober-faced butler. "He insisted I save our best room for you, Mrs. Darlington."

Clarissa reached up and pinched Winters's cheek. "He is a little darling, isn't he?"

Caleb missed the grand lady's effort to center the attention on herself. "If you want an adventure, Mrs. Darlington, try traveling by wagon all the way from Maine. That's how the Chambers got here. It is one grueling trip."

"And the worst is yet to come, so I hear," Evan added, sending his wife an encouraging smile. "But it will be worth it when we reach the great Willamette Valley in Oregon, where the trees touch the clouds and the rivers run with salmon."

Abigail had heard Mr. Farnsworth's stories of easy living in Oregon and of California madmen greedy for gold. Newspapers as well printed the tales of an idyllic life on the West Coast. Even she, who was as sensible as a pair of brown lace-up shoes, found it romantic.

Abigail could see that Sara was a woman who protested having her world upended by moving west. Abigail surmised that Sara and her husband had had several arguments regarding the trip and still fought over it.

To women like Sara, the frontier was a man's world with no respite for females. While the decisions were made by the male species, a woman was doomed to follow her spouse wherever he led. *That will never happen to me,* Abigail vowed. *I will never allow some man to—*

"In the middle of the night, mind you. Dear Abigail barged out of the cabin. Didn't you, Abigail? Abigail?" Clarissa called to Abigail while the rest of the group glanced curiously at her. "Abigail?"

"Huh? What? Oh, excuse me, woolgathering, I fear. What was it you asked, Clarissa dear?"

The woman smiled. "I was telling them about our little adventure on the riverboat."

Abigail opened her mouth but couldn't think of a thing to say. Nell, however, was not at a loss for words. She told the story with bells and flourishes worthy of being Irish. Abigail gave a relieved sigh, relieved to not be the center of attention.

"Miss Sherwood," Tyler whispered, tugging at her skirt. "Did you really fight off a bad man with your umbrella?"

Abigail chuckled. "Well, yes, with the help of a Mr. Lassiter, that is. It was his arrival that frightened Nell's attackers away, I fear, not my umbrella."

Abigail was relieved to have their hostess announce supper was on the table. They all gathered around the long oak trestle table. Caleb invited everyone to join hands and bow their heads for the blessing.

Abigail smiled. This was how she always imagined a good Christian family would behave. As she watched the interplay between the Cunard couple, she vowed that if she ever did have a home and family, blessings at meals would be part of it. Whether or not she hoped her dream would include a husband, Abigail wasn't too sure. Very few men she'd met were as gentle and refined as her host, Mr. Cunard, appeared to be.

Conversation at the table flowed freely as it always did when Clarissa Darlington was present. One of the benefits of traveling with Clarissa was that Abigail didn't feel obliged to participate in the interaction. She could maintain a look of peaceful acquiescence, and no one would be the wiser as to her personal opinions on the topic at hand. She'd learned this well when dealing with her sister's husband. It was so much easier than arguing over issues neither could control.

After the meal, the men retired to the great room while the women—except for Clarissa, of course—cleaned up the dinner dishes. No one expected her to volunteer for such servile duties.

Abigail would have preferred listening to the men's political discussions rather than enduring the mundane topics most women discussed, subjects like getting grease stains out of silk, toilet training toddlers, and the agonies of childbirth. But while the men were discussing grave political issues such as the Fugitive Slave Law of 1850 and the possible abolishment of the Missouri Compromise, Abigail caught an insight into the personality of her hostess.

As young as Serenity Cunard appeared to be, the woman had a knack for bringing people out of themselves. Abigail had barely dried a platter before she found herself telling Serenity and the other women about her life in England, her father, and even her dear Bessy.

"You're an artist?" Nell exclaimed. "I didn't know that. So that's what you've been doing sitting in corners and scribbling in your brown notebook!"

"Please," Serenity began, "could you show us some of your work?"

Abigail lifted her hands in mild protest. "I am not an artist. I draw for my own enjoyment."

From the other side of the kitchen, Sara Chambers spoke up. "It must be nice to have the time and luxury of dabbling in one's little hobbies. With three children, I barely have time to keep my hair brushed and combed."

Before Abigail could respond, Nell interjected, "Oh, but Abigail cared for her sister's five children every day before she started west. But then, dear Abigail is a remarkable woman!"

Abigail stared at Nell in surprise. The adoration on the Irish lass's face was genuine. Serenity took the dish towel from Abigail's hands. "Please, Abigail, could we see a few of your drawings?"

Backed into a corner, Abigail couldn't refuse. She hurried into the room she would be sharing with Nell and returned with her newest collection of sketches, those done on board the trains and riverboats.

The women and children gathered around the oak table to view the sketches Abigail had made of the life and people during her trip. It wasn't long before the men joined them. Abigail was relieved when Clarissa took over identifying the different scenes, elaborating on each event drawn. The woman spent much time talking about the dashing Mr. Lassiter.

No one noticed when Abigail stepped back from the circle. They were too busy admiring her work. Taking a stick of artist's charcoal from her apron pocket, she sketched the scene before her, the walls, the fireplace, the oak table, and the people.

She was adding the finishing touches when Tyler, the youngest of the Chambers children sidled over to her to take a peek. "Mama, look!" the child exclaimed. "It's me! Miss Sherwood drew a picture of me and Chip and here's Amy and—"

"This is incredible!" Clarissa shrieked. "I didn't know you were so good. But, darling, you are really good. What I could do with these sketches in New York City. With the current craze for anything western, we could make a mint!"

Abigail laughed uncomfortably.

"Miss Sherwood, you must do more," Caleb insisted. "You really are good, you know."

"Yes, Miss Sherwood," the children clamored, dragging her by the arms to the table. "Do more. Do more."

"All right, I'll sketch one of each of you children. How will that be? But you'll have to sit still when I'm sketching you."

The children eagerly agreed. One by one, starting with Chip, the eldest, she sketched their excited faces, neatly autographing each one. She managed to capture the defiant tilt of Chip's head, the devilish glint in Amy's eyes, and the wide-eyed wonder in Tyler's face.

"Be careful," she warned, "of the charcoal smudges," as she handed each child his or her own sketch.

A mantel clock over the fireplace gonged nine o'clock when Mr. Chambers announced, "All right, children, it's time for bed. Tomorrow is going to be a busy day."

A groan followed. Mrs. Chambers made a feeble attempt to rise from the table. Her husband kissed her atop the head. "You rest, my dear, I'll get them ready for bed tonight. Kiss your mother, children, and off to bed with you."

Once Mr. Chambers and the children left the room, the topic of conversation returned to Clarissa as she described her designer model Conestoga wagon.

"The minute I made up my mind to join the trek to Oregon, I knew I could make the trip in nothing less than a genuine Conestoga wagon. I did my research, you see. I immediately sent Winters to Pennsylvania to commission a wagon designed for the optimum comfort possible for the journey."

Caleb whistled through his teeth. "I've seen the wagon, and it is mighty impressive, Mrs. Darlington. Its unique boat shape is said to be able to carry as much as ten tons of cargo without slipping on slanted terrain."

"That's right, Mr. Cunard. Its underbody is fourteen feet long and the upper body, the red part, is nineteen feet in length. And the canvas top has been seasoned with linseed oil to prevent leaking in a rainstorm."

Mr. Chambers reappeared in the doorway to the sleeping quarters. "What will you have pulling it, Mrs. Darlington?"

Clarissa's eyes twinkled. "Winters purchased six Conestoga horses. They're a special breed, you know, sixteen hands high. Dapple gray, I believe."

Evan Chambers shook his head and clicked his tongue. "Must be quite the sight, the red-and-blue wagon with its white sails billowing in the wind, being pulled by such powerful, elegant beasts."

Sara gave her husband a sour look. "I'm afraid our wagon is a much simpler construction, a farm wagon, actually, no paint, no frills, no creature comforts."

"Ah, but Mrs. Chambers, you'll fit right in with your neighbors," Caleb encouraged. "Not many pioneers can afford the luxury of a genuine prairie schooner. I've seen wagons, hardly more than pony carts pass through Independence on their way westward. It's not the size of the wagon that determines the success of the journey. It's the grit and determination of the pioneer, and perhaps the grace of God that makes the greater difference."

Abigail watched and listened to the interplay between the individuals gathered around the fireplace. She studied their faces. *Perhaps it is the artist in me,* she thought, *that helps me observe character in a person.* She found Clarissa entertaining; the Chambers interesting; and Nell and Winters confusing. But the ones she wished she could get to know better were the Cunards. She could easily see herself becoming good friends with Serenity.

They didn't talk much longer. The guests were eager to retire for the night, as on the morrow they'd attend a meeting with their wagon train's organizer and meet some of those who would accompany them to Oregon, the promised land. Before going to her room, Abigail slipped a sketch she'd charcoaled of her host and hostess into their family Bible as a thank-you note.

CHAPTER SIX

LAST-MINUTE CHANGES

ABIGAIL WAS UP WITH THE BIRDS AND THE children the next morning. Surprised to find her hostess in the kitchen making bread before the first streaks of dawn lightened the eastern sky, Abigail volunteered to help.

"How's your coffee?" Serenity asked, pointing to the coffee grinder on the shelf in the pantry.

Abigail laughed. "My brother-in-law never had any complaints. And if Ralph didn't complain, it must have been all right."

"So, you've caught the call of the westward movement." Serenity sprinkled more flour on her hands and continued kneading the lump of dough on the pastry board. "I went to school in Boston."

"Really?"

"Martha Van Horne's Finishing Academy for Young Ladies."

Abigail gasped. "I've heard of that place. It serves a wealthy clientele."

"I suppose. But tell me, why would you leave Boston for Oregon? It is Oregon where you're going, isn't it?"

"Yes, it's Oregon. I heard a missionary talk about the need to settle Oregon and I . . ." Abigail paused for a moment. "No, that's not quite true. If Mr. Farnsworth, that's the missionary's name, were speaking of the darkest of Africa, I would have responded, I think. I'm running away more than I'm running toward, I think."

"Running away? That's sounds intriguing." Serenity's tone made

Abigail comfortable enough to speak about herself.

Abigail chuckled. "Intriguing? Hardly. I'm a bit 'long in the tooth' as the British say. Since having a family of my own doesn't seem to be an option for me, I decided I needed a life beyond serving my sister's tea parties and raising her children."

Serenity threw back her head and laughed out loud. " 'Long in the tooth,' I haven't heard that one since my mother died. And I hardly think you qualify for the euphemism, especially in the west. It's rumored that there are seven men for every woman, you know."

Abigail blushed. "I didn't come west for that purpose!"

"I'm sure you didn't. I'm sorry. I didn't mean to imply such a thing either. But don't be surprised if the good Lord isn't preparing a mate for you as we speak." Serenity's eyes twinkled with devilry. "If you were staying around a while, I could help Him along by introducing you to a few of my single male friends. How does a cultured attorney sound?"

Abigail raised her hands in protest. "Please, no. No matchmaking. My sister's done enough of that to last me several lifetimes."

As she talked, Serenity shaped the balls of dough in their tins, carried the tins to the stove, and placed them on the back to rise before baking. "I never had a sister, so I can't fully appreciate your predicament."

While the three Chambers children played with the Cunards' dog, Onyx, outside the front door, the two women chatted as they prepared the morning meal. When Serenity went to collect eggs for breakfast, Abigail joined the children in the yard. They were playing fetch with the dog.

"Come, Miss Sherwood," Amy Chambers called. "Watch Onyx chase the stick."

Over and over, the dog chased the stick until both he and the children were exhausted. The big black mutt nuzzled up to Abigail's skirts, begging to be petted. Abigail obliged. The three children gathered about her as well. Serenity slipped by them and into the house without a word.

"Miss Sherwood," Chip began, "tell us about the bad men on the boat again?"

Sitting down on the doorstep, Abigail retold the story of the men accosting Nell aboard the riverboat. They laughed when she demonstrated how she'd come after the bigger man with her umbrella. It wasn't until she saw Caleb coming in from the barn with the morning supply of milk that she realized she'd forgotten all about helping Serenity with breakfast.

The tantalizing aromas coming out of the kitchen had awakened the rest of the household. And the food tasted as good as it smelled, especially the honey walnut biscuits. After they finished eating, Caleb opened the family Bible as he had the evening before, and read several verses from the one-hundred-and-twenty-first psalm. " 'I will lift up mine eyes unto the hills, from whence cometh my help. My help cometh from the LORD, which made heaven and earth.' "

The familiar psalm reminded Abigail of her gentle father. She closed her eyes and imagined it was her father's voice she heard. " 'The LORD shall preserve thy going out and thy coming in from this time forth, and even for evermore.' "

"Well, that was certainly appropriate, Mr. Cunard," Clarissa reminded. "We are all about to set out on a dangerous journey into heathen territory. It is comforting to know that the good Lord will be going with us."

Winters nodded his head and said, "Amen." Mr. Chambers remained silent.

"Let's pray together, shall we?" Caleb led his guests in prayer for guidance and for protection throughout the new day. "Lord, we give ourselves to Thee today. May Thy light shine through us on to everyone we meet. Amen."

Her host's prayer made Abigail feel warm and safe. She hadn't felt so protected since her father's death.

"Well," Clarissa rose to her feet, "if that's finished, we need to be on our way into town. Winters, I want to speak with the wagon master, the teamsters you hired, and of course, Mr. Farnsworth. Also, we should recheck the list of supplies to make certain we're missing nothing essential." She crossed the room toward the sleeping quarters. "Winters, if you would please ready the carriage. Abigail, I will need you to help me repack my clothing, of course."

As she walked toward the hall, her instructions continued. "Mr. and Mrs. Chambers, you are welcome to ride into town with us. Nell will stay here with the children. I'm sure you don't mind, Mrs. Cunard."

Abigail caught the bemused smile that passed between the Cunards and Winters, the butler. Realizing she had her marching orders for the day, Abigail sighed, then hurried after Clarissa. Repacking took no time at all. With the latches on the trunks fastened and locked, Abigail hurried to her room to fetch her coat, gloves, and bonnet. She barely had time to check her hair and put on her bonnet when Clarissa's brougham pulled up by the side of the house and Clarissa knocked on her door, urging her to hurry.

The ride into town passed quickly as Clarissa entertained her guests. Abigail had to admit the extra conveniences on the carriage did make for a smoother ride. She wondered how the velvet curtains would hold up in the heat and dust of a prairie summer.

On the outskirts of town, they saw the caravan readying to roll westward. Children scurried in and out of the vehicles. Haggard women sitting on the wagon seats stared numbly into nothing as their men brought their rigs into the milieu. Abigail knew that these were the poor immigrants like the Chambers family who'd traveled to Missouri by land because they lacked the funds for steamboat passage.

Abigail politely looked away as they passed a wagon of prostitutes setting up camp. Gambling tents and whiskey sellers hawked their wares to anyone who would listen. Swindlers, charlatans, and bunco artists of all kinds were busy making fast bucks before being ordered from the camp.

Winters parked the Darlington carriage beside Clarissa's monstrous Conestoga wagon. Abigail couldn't believe the size of the behemoth, though she had to admit that it lacked for nothing.

They'd arrived in time to hear the train organizer's speech. The leader stood on a hastily constructed wooden platform. His dusty, well-worn canvas clothes and his wide-brimmed, nondescript, brown felt hat had seen better days. An unkempt mustache tickled the sides of his mouth. Abigail suspected that he could strain soup through it. But when he spoke, everyone listened.

"We will set up a governing tribunal, though each immigrant is responsible for his own security and that of his belongings. Punishment for theft will be banishment from camp after the thief makes appropriate restitution. Adultery and murder are hanging offenses." The grizzly bear of a man scanned the upturned faces before him. He paused for a moment on Clarissa and her feathered bonnet and then continued.

"Once you leave here, you enter the wilderness. There is no law on the prairie. Might makes right. The grass is greening up, gentlemen and ladies. The first rains will begin within the next three days. Then, it will be time to roll."

Again the speaker's eye caught the bobbing feathers on Clarissa's bonnet. "Lady," he called over the heads of the crowd, "remove that feather from your bonnet, and all other feathers that might be attached to your bonnets! You'll spook every horse from here to Council Grove! Now, as I was saying . . ."

Clarissa's face reddened with anger and embarrassment. "Who does he think he is?"

"*Ssh,* Mrs. Darlington," Winters hissed. "He is the high court judge and jury from here to Oregon."

Sputtering, she removed the offending hat. The darts of fury from her gaze missed their mark as the grizzled man continued his list of instructions. "We will travel in companies. Begin thinking about those companies. You can do it geologically, by nationality, by religion, however you wish, but choose wisely. A bad leader can be worse than no leader at all."

Clarissa listened to the man in spite of herself, as did every other traveler gathered there.

"Each company needs to hire a guide. You can follow the ruts until you reach South Pass, but after that the ground gets rocky and desert-like, and the ruts won't always show. A good guide knows the Indian tribes, which to trust and which to fear. He can speak their languages. That's important."

A man who appeared to be second in command whispered something in the speaker's ear. The speaker straightened. "We have enough army guides for everyone. Two hundred dollars is the going rate for here to Oregon. If anyone tries to charge you more, tell me. And if he talks about taking shortcuts, don't hire him. Two years ago we lost thirty families when their guide took them on a supposed shortcut, smack into a band of Sioux."

The hairs on Abigail's neck rose. She'd read stories about Indian massacres, women and children being taken captive, men being scalped. The speaker continued, "Going west is not a Sunday afternoon picnic, folks. It is deadly serious. You must be alert and on your guard at all times. One careless act can put you and your family, and perhaps many families, in jeopardy for their lives." Again he paused to scan the faces of the audience. This time even Clarissa looked dutifully serious.

"If you forget everything else I say, remember this: always keep your goal in mind—to reach Oregon. Any decision that interferes with that goal is the wrong decision. May God be with you."

The man stepped down from the raised platform into a hive of questioners and a battery of questions. Abigail followed his progress until he disappeared into the crowd. As she gazed at the faces of her fellow travelers, Abigail fought a rising fear in her chest. *Which of the immigrants will make it to Oregon and which will die along the way? Which will I be? How many can survive in these conditions?*

Abigail was disgusted with the lack of sanitation in the camp. From the reading she'd done, she knew that the immigrants were courting sickness by keeping their slop pails in their wagons, not washing their hands, and letting their children defecate wherever and whenever urged to do so. The manure from horses, oxen, dogs, cats, and humans set up an environment ripe for a disease epidemic.

She mentioned her concerns to Clarissa. Clarissa's reply surprised Abigail. "Keep your opinions to yourself, woman. If you want to make enemies on your first day here, try telling these God-fearing Christian women that they're dirty housewives."

Abigail could see the wisdom in the woman's words and bit her tongue until she was sure she'd develop scar tissue. When Winters returned from searching for Mr. Farnsworth as ordered, the missionary and Mrs. Darlington strolled off together.

Winters looked at Abigail and shrugged his shoulders. "I guess I'd better check on the teamsters that will be driving the carriage and the wagon. Would you care to come along?"

"No, thank you. I'm sure I'll see enough of them on the trail." She laughed self-consciously. "I think I'll stay here and get acquainted with the cooking supplies."

Abigail walked to the rear of the wagon, hiked her skirts, and lifted one foot to the lowest step on the ladder at the back of the Conestoga.

"Madam, we meet again."

She whirled about at the sound of the familiar voice. "Mr. Lassiter! What a surprise. I thought we lost you in St. Louis." She stepped down and extended her hand.

"Miss—oh, yes, I still don't know your name." His eyes twinkled with merriment. "Don't you think it's time I know what to call you, especially since we're to be neighbors?" He pointed to the wagon behind the Conestoga.

She blushed and gave him a coy smile. "I suppose so. I'm Abigail Sherwood from Chelsea, Massachusetts, originally from London, England."

"Well, Miss Abigail Sherwood from Chelsea, Massachusetts, originally from London, England, it is a pleasure to make your acquaintance." He removed his hat and took her gloved hand in his, touching the back of her fingers to his lips. She couldn't believe the incongruity of the man's English manners and his clothing of buckskin and fringe.

He cocked his head to one side and arched an eyebrow. "Do I amuse you?"

"Oh, sorry. I didn't mean—"

"It's all right, Miss Sherwood. I'm always happy to amuse a pretty woman." He bowed from the waist.

Abigail grimaced at his word choice. Was he making fun of her? She had a perfectly clear looking glass. She knew she might be comely perhaps, but hardly pretty.

She couldn't miss the bemused look in his eyes when he released her hand. "Now, if you will excuse me, I have appointments to keep. Give my regards to your employer, Mrs. Darlington." He put on his hat and strode away.

She had insulted him, she was sure. *Bite my tongue!* She muttered as she climbed into the Conestoga. The thought saddened her. He seemed to be a nice man, despite his tendency toward hyperbole.

CHAPTER SEVEN

LEAVING MISSOURI

T HE RAINS CAME AS PREDICTED. THE NIGHT the clouds broke and Abigail could see the moon, she knew the wagon train would be pulling out of Independence come morning. Her emotions were confused about leaving Serenity Inn so soon. She felt like she'd just gained a friend in Serenity.

From a small family cemetery at the top of the only rise for miles around the inn, Abigail gazed at the wide expanse of prairie—her destiny. While the others packed their belongings for the short journey to the camp where the wagons waited, she craved some time alone. Earlier in the afternoon, she had chatted with Serenity in the parlor while the woman sewed a patch on her husband's favorite plaid shirtsleeve.

"Did you and Caleb ever consider going west?" Abigail asked as she slipped her feet under her skirts and snuggled down in the cushion of Serenity's blue upholstered, overstuffed winged-back chair. Though Serenity Cunard was almost ten years her junior, Abigail felt like a little sister listening to an older, wiser woman.

Serenity bit off the thread and placed the needle in her sewing basket. "Yes, as a matter of fact, we did. When Caleb's parents headed for California, they wanted us to go with them. But both Caleb and I had caught the vision of Serenity Inn, a safe place for travelers to rest from their journey."

"The inn kept you here?" Abigail was surprised.

Serenity smiled, her eyes twinkling with kindness. "No, not the inn. It was more like, how do I say it? You were a preacher's daughter, right?"

Abigail nodded, pleased that the young woman remembered information she'd shared during one of their previous talks.

"Both Caleb and I are convinced that we are where God wants us to be at this time in our lives. Tomorrow? Who knows where our Lord will lead us."

Abigail studied Serenity's face for several seconds. "You are so young to have such a deep faith."

Serenity laughed. "Any faith I have has come because of trials. God has been so faithful, leading me like He promised in His Word."

Flames crackled in the fireplace, warming the large great room and keeping the dampness outside the soddy's doors. The glow of the fire softened the starkness of the whitewashed walls and the well-worn furniture.

"How do you know that you're where you are supposed to be?" Not wanting to miss a word, Abigail leaned forward.

Serenity paused, the threaded needle poised in her hand. "As you know, God promised that if we acknowledge Him, He will direct us in all our ways. Caleb and I believe His promises completely. When we have a decision to make, we pray together, and we pray separately, asking Him for direction. Then we sleep on the problem.

"In the morning, we share our feelings on the matter. If we are in agreement and are at peace with the decision, we move forward, all the while praying that if we misunderstood God's direction, He will stop us."

Abigail smiled at the simplicity of the young woman seated across the coffee table from her. "And if you aren't in agreement? What do you do then?"

"Then we go back to our knees in prayer."

"What if you cannot agree, no matter how hard you try?" Abigail was thinking of the autocratic rule of her brother-in-law, Ralph. In his house, his will was law regardless of how Rebecca might feel.

Serenity shrugged and gave a wry smile. "That hasn't happened yet. God has always made His will plain enough for us."

"But if it did?"

The young innkeeper straightened her back and gazed directly at her guest. "Caleb and I have never discussed that possibility. But for me, there would be only one possibility. I'd submit to my husband's judgment."

Abigail didn't like Serenity's answer. "But you seem like such an independent woman, running the inn and all." Caleb Cunard had made it clear to Clarissa and her entourage that the inn was his wife's business. He was a blacksmith.

"For me, God's Word is clear on the matter. I want my husband to lead in our home. Having said that, I know that I can safely trust my husband to honor me and my opinions." Serenity's smile broadened. She gave a pleasurable sigh. "Caleb's a gentle leader and wise."

Abigail stared in disbelief. She had never seen such an arrangement work. In her parents' home, her mother ruled the nest, and her meek and gentle father went along with whatever plans had been made. In Rebecca's marriage, it was the opposite.

Serenity stitched carefully around the second elbow patch. "Have you ever seen a chicken born with two heads?"

Abigail shook her head.

"Believe it or not, it can happen. Anyway, the animal runs around the yard in confusion, not knowing which direction to turn and which brain to obey." Serenity chuckled before continuing, "I believe marriage only works when God is the head and the couple lovingly espouse their roles in that relationship."

"Well, I can never imagine cowing to a man," Abigail sputtered. "Not that I'll ever have to worry about such things." She picked at the folds of her gray cotton batiste skirt with one hand.

Serenity looked up in surprise. "Why do you say that? Can you read God's mind? Are you privy to God's plan for your life?"

"Well, no. But I'm twenty-eight years old."

Serenity waved a hand, dismissing Abigail's announcement. "Nonsense! Without thinking about it, I could line up seven single men who would eagerly court you. Eligible women are as scarce as hen's teeth in these parts."

Abigail laughed in spite of herself. "Please! Do me no favors!"

Serenity's face grew serious. "Seriously, I wish you were going to be around these parts. I'm going to miss you."

Abigail's eyes misted. "And I you, Serenity."

That evening on the crest of the knoll, with a quarter moon shining overhead, Abigail again acknowledged how fond she'd become of Serenity Cunard and the comfortable little inn on the edge of the great American wilderness.

When she saw Winters harness the horses to the carriage and bring the vehicle around to the front of the inn, Abigail knew it was time to leave. They would be spending the last night in the Conestoga so as to get an early start come morning.

Abigail was quickly absorbed into the flurry of activity inside the inn. Like a military officer, Clarissa stood in the middle of the great room issuing orders. She'd even managed to include directions for the Chambers children.

As Abigail fastened the bow of her bonnet beneath her chin, Serenity came up to her and whispered in her ear, "Thank you so much for the sketch. Caleb just showed it to me. We will treasure it always." She held the eleven-by-fourteen-inch sheet of paper in her hands.

Abigail eyed the sketch too. She was pleased to see that she'd captured the love and the peace in the couple's eyes.

"I know this might be asking too much," Serenity said, "but keep in touch, at least at Christmas?"

It warmed Abigail's heart to learn that Serenity had seen the potential in their friendship as well. "I will. I promise. Besides I'm dying to know if you're carrying a boy or a girl." Abigail chuckled at the surprised look on the younger woman's face.

"How did you know?"

"My sister was perpetually pregnant, or so it seemed."

Taking Abigail's hand in hers, Serenity said, "Abigail, always remember that God is leading in your life. He loves you and wants the very best for you."

Tears glistened in both women's eyes as they embraced. Abigail watched from the carriage wagon as the little sod inn and her new friends disappeared in the darkness.

* * * * *

With the rising of the sun, the bland brown and gray of the prairie was transformed into a vivid green carpet of new grass. Other signs of spring burst forth along the Missouri River. Tree branches swelled with buds. An occasional patch of daffodils planted by a housewife who'd since moved on to other places threatened to bloom at any moment. The new life signaled the beginning of the westward movement for the new year.

At dawn, the first wagon wheels began to roll. Slowly at first and reluctantly, the lumbering, cumbersome wagons inched forward in single file. Clarissa Darlington's Conestoga wagon loomed high above the rugged farm wagons like a clipper ship dominates a harbor full of fishing boats, her canvas sails shining in the brilliant sunlight.

From her vantage point on the brougham, Abigail counted twelve continuous lines of canvas-topped wagons, running abreast, pursuing their own course across the prairie. Abigail's hands tingled with excitement as she took the reins of Clarissa's brougham in her hands and waited for the signal to join the line of wagons inching westward.

Two nights earlier Clarissa caught the hired carriage driver mistreating one of her horses. She fired him on the spot, leaving her without a driver for the carriage. That's when Abigail volunteered. "I used to drive our carriage when my father visited his parishioners. He would study his theology books while I drove the team of horses."

Clarissa leaped at the suggestion, instructing Winters to train Abigail on the intricacies of driving the sleek brougham. This would free him to care for the animals and the other equipment.

After the long journey from Massachusetts, Abigail could barely believe she was actually leaving civilization behind and heading into the unknown. She'd spent her first night sleeping in the Conestoga with Nell and Clarissa, while Winters slept in a small tent beside the carriage. The teamsters were consigned to sleep with the animals and with the other hired help.

Clarissa had arranged for her wagon and prairie schooner to follow directly behind Mr. Farnsworth's pair of wagons. From Abigail's perspective, it seemed that Mr. Farnsworth spent little time and attention on Mrs. Darlington. *That will prove to be a big mistake for the young missionary,* she thought.

Sitting in the driver's seat of the carriage, Abigail's face was wreathed with smiles. The sky had never been so blue and the tiny, puffy clouds so white. Mr. Lassiter waved to her from his horse as she sat poised with reins in hand, waiting for the signal to begin the journey. Behind her, inside the carriage, she could hear Clarissa fussing with Nell. For a moment, Abigail felt a twinge of guilt for not having to ride with her complaining benefactor. She'd learned from experience that no one could please Clarissa at this hour of the morning.

It was late morning before Abigail received the signal to roll out. She glanced over her shoulder to give Clarissa the word, then glanced over her left shoulder to see the driver of Clarissa's Conestoga easing into line behind her, followed by Mr. Lassiter's wagons. By the length of the line of white-topped wagons rolling behind her, Abigail imagined that the rigs would continue rolling out of Independence throughout the rest of the day.

She spied a hawk soaring overhead. *What must the caravan of wagons look like to him? Long white snakes winding across the prairie?* Because of the rains, the dust stirred up by the wagon wheels wasn't as bad as she'd expected.

The carriage rumbled past a village of prairie dogs lined up outside their homes, curious about the strange invasion. Periodically, jackrabbits dashed in front of the horses. Occasionally, a rattlesnake slithered away from the wagon ruts and into the rich green carpet of spring grass.

Abigail listened to the rhythmic rumble of heavy wagon wheels, the creak of straining axles, and the *clop-clop* of horses' hooves. The team of horses hitched to Clarissa's carriage didn't break a sweat keeping pace with the slow, patient movement of the caravan.

A lump filled Abigail's throat as she realized she was part of American history in the making. The hundreds of wagons each carried a cargo of hope for a better life, for riches, and for a place to call their own. Abigail bit her lip as her vehicle rolled past what looked to be the last soddy in Missouri. Two small boys stood by the front door waving to the travelers.

Following the well-worn ruts through the sea of grass took very little concentration. As she stared out across the flat land, her thoughts returned to her sister and to the children she'd left behind. Abigail wondered if her mother, when she went off to the Caribbean with her sea captain, had the same hollow feeling inside.

Once the newness of the situation dulled, boredom set in as the lightly sprung carriage bounced over ruts and rocks. A cool breeze blew her poke bonnet off her head and on to her shoulders. Before long, her braid came loose from where she had it pinned at the nape of her neck. The long braid bounced freely on her back, making her feel like a schoolgirl again. Stray strands of hair tickled her face and nose.

She continued to study the immense flatlands. Two-thirds of the world ahead was pale blue and the rest a soft green. Abigail guessed it would be many days before the scenery changed.

When the wagon master halted for the noon meal, Abigail devoured the freshly made bread, cheese, cookies, and hot coffee Nell had prepared. While she didn't particularly enjoy the taste of coffee, she'd heard that people who drank the stuff didn't catch the dreaded cholera. She wasn't sure her teas would function in the same way, so she drank the prescribed drink.

Clarissa was cranky and tired of traveling inside the carriage. She joined Abigail on the driver's seat for the afternoon run. Clarissa limped about the camp that night. Sitting on the driver's bench as the carriage bounced over the ruts caused aches and pains to develop in muscles Abigail didn't know she had. She imagined that Clarissa had learned the same thing.

Though dusty and stiff from long hours in the hot sun, Abigail helped Nell prepare the evening meal while Clarissa went to speak with Mr. Farnsworth. The dowager returned a few minutes later irritated that the man had gone to some other family's camp to dine.

After they ate, Abigail wandered through the camp with her sketchpad and pencil case, making brief sketches of the sights of life on the trail. When the Chambers children saw her coming, they ran to greet her. Delighted, she swept little Tyler into her arms. All three had to tell her about their adventurous day. Abigail found a rock on which to sit while the children gathered around her.

"Tell us a story, Miss Sherwood," Amy begged, "the one about the bad men on the riverboat."

"We've already heard that one. I want her to tell a story about where she used to live in England," Chip interjected.

"All right." Deep furrows creased Abigail's brow for several seconds. "Um, let's see. How would you like to hear about the time the neighborhood bully fell into Mrs. Brody's well?"

"Yeah, yeah. That sounds good." Chip's eyed danced with excitement.

Thanks to her niece and nephews, Abigail had become a great storyteller. Along with stories of growing up in a parsonage, she was well acquainted with classic English narratives and fairy tales. As she related her tale, other children from neighboring camps wandered over to the campfire to listen. Several adults joined their children as well.

The word spread through camp about the "story lady." The next evening, Abigail's audience had grown to more than fifty children. She had no idea how many adults listened from the shadows. By the fifth night out of Independence, more than a hundred children gathered in the Chamberses' camp before Abigail had finished helping Nell clean up after dinner.

"Go! Go!" Nell pushed Abigail toward her fans. "I can take care of this. Besides, I want to hear what happened to the little princess of Windsor."

Abigail laughed. Her skirts whirled about her ankles as she hurried to the waiting children. She was glad Clarissa kept herself occupied with either Mr. Farnsworth or Mr. Lassiter in the evenings and didn't need her to write business letters.

When Abigail arrived, she discovered that Evan Chambers had hammered together a small podium on which she could stand so the children could see her better. After she finished the story about the little English princess, the children reluctantly returned to their wagons. Wanting to thank him for constructing the podium for her, Abigail went searching for Mr. Chambers. She found Sara, his wife, woodenly going through the motions of repacking the supper dishes. The woman seemed preoccupied.

"Sara, how are you doing?" When the woman turned to see who was calling, her face contorted and she doubled over with pain. Abigail ran to her. "Sara! What's wrong?"

The woman took a deep breath, and then straightened. "It must be something I ate," she gasped in a weak whisper. "The pain in my side started yesterday at breakfast. It comes and goes."

"Have you told your husband? Maybe you should see the doctor." While she hoped she'd never need his services, Abigail had been pleased to learn that the only physician on the train, Doc Reese, an herbal doctor, was five wagons behind Clarissa's.

The woman shook her head. "No! No, I'm sure it will pass. Besides I don't want to ruin things for Evan. He's so excited about this trip. Even after a hard day on the trail, all he can talk about is reaching Oregon."

A worried frown coursed Abigail's brow as she helped Sara sit down.

"But the doctor may have something that would help," Abigail urged.

"And he might report my illness to the wagon master who could ban us from the train. No, I can't risk that." Sara took a deep breath. "Besides, I'm fine now. As I said, it comes and goes."

"I have some comfrey tea in the wagon. It works well with dyspepsia," Abigail insisted. "It would be no trouble to make."

"That does sound refreshing." With one hand, Sara wiped away the beads of sweat accumulating on her forehead, and with the other, she gripped her stomach. "Please don't say anything to Evan or the children?"

Abigail hated making such a promise, so she said, "Let me know if your pain gets worse."

Sara nodded, closing her eyes for a minute.

"Where are Evan and the children?" Abigail asked.

Sara lifted her face to the cool breeze. "Evan took the children with him to the corral to bed down the animals. He'll be back soon."

Abigail glanced in the direction of the roped-off area referred to as a corral. "Please tell him thank you for building the podium. It does make it easier for me to be heard and seen."

Rivulets of pain crossed Sara's face.

Abigail touched the ailing woman's shoulder. "Are you sure I can't do something for you?"

Sara struggled to her feet. "You can help me into the wagon so I can lie down."

"Of course. And the tea. I can make you a cup of tea."

Sara had barely climbed into the wagon and onto the narrow mattress she and her husband shared when she insisted Abigail leave. Not knowing what else to do, Abigail obeyed. "I'll be right back with the tea," she called.

Walking to the Conestoga, she ran into Evan and the children. After she thanked him for building the podium, she started to tell him about Sara's malady but remembered in time to keep her word.

"It's a big help having you tell your stories each evening to the children, Miss Sherwood." Evan gave her a warm smile. Tyler, the youngest hung on to his father's pant leg. The other two children had run ahead to their wagon.

"We parents appreciate not having to worry where our children might be as the sun goes down. And you do such a good job. I hate to miss a minute of it to do my evening chores."

"Thank you. Fortunately, I love children and I love storytelling. My father was the greatest storyteller I've ever known." She glanced worriedly toward the Chamberses' wagon. "I'm going to brew a cup of comfrey tea for your wife. She's looking a little peaked this evening, don't you think?"

"*Hmm,* I hadn't noticed. But now that you mention it, she's not been feeling well since we left Maine."

Abigail hurried to her wagon, brewed the tea, and took it to Sara. Evan met her at the canvas door of the wagon. He thanked her and promised to return the porcelain teacup and saucer in the morning.

Knowing how much Clarissa hated to be disturbed after going to bed, Abigail doused the fire and climbed into the back of the Conestoga. A string of complaints from Clarissa greeted her. The heat, the dust, the smelly animals, the crusty teamsters—everything was wrong as far as the wealthy dowager was concerned. Her litany lengthened with every mile westward. Nell, who was sitting on her mattress at the far end of the wagon brushing her hair, rolled her eyes heavenward.

Abigail inwardly groaned. How many more evenings of the woman's complaining and harping could she take? She felt like asking which of the woman's admirers had shunned her that evening, but she held her tongue. Knowing Clarissa as well as she did, the dowager's irritation had something to do with some man. Abigail wondered, as she slipped out of her clothing and into her nightgown, how dear, sweet, patient Winters had put up with the woman for so many years.

As the widow continued her string of gripes, Abigail slipped beneath her downy quilt and decided Oregon couldn't come soon enough. Welcomed darkness filled the Conestoga after Clarissa lowered the wick on the oil lantern and curled into a ball facing the wagon's highly polished oak wall.

Sounds outside wafted through the canvas. Mules brayed. Horses snickered. A group of teamsters played cards by the light of their campfire. The young woman sighed. After a while, Abigail heard a gentle snore come from the mighty Mrs. Darlington.

Abigail chuckled quietly. *Who would have guessed that the Lord was preparing me to deal with Clarissa by teaching me how to mind my tongue with Ralph?*

CHAPTER EIGHT

ON THE TRAIL

EARLY THE NEXT MORNING THE PIONEERS broke camp and the wagons rolled westward over the flat and monotonous, green-gray prairie toward Council Grove. They'd been told that this leg of the journey would take twelve days. Once the pioneers reached Council Grove, the trains would divide, one group heading southwest for Santa Fe and the other heading northwest and following the Oregon Trail along the Platte River. Before leaving Council Grove, the people would elect officers for their company of wagons.

Abigail leaned her aching back against the padded driver's seat and sighed. There would be many more miles of this terrain before they reached the mountains. No matter how fast they traveled or how far, the scenery didn't change.

As driver's seats went, Clarissa's carriage had one of the best. But even with the best carriage springs money could buy, the bone-jarring ruts took their toll on Abigail's angular frame. Hours later, when they stopped for the night, she thought she'd never be able to walk again without pain.

Clarissa's attitude darkened with each passing day that Mr. Farnsworth managed to be some place other than by her side. The even-tempered Nell was finding it difficult to be in the woman's presence. Abigail knew why the biggest problem on the trail wasn't Indian attacks or even cholera. The most destructive problem was people not getting along with other people, especially someone in their own family. Traveling in such close quarters and for long hours brought out the worst in the most tranquil of individuals.

As the carriage bounced over ruts and clods of soil, Abigail wondered about Sara Chambers. The pain in her side hadn't lessened. Abigail was relieved when Evan sent for the doctor. However, Abigail didn't like the look in the physician's face when he left the wagon. She tried to put her concern aside as she gathered the children for their nightly story, but her mind kept returning to the ailing woman in the wagon behind her.

Before morning, rumors darted through the camp. *Cholera!* Nothing on the prairie was more feared than this dreaded disease. Abigail couldn't believe the ridiculous tales flying through the camp during each break. Despite the doctor's assurance that the woman didn't exhibit the symptoms of cholera, some of the travelers were demanding that the Chambers family leave the wagon train.

After supper, while the children were gathering for the evening story, a scream from the direction of the Chamberses' wagon pierced the air. Abigail and several other women rushed toward the wagon. The doctor was ten steps behind.

They found Evan Chambers holding the fevered body of his suddenly comatose wife. The doctor cleared the area of curious onlookers, except for Granny Parker, a woman who was traveling to Oregon from Ohio with her only son, Perry. While Granny had been widowed since her early thirties, Perry's wife and infant son had died of influenza in November of the previous year. When, in his grief, the young farmer threatened to "chuck it all" and move to Oregon, Granny leaped at the chance for adventure. Like so many other travelers, they sold their land and possessions, packed the essentials into a farm wagon, hitched up the team, and headed west.

Since leaving Independence, Granny had demonstrated extensive knowledge in the healing arts. She was an easy listener as well. The travelers sought her out before they did Doc Reese. The medically trained man appreciated Granny's skills as much as those she helped.

"Go, Miss Sherwood," the doctor charged, "go and conduct your story hour for the children. You can prevent everyone from getting into a panic."

Abigail did as she was told. The children, wide-eyed and afraid, slowly gathered about the podium and the storyteller. *Oh, dear God,* she silently prayed, *what story shall I tell? Everyone is frightened. How can I keep the children's attention focused on me instead of Mrs. Chambers?*

"Long ago," she began, "in a faraway land, there lived a man named Abraham." The children listened intently to the biblical story that sounded strangely like their own lives. They understood the pain of leaving their homes behind to head for an unknown land. "Instead of teams of horses or mules or oxen," Abigail said, "Abraham had camels. How many of you have ever seen a camel?" No one raised a hand. Abigail described the strange beasts. "In Arabia, they are called the 'ships of the desert.' "

The children had no trouble relating to the rest of the story. They understood the discomfort of riding across hot, arid land all day and sleeping on hard wooden pallets at night. When it grew too dark to see the children's faces, Abigail concluded the day's portion of the story and the children reluctantly returned to their wagons.

By the light glowing through the Chamberses' wagon canvas, Abigail knew that the doctor was still inside the wagon. At one point, Evan had come out for a pan of water.

"Chip, please take your sister and brother to my wagon for the night. It will make it easier for Doc Reese to help your mother. I'll tell your father where you are," Abigail promised. Reluctantly, the boy agreed. The two younger children were excited about seeing inside the impressive Conestoga wagon.

Abigail worried how Clarissa would react to the children's arrival. But when she explained her hasty invitation, she was surprised at Clarissa's response. The woman obviously welcomed the diversion. Abigail stared after her, dumbfounded that the wealthy widow could be a witch one moment and so absolutely charming the next.

During the night, Sara Chambers died. Later the doctor said that was a blessing from God. She had been in excruciating pain. When Doc Reese announced the woman's demise to the rest of the wagon train, he assured the people that Sara Chambers hadn't died from cholera but from a burst appendix.

Upon hearing the news, Clarissa did what Abigail hoped she'd do. She arranged to have the Chambers children ride with her and Nell in her fancy carriage for the next few days.

Abigail fought back tears as she made her way to the Chamberses' wagon. *Why God?* she cried. *Why must this mother die when her children need her so much? How can Sara's death be a part of Your divine plan?*

Sara wasn't the kind of woman Abigail would normally be attracted to as a friend. But she had come to know and like the tiny brown wren of a woman in the few short days they'd spent together at the inn, then later on the trail, despite Sara's penchant for whining.

At the wagon, Abigail found Granny and another woman washing and dressing Sara's body for burial. Realizing she was more in the way than of use, Abigail climbed out of the wagon and rounded the corner, slamming into Evan Chambers. The armload of blankets he'd been carrying tumbled to the ground. She scrambled to help him pick them up.

Folding a blue-and-white print quilt, she handed it to the grieving man. Their eyes met for an instant. The emptiness she saw touched her heart. Abigail placed her hand on his forearm. "I am so sorry, Mr. Chambers. I'm so sorry."

"Thank you, Miss Sherwood. That's what everyone says." He gazed beyond her at some distant point. "What am I suppose to do now without Sara? The children and I can't go on . . ."

Is he talking about going on to Oregon or going on living? She wasn't sure. Abigail nibbled nervously on her lower lip. "The children need you," she whispered.

A wild, tormented look emerged in his eyes. Without a word, he brushed past her, dumped the armload of quilts on to the wagon tongue, and stormed out of the camp. He was gone for several hours.

The same day she died, Sara Chambers's canvas-wrapped body was lowered into a quickly dug grave. There wasn't any wood available for a proper coffin, so Sara was wrapped in a white cotton sheet. Mr. Farnsworth read from the twenty-third psalm and offered a prayer. At the head of the grave, Evan placed a roughly constructed cross on which he'd scratched Sara's name. To Abigail, the sorrowing husband looked more like a lost little boy than either of his two sons. After they sang a hymn, the wagon master gave the signal for the wagons to begin rolling once again.

Abigail herded the children into Clarissa's carriage. The three children huddled together, their faces ashen and frightened. Chip tried to be brave, but large tears filled his eyes. Abigail searched for something to say but found nothing. For once, Clarissa had nothing to say as well. Even Nell was silent.

As Abigail climbed up on to the driver's bench, she glanced over her shoulder in time to see a group of men cover the lonely little grave with soil and pile stones atop. She'd been told that the stones would keep wild animals from digging up the body. She remembered passing other graves along the trail, but they belonged to strangers. Sara Chambers she knew. They'd talked. They'd shared comfrey tea.

* * * * *

Regardless of the mourning, regardless of the pain, the wagons continued to roll westward. They had a schedule to keep if they were to reach their destination before the first snowfall. In the nights following Sara's death, Granny Parker and Abigail took turns sleeping with the children in the Chamberses' wagon while Evan Chambers roamed the hillside, alone in the darkness. During the day, the three Chambers children rode in the carriage with Clarissa and Nell. With the children present, Clarissa didn't snap at Nell or Abigail as much.

The trees were the first signs of civilization as the wagon train approached Council Grove. A broad strip of oak and walnut, cottonwood and ash grew along Council Grove Creek, the main branch of the Neosho River. *Or is it a mirage?* Abigail wondered. She'd seen many dancing, shimmering ghosts in the heat of the prairie sun. But no, it became obvious that the trees were real. The anticipation of a respite from the pain caused by the jarring carriage seat brought a smile to her face. *Rest, finally, a few days' rest.*

Gnats and flies pestered her nose and face as she guided the team over the rutted ground. With her free hand, she slapped at the pests in irritation. Behind her, she could hear Clarissa doing battle with the pesky creatures as well. Whatever the woman was doing, it was making the Chambers children laugh. Abigail smiled. It was nice to hear their laughter once again.

The Farnsworth wagon, directly in front of the Darlington carriage, rolled to a stop. An army officer strode to the carriage and instructed Abigail to park her vehicle beside Farnsworth's second wagon. The

Conestoga, with Winters driving, eased into the space next to hers, and likewise down the line.

Hordes of people swarmed the area. Their noise and their close proximity to the carriage spooked her team of horses. Alarmed, the front animals snorted and attempted to rear. Abigail hauled in the reins. "It's all right. It's all right!" she shouted. The lead horse settled down at the sound of the woman's voice.

Abigail stood up in the driver's box and gazed out over the beehive of people shouting, laughing, greeting friends, and running in every direction. In the distance, she could see the tents of whiskey sellers and fancy ladies of the night, as her mother called such women. Peddlers promising to cure everything from a backache to psoriasis hawked their tonics from the back of squared off, brightly painted wagons, while peddlers of fabric and needles brandished their wares to the ladies. Abigail's ears rang from the noise of the celebrating travelers and their hosts.

On the northern side of the camp, there was a strange mixture of bearded trappers and gaily dressed Shawnee and Osage Indians. She'd read about the treaty the Osage Indians had signed with the United States a few years back. The Indians had agreed to allow the wagons to pass through the area safely in exchange for eight hundred dollars' worth of goods sold by the traders at Council Grove.

Abigail wondered if, as the Indians stoically watched wave upon wave of wagons roll into the grove beside their river, they ever regretted signing that treaty. Army dragoons strolled through the rows of wagons, ostensibly maintaining order but overtly flirting with any pretty young woman they came across.

An unexpected tap on Abigail's ankle drew her attention to Winters, who was standing beside the carriage offering her assistance in climbing down from the wagon. Clarissa and Nell, with the Chambers children safely in hand, were eagerly rushing into the din of humanity.

"This is unbelievable," she shouted as Winters lowered her by her waist to the ground.

The ever-proper butler cupped his ear and bent toward her. "Begging your pardon, miss, but I cannot make out what you are saying."

Abigail laughed and mouthed, "I understand. Thank you." She turned and walked toward the rear of the carriage.

"Miss Sherwood. Miss Sherwood, I was hoping to catch you," a voice called. She glanced over her shoulder to see Mr. Lassiter running toward her. "May I offer my services as your protector and guide?"

She laughed and cocked her head to one side. "Do I need a protector, sir?"

The suave gentleman's face grew grave. "Indeed you do, Miss Sherwood. Who is to know what might happen when some of these soldiers get a few drinks under their belts?"

"You are very persuasive, kind sir." Abigail laughed and slipped her hand in the crook of his arm.

He laughed and started toward the army camp. The closer they came to the center of the encampment, the more Abigail could smell the tantalizing aroma of meat cooking over an open fire.

"Smells great, huh? It tastes even better," Mr. Lassiter confided.

She nodded as they came upon a huge ditch filled with hot coals. Deer, buffalo, bear, and wild turkeys turned on spits over the fire. At the far end of the fiery ditch, giant kettles of beans simmered on tripods above the hot coals.

"The meat was brought in by hunters in the area for the occasion," he explained. "It's a tradition to hold a feast celebrating the arrival of the first wagons of each season. Wait until you taste the soda biscuits—*aah,* a culinary delight."

"Oh? That good, huh?" Abigail had to admit that the man certainly was entertaining.

Mr. Lassiter dramatically licked his lips. "Indubitably delicious. Everyone attends—whites, red, soldiers, traders, trappers, travelers. The only requirement is that you bring a good appetite."

Abigail laughed aloud. "How could you do otherwise? Everything smells so delicious."

"It's a feast you will never forget," her escort promised.

She squinted her eyes toward him. "How do you know so much about all of this?"

"This isn't my first trip across the country. My brother and I own a little claim in the Sierra Nevada range. He's working it as we speak."

"A claim?"

"Gold, I guess. He's the prospector, not me. I put up the capital."

Abigail nodded. "Then why are you heading for Oregon?"

Mr. Lassiter cast a teasing grin at the young woman. "Gold, of course."

"In Oregon?"

He nodded slowly. "More than you can ever imagine."

Abigail had met several people who were heading west to search for gold, but she'd never spoken to anyone who'd actually found any. She suspected that much of the gold had been panned out with the first wave of prospectors. Yet the prospect of riches continued to lure men by the hundreds.

Mr. Lassiter patted her arm gently. "Gold is a boring subject. Let's talk about something more interesting—you and me. After the feast, there is going to be a dance, Miss Sherwood. Would you do me the honor of attending it with me?"

Suddenly, the face of Clarissa Darlington flashed into her mind, and she hesitated. A blush skittered up past her pristine collar. "I appreciate your asking; however, I'd better not. I have several letters to finish for my benefactress. But I'm sure that Mrs. Darlington would enjoy receiving such an invitation from you." She glanced at the man shyly.

Mr. Lassiter arched an eyebrow and grinned knowingly. "You are a diplomat, Miss Sherwood." He patted her hand and urged her past the rows of wagons until they arrived at the center of the camp, where they found a trio of young soldiers strumming guitars and singing songs about unrequited love and star-crossed lovers.

Outside the army headquarters, a shooting contest was in progress. Before she thought about it, Abigail found herself rooting for a sixteen-year-old Southern boy with red hair and freckles; yet all the while, she hoped he wouldn't win the dubious prize of a keg of whiskey. A cheer went up when the points were counted and the winner was announced—a leather-faced trapper, gray and weather scarred.

When the couple finished their tour, Mr. Lassiter returned Abigail to Clarissa's Conestoga, where they found the wealthy dowager pacing in front of the wagon and fanning at the pesky flies. The glare Abigail received from Clarissa could have scorched dinner, or so Abigail believed. She could only imagine what had irritated the woman this time. From the woman's blistering comments on the previous night, Abigail suspected her foul mood was related somehow to the continued absence of Mr. Farnsworth.

Abigail thanked her escort, and then hurried to the Conestoga to find Nell. As she rounded the back of the wagon, she saw Mr. Lassiter tip his hat to Clarissa. The angry expression on Clarissa's face instantly softened.

During the evening meal, Abigail avoided the charming gentleman from England by taking charge of the Chambers children since no one knew where their father was. As she took Chip for a second helping of meat at the barbecue ditch, she saw Clarissa dining with Mr. Lassiter.

She smiled at the scene. The elegantly dressed couple picnicked on a linen tablecloth spread on the grass, complete with Limoges china and Revere utensils. Those around them ate with their fingers and barely bothered to wipe the juices of meat from their dripping chins and hands. And standing at a discreet distance was Clarissa's faithful butler, Winters.

Relieved from having to prepare the meal that evening, Nell disappeared into the crowd with a pockmarked army lieutenant she'd met that afternoon. As Abigail nibbled on a second soda biscuit, she searched the crowd for Mr. Chambers, but he was nowhere to be seen. She knew the children had been doing the same. Only Tyler had the courage to speak of his absent father.

"Too bad Dad is missing this great supper! This turkey leg is delicious!" The two other children looked away without comment.

As the fiery sun disappeared beyond the horizon, a couple of men brought out their fiddles and began playing familiar songs. The crowd cleared a large circle in the middle of the meadow where several people began to dance.

Before long the music had Abigail's toes tapping as well. When a young officer asked her to dance, she could feel her face flush with color. "No, thank you, but thank you for asking," she said. The truth was Abigail had never learned how to dance. Rebecca had. Their mother had overridden their father's objections and taught her youngest to do all the popular steps of the day. But Abigail couldn't bring herself to disappoint her father.

By midnight the celebration was in full swing when someone rolled out the barrels of whiskey. The atmosphere was getting rowdy. Mothers began taking their exhausted and protesting children to their wagons to send them to bed for the night. Older people were retiring as well.

Granny Parker offered to help Abigail with the Chambers children. "They're falling asleep on their feet," she said.

"Thanks." Abigail cast a relieved glance at the older woman who seemed to have read her own thoughts. Scooping the groggy Tyler into her arms, she followed Granny and the two older Chambers children silently through the partying crowd. Flaming torches on poles lit the way back to their company of wagons.

The braying of donkeys and the lowing of cattle came from beyond the glow of several lanterns dotting the darkness. On one side of Abigail, as she led the children toward their wagon, the fiddlers squeaked and squawked their discordant music, and on the other, the animals called out into the night.

At the Chamberses' wagon, Granny Parker said good night to Abigail and the children and left for her own wagon. Chip climbed into a bed sack under the wagon without any urging from Abigail. The other two climbed inside the wagon and dressed for bed. As Tyler pulled an oversized nightshirt over his head, his face grew somber. "My mama promised to make me my very own nightshirt. This one was Chip's."

Tears threatened to spill from Abigail's eyes as she scooped the boy into her arms. "Chip's nightshirt looks very handsome on you."

Indignant at her display of emotions, he wriggled free of her grasp. "I'm not a baby, Miss Sherwood. I understand what happened to my mama. But one thing I don't understand."

"What's that, Tyler?" Abigail asked.

"I don't understand why God needed my mama more than me, do you?"

Abigail took his hands in hers. "I don't understand either. Maybe we can't understand such things because we're human and we think human thoughts, while God is God and He thinks God thoughts."

The boy scowled. "I reckon you're right, Miss Sherwood. But someday, I'm gonna ask Him, I am, face-to-face! Do you think He'll get mad at me if I do?"

Abigail shook her head. "Not at all." She knew Tyler's brother and sister were listening. She wondered what they thought of their little brother's wise question. "You know, Tyler. I have a lot of questions I want to ask Him too."

From the darkness came a soft, feminine voice and a sniffle, "Me too."

Chip, the eldest of the three, said nothing.

"Would you like it if I told you a story before you go to sleep?" Abigail asked the two younger children.

"Oh, yes. Would you?" Amy sniffed. "I feel a little lonely. I wish my father were here."

"Where is my father, Miss Sherwood?" Chip's voice was filled with anger. "I haven't seen him all day."

"I, ah, I imagine he needs time to be alone right now after losing your mother the way he did. He loved her very much." Her answer sounded hollow. She sensed that the children didn't accept it either.

"Well, he should have been here with Tyler. Tyler needed him!" Chip charged.

"When he returns, and I think he will soon," Abigail volunteered, "I think you should remind him of how much you need him right now."

"I don't need him!" Chip snapped. "He's the reason my mother died."

"No, Chip, no. That's not true." Abigail rose to her feet and climbed out of the wagon to where he lay.

"Yes it is. I heard them arguing in the night. You didn't, so you don't know!" When she reached out her hand to comfort him, the boy jerked free of her touch.

"Chip, parents argue. That's life. They often have differing opinions. You'll discover that as you get older. I am sure that your father and mother—"

The boy whirled about to face Abigail. "My mama didn't want to go to Oregon. She didn't want to leave Grandma Fletcher and Aunt Faith. Now, she'll never see them again, just like she said would happen."

Again Abigail tried to reach out to the boy; again the child pulled away. "Chip, your mother died from an appendicitis attack. That probably would have happened wherever she was at the time. Your father, your grandmother, your aunt, no one could have prevented it from occurring. It's not fair to blame your father for something he could do nothing about."

Chip yanked his blanket over his head. From inside the wagon, Abigail could hear Amy sobbing. Climbing back inside, she sat on the edge of Amy's bedding. "Cry, honey. Cry as much as you like. It's all right."

The little girl threw herself into the woman's arms. Tyler slipped from his bed and wrapped his little arms about Abigail's neck. As the children's tears subsided, Abigail brushed a wet curl from Amy's cheek. "I lost my papa. I remember how it feels. Would you like me to tell you about my father?"

The two children nodded and sniffed. Taking an extra handkerchief from her pocket, she dotted Amy's nose. Before she could get to Tyler's, he'd solved the problem with the sleeve of his nightgown.

She gathered the children, one in each arm. "My daddy was a preacher, not one of those fiery preachers who scare people into repenting with violent tales of hellfire. He was too gentle for that. The people of his church loved him, and they knew he loved them." She smiled at the memory. "When Billy Flagg got arrested for stealing a pint of ale from the local pub, my father went to him in his jail cell. And with tears, my daddy reminded the boy that he loved him and that God loved him so much that He sent His Son to die so that He would never again be separated from His precious children. 'And you're one of those children, Billy,' he said."

"Then what happened to Billy?" Amy asked.

"Well, I think he saw in my father a tiny glimpse of the love God had for him because he gave his heart to the Lord and promised to be baptized once he was released from jail."

Tyler leaned his head against Abigail's heart. "Then what happened?" he whispered.

"My father convinced the bar owner, Mr. McDougal, to drop the charges, and Billy was set free. Billy kept his word and was baptized. My daddy gave Billy the job of tending the grounds around the church. And a few years later, Billy went away to college to become a minister like my father."

"That's a nice story," Amy admitted. "I like stories with happy endings."

"I do too." Abigail placed a kiss on the girl's forehead. "And now, it is time for you to sleep. Tomorrow's going to be an exciting day. They're holding more shooting contests and several footraces you won't want to miss."

"Will you take us to the races?" Tyler asked as Abigail tucked him into bed.

"I certainly will. And maybe, if you're extra good, young man, I'll take you on a tour of the fort."

Abigail smiled at the gentle *"ooh"* that came from the little boy as he climbed beneath his rough cotton sheet. "If you need me," she said, "I'll be right outside. Good night now."

Thousands of stars twinkled in the sky above her as Abigail walked a few paces to her own wagons. To her right, she spotted a shooting star and shuddered even though she didn't believe the old wives' tale about shooting stars and death. She removed her bonnet and laid it on the top step of the Conestoga. She wiped the sweat from her neck and face with her handkerchief.

Slowly, Abigail removed the pins from the bun at the nape of her neck and slipped them into her skirt pocket. Drawing the braid over her shoulder, she freed her long brown tresses. She sighed as the cooling prairie breeze ruffled her hair about her face.

Abigail moistened her lips. The night air was hot and dry. Deciding she was thirsty, she strode to the barrel of drinking water near the front of the Conestoga wagon. Her steps were firm; her back was straight, a habit she'd developed as a child. She walked with the confidence and grace of royalty, or so she'd often been told. Men, however, found her stride intimidating, so she had also been told.

Upon reaching for the wooden communal dipper, Abigail suddenly felt a hard, callused hand clamp over hers. She gasped in surprise and whirled to face the hand's owner. When she did, he released her hand.

"Miss Sherwood." She recognized Evan Chambers's voice though his face was shrouded in shadows. "I owe you an apology."

"An apology?" She was surprised to discover that he was taller than she. Few men were. She'd never thought of the muscular carpenter as being that tall.

"Yes, for neglecting my responsibility to care for the children today. I am sorry to have presumed that someone would care for them in my absence. And I want to thank you for doing so."

"It was a pleasure, Mr. Chambers. You have three darling children, you know." A horse whinnied somewhere to the right of where they stood. The voices of two teamsters arguing near the makeshift corral rose in anger, and then subsided. "It isn't me who needs your apology, you know."

"I know." His face was silhouetted in the moonlight, successfully hiding the evidence of his pain.

"Where were you, if I may be so bold?" She expected him to say his whereabouts were none of her business.

"I took a long walk along the river." He jammed his hands in his pants' pockets. "I needed to be alone."

"I understand, Mr. Chambers." Her heart softened, remembering how empty she felt after her father's death. The victim of a heart attack, Abigail's father had died at his desk while working on his next sermon. Her mother had found him. "I've lost loved ones too."

A raspy edge entered the man's voice. "Yes, I suppose you have. Hasn't everyone?" He tried to clear it, but to no avail.

"Yes, I suppose so, but it never gets easy, does it?" she mused to herself as much as to the grieving husband.

They lapsed into a comfortable silence. Evan and Abigail stood side by side for several minutes. She folded her arms across her chest and listened to the night breezes play haunting melodies across the prairie. A lone coyote howled from some distant point. A night owl nesting down by the river hooted once, twice, and then fell silent.

"I suppose the children hate me for not being here for them." The pain in his voice brought tears to her eyes.

She studied the angles of his face, his aquiline nose, and his strong, determined chin. The brim of his hat hid the rest of his face and head in shadows. "No, Mr. Chambers, your children don't hate you. They're hurting from the loss of their mother just like you are. You need each other."

"I've dreamed of going to Oregon since I was a teenager after reading reports about the Lewis and Clarke expedition across the Northwest. Sara knew of my dream before she married me, you know. I thought it was her dream too." He bowed his head for several seconds before continuing, "Once I met a trapper returning to his family in Maine. He'd visited the Willamette Valley, on the west side of the Cascade Mountains. The man said there was a ribbon of black loam soil running along the Willamette River and stretching all the way to the foothills of the Cascades." The man gestured with one hand to show the graceful sweep of the fertile valley.

"With God's help and a lot of hard work, the trapper said, one could carve out a farm and raise a family in that valley." His voice broke when he mentioned the word *family*. Silence followed. Abigail could hear the strains of the English ballad "Black Is the Color of My True Love's Hair" being played on a harmonica by some teamster who'd drawn night duty down at the corral.

Evan's hand dropped hopelessly to his side. "But what does it matter now?"

Abigail had no pat little answers to give him. Her heart ached over the man's lost dream and lost wife. She assumed that most likely he'd head back to Maine with the first eastbound wagon train.

"Mr. Farnsworth conducted a nice service today for Sara," Evan said.

Abigail agreed. "God is the Source of our only strength on days like today," she mused.

"When it comes to God, I don't understand any more about His mind than a prairie dog popping out of a hole in the ground can comprehend the wagons rolling past and disrupting the little creature's quiet life."

She couldn't mistake the brittle edge in his voice. "Tyler said much the same thing when I put them to bed in your wagon tonight."

"He did?" The grieving man sounded surprised.

"He couldn't understand how God could need his mother more than he did."

Upon hearing his son's remark, Even Chambers cleared the emotion from his throat. "And what did you tell him?"

"I told him that presuming to understand God's mind with our human minds was impossible." Abigail gave a small chuckle. "Tyler said that when he gets to meet God face-to-face, he had a bunch of questions to ask."

The man laughed.

"You know, Mr. Chambers," Abigail ventured, "I believe that one day we will understand God's plan for each of us, your wife included. In the meantime, when we can't read His mind, we can trust His love for us."

A moment of silence followed before he replied. "*Hmm,* you're quite a talker, Miss Sherwood. Are you some kind of preacher?"

She could feel him studying her face. It made her nervous whenever she became the focus of a man's attention. She stared down at her feet.

"No, but I'm the daughter of a faithful man of the cloth."

"And did he approve of your leaving home to travel to Oregon?"

If only . . . She smiled at the thought of asking her father's permission to make the arduous journey. "He died several years ago."

"I'm sorry."

"So am I."

The voices of the camp's night watchmen interrupted their conversation. As the interlopers passed, Abigail and Evan silently stared into the dying embers of their campfire.

After several minutes, Evan heaved a deep, ragged sigh. "Thank you for listening, Miss Sherwood. And for watching over my children. I promise that tomorrow I'll be back, and I'll talk to them about what has happened."

The man respectfully touched the brim of his hat, and then disappeared back into the night seconds before Clarissa strode out of the darkness on the arm of Mr. Lassiter.

"Abigail, whatever are you doing awake? I thought you'd be asleep by now." Clarissa patted her escort's arm possessively. "Dear Mr. Lassiter has been so entertaining this evening. I don't know when I've enjoyed myself so much, hearing about his escapades in Queen Victoria's court." The woman gazed up lovingly into the man's decidedly uncomfortable face. "And tomorrow, he's promised to escort me to the fort to take care of a little business I have," Clarissa cooed, snuggling her body against his arm.

"Mrs. Darlington, remember, I said I'd try. I have business to take care of as well."

A pout formed on Clarissa's lips. She gazed up at him with pleading eyes. "But, Mr. Lassiter, I am counting on you."

Abigail imagined that the illustrious pint of energy known as Clarissa Darlington had used that pout since she was a wee girl on her father's knee. Nary a man seemed capable of resisting it. Only age threatened to loosen its power.

Untangling the dowager's hand from the crook of his arm, the man gave Clarissa a curt bow. "Madam, I will do my best."

The wealthy dowager clapped her hands like a delighted child. "Oh, you are such a dear, sweet man."

The debonair Mr. Lassiter quickly said, "Good night" and escaped.

With her male companion gone, Clarissa bade Abigail good night and climbed into the Conestoga to sleep.

Abigail sat down on a rock near the fire pit and stared into the glowing coals. *Today Council Grove, then on to Fort Kearny, Chimney Rock, Scotts Bluff, and Fort Laramie.* The names sounded so western and so wild to the English-born lass, sending shivers of excitement up and down her spine. As she drew her knees to her and rested her chin on her arms, Abigail wondered what it would be like if she, like Evan Chambers, had to abandon her dreams and return to the East. She smiled to herself and thanked God for her good fortune.

CHAPTER NINE

LIFE'S CHANGING TIDES

WHEN ABIGAIL FINALLY CRAWLED BETWEEN the cotton sheets on a pallet mattress to sleep, she had no idea of the decisions being made by others that would affect her destiny. At daybreak she awoke with sweat trickling down the side of her face. The temperatures had remained high throughout the night. The next thing she felt was Tyler tugging at her arm.

"Miss Sherwood, Miss Sherwood, I need to go—" Agony filled the boy's eyes as he stared down at a puddle growing around his bare feet. "Oops! I'm sorry," he whispered, his face wreathed with agony. "I couldn't find the chamber pot. I tried to wait."

"I'm sure you did, honey." Abigail placed a reassuring kiss on the child's forehead. "I'll clean it up while you hop onto your bed, all right?"

She dried the floor, slipped on her pink cotton plissé robe, and hurried toward Clarissa's Conestoga for a change of clothing. When she opened the canvas, the first thing she noticed was that Nell's bed hadn't been slept in. Surprised, Abigail glanced toward Clarissa's bed. While it had been occupied during the night, it was now empty as well. *Curious,* she thought as she climbed up the steps. Dressing as quickly as possible, she returned to the Chamberses' wagon where she'd left the soiled cloth she'd used to clean the floor draped over a rear wheel. After rinsing out the cloth with clean water, she placed it on the wagon tongue to dry.

She paused to take in the beauty of the eastern sky. Streaks of sunlight bathed the immense prairie with hues of gold. She could hear her neighbors. In a nearby wagon a man snorted and coughed. Another mumbled a string of curses. *Probably hung over from too much partying,* she surmised.

Her hair still hanging loose about her shoulders, Abigail stretched and yawned. Getting to bed after midnight was something she'd seldom done. Also, she felt that familiar stiffness in her muscles from driving the carriage. As trained as the teams of horse were, they took her constant attention. With her hands on her hips, she twisted her body from one side to the other several times to loosen the pesky knots that had formed in her back muscles.

The campfire Winters had built the night before in front of the Conestoga lay ready to be lit. She decided to start the morning coffee. After locating a match in the kitchen supply trunk, she struck it against the wagon hub and tossed it into the stack of wood. She strode to the water barrel, not waiting until the fire took, for she trusted Winters's fire-building abilities. She dipped water from the barrel into the cast-iron kettle. After placing the kettle on the iron over the fledgling fire, she straightened and glanced about the area.

No one stirred at either of her neighbors' wagons, including the Chamberses' wagon. She waved to Mrs. Simmons, who was stacking wood for her morning fire three wagons down the line. The two women exchanged greetings. Before long Tyler poked his head out of the Chamberses' wagon. "Can I get up now?" he asked.

"Of course you may. Get dressed and come and help me make our breakfast porridge."

The boy ducked back inside the wagon. Their voices must have awakened Chip; for seconds later, the older boy crawled out from under their wagon and mumbled something about going to see Mr. John. He disappeared behind the wagon. Fully dressed, Tyler and Amy tumbled out of their wagon, ready for another day. That's when Abigail remembered she hadn't pinned up her hair. "Amy, would you please measure out two cups of oatmeal into the medium-sized, black pot in the trunk while I finish getting dressed?"

"Yes, ma'am." The girl seemed delighted to be given a grown-up job.

Abigail hurried to the Conestoga, climbed the ladder, and drew the canvas closed behind her. Her silver-handled brush and matching mirror lay on top of her clothing inside her footlocker. After brushing out the snarls from her tresses, she quickly wound her hair into a knot and pinned it in place at the nape of her neck. As she left the wagon, a few strands of hair fell across her eyes. She blew them away from her face.

The girl stood with the iron pot in hand beside the fire, waiting for further instructions. Abigail took the heavy pot from the child's hands and strode to the water barrel where she added several ladles full of water to the mixture.

"Next, we toss in a dash of salt," Abigail instructed. The two children watched her every move. "And a piece of cinnamon stick. There. Now let's cook it, shall we?"

The children followed her to the fire and watched as she hooked the pot on the fire grate. The water for the coffee boiled first. Since no one was waiting for coffee, Abigail ran to the food trunk and located a package of cocoa she'd packed before leaving Boston. After a rough day like the previous one, hot cocoa would help soothe the children's exhausted nerves.

Within minutes, the trio was perched on a rock beside the fire, drinking their hot cocoa. Even Chip wandered back into the camp when he smelled the sweet aroma of chocolate. One of Clarissa's teamsters came by with a bucket of fresh milk for their hot, steamy oatmeal.

They'd barely washed and dried their breakfast dishes when Clarissa and Winters arrived at the wagon, followed by a distraught Mr. Farnsworth. Abigail wondered where they'd been so early in the morning.

"Where's Nell?" the woman demanded. "Is she still in bed?"

Abigail gulped. "Uh, no, ma'am."

"Then where is she, pray tell! Performing her morning toilet?"

"I-I-I don't know, ma'am. She didn't come home last night." Abigail wished the ground would open up and swallow her.

"Didn't come home? Why, that slut!" Clarissa whirled about to face the mild-mannered Winters. "Find her immediately and fire her!"

"Are you sure?" the butler asked in the gentlest of tones.

"Of course I'm sure. Do you question my judgment?" Anger oozed from the woman's pores.

"Madam, if I may be so bold as to suggest—"

Mrs. Darlington straightened her shoulders and glared down her nose. "Winters, must I remind you of your station in life?"

The man reddened. "No, ma'am."

"Then do as I say without questioning me. You know how I hate to be second-guessed!" The woman whipped about to face the strangely silent Mr. Farnsworth. "As for you, I have made up my mind, Mr. Farnsworth. Your ministry in Oregon is going to have to do without the likes of me!"

Abigail's eyes widened in surprise. *What is going on?*

"I am not going one step farther with you and your—your fiancée! To think a man of God would, would . . ." The woman left the end of her thought unspoken.

What is happening? Abigail looked from Clarissa to the missionary, and then back again. Whatever had happened since the previous night at the party? Dismissing Mr. Farnsworth with a flick of her wrist, Clarissa whirled to face Abigail. "I want you to pack up our belongings. I've hired a guide to take us back to Independence, where we'll board a riverboat for Boston."

Abigail stared in amazement. She didn't know what to say.

"Are you going to betray me, too, young lady?" She whirled about and stormed toward the Conestoga. "What is this world coming to when the lower class wantonly ignores the commands of the wealthy?"

Abigail turned slowly toward the three stunned children.

Amy rushed to Abigail and wrapped her arms about the woman's hips. "Are you leaving us, Miss Sherwood? Are you leaving us like Mrs. Darlington said?"

"I don't know." What else could she say? Her mind was in turmoil. *Go back to Boston? Abandon my dream? Is Clarissa serious? Or will she change her mind as quickly as she changes her moods?* Abigail didn't know.

Like a woman in a trance, she moved about the camp. To call the place rustic would be a compliment to be sure. Even with all the added little conveniences Clarissa had insisted upon, life on the trail was rough. It would be nice to have clean fingernails again, to be able to soak her body in a soothing bath of baking soda and lemon verbena oils. She was lost in her quandary when Evan Chambers rounded the corner of the Conestoga.

"Daddy! Daddy!" The two younger children shouted and ran to their father's outstretched arms. While Chip held back, he couldn't hide the look of relief on his face to see his father once more.

Abigail forgot her own pain as she watched the touching reunion.

"Daddy!" Tyler freed himself of his father's arms and planted his hands on his hips. "We have a lot to talk about."

Evan tousled the boy's tangled thatch of blond hair, so like his own. "Yes, son, we surely do."

"Have you eaten, Mr. Chambers?" Abigail asked. "I'm brewing a pot of hot coffee as we speak."

"Oh, thank you, but I've been bunking with the teamsters, and they keep me well fed." The man grinned. In his eyes, Abigail could see that the teamsters also gave him the solitude he needed. "Chip, I need you to grab my cigar box of important papers from under the driver's seat and bring them to me if you will." Turning to Abigail, he added, "I need to go to army headquarters to ask about the logistics of returning to Independence." The sadness in his eyes broke the woman's heart. He'd revealed so much about himself the night before in the moonlight.

"I'm so sorry, Mr. Chambers." She glanced down at her hands for a moment. "It seems we may be traveling companions once again, however. My employer announced this morning that she is abandoning the wagon train and returning to Boston." A tear trickled unbidden down the side of Abigail's face.

The grieving man reached out as if to brush away her tear but thought better of doing so. "I'm sorry, Miss Sherwood. I know how disappointed you must feel."

She sniffed, her voice catching as she spoke, "Yes, I know you do."

"Oh, Miss Sherwood," Amy cried in delight. "We'll be almost neighbors, with us living in Maine and you in Massachusetts. Why my grammy took me to Boston for my birthday last year."

Abigail knelt down and hugged the little girl. "You're right. We'll almost be neighbors."

When she rose to her feet, Evan Chambers took her hand in his. "I hope I am not being forward, but you have been so kind to care for my children during my wife's illness and since her death. I can never thank you enough."

"I didn't do it alone. Mrs. Darlington helped. So did Granny Parker and Nell. If Clarissa hadn't volunteered for the children . . ." His gaze distracted her. "If, if Clarissa, er, Mrs. Darlington hadn't . . ." For the first time she noticed the warmth in his gray-blue eyes and the smattering of freckles across his nose, just like Amy's.

Disgusted with herself for being attracted to any man's eyes, let alone this man, Abigail snatched her hand from his. "Would you like that cup of coffee or not, Mr. Chambers?"

"No, the children and I need to be going. I want to get to the headquarters before the line forms. Thanks again for everything. I'm sure we'll be seeing more of each other later."

Poised beside the fire pit, she listened to their footsteps and voices grow dimmer. She closed her eyes and counted to ten as she always did when her life threatened to spin out of her control.

"He has a thing for you, Miss Sherwood," a decidedly masculine voice with a clipped British accent called from the next campsite. Abigail turned to see Mr. Lassiter ambling toward her.

Anger rose inside her. "Mr. Lassiter! Your remark was ill timed and out of place. The man just buried his wife, remember?"

A crooked grin formed on the man's lips as he swaggered to where she stood. "He's still a man, and he needs a good woman to help him raise those children."

"Mr. Lassiter, for a man of refinement and class, you are displaying an odious lack of good taste!" As she reached for her skirts to whip away from him, he grabbed her forearm. She tried to pull free, but he refused to release her.

"I heard what Clarissa, er, Mrs. Darlington said about returning to Boston. I fear I might be partly to blame." A scowl on his forehead deepened.

"You?" Abigail was disgusted. Did his ego ever stop?

"Yes, last night we ran into Mr. Farnsworth and his fiancée. She's the general's daughter here in Council Grove. They'd met during his last visit to the fort on his way east. They'd been waiting to marry until he returned from his East Coast tour to raise money for the expedition."

Abigail couldn't have been more surprised. The way Mr. Farnsworth acted around the wealthy dowagers of Boston, especially Mrs. Darlington, Abigail would never have guessed the man had a fiancée somewhere in the West. "And how does that involve you, sir?"

Mr. Lassiter swallowed hard, like a schoolboy repenting for breaking a school window. "Well, toward the end of the evening when Mr. Farnsworth introduced his fiancée to Clarissa and me, I made a smart remark. I equated marriage to breaking the spirit of a wild horse."

"And?"

"And, I guess I said too much, especially about my own aversion to the holy state. I knew something was wrong when I escorted her back to the Conestoga."

Abigail couldn't believe the man's arrogance. "So between Mr. Farnsworth's engagement and your aversion to marriage, you think Clarissa decided to abandon the journey and return east?"

The man pushed the rim of his hat back from his face. "Well, it seems that might be the case. Of course, many travelers change their minds by the time they reach Council Grove, for numerous reasons. It's not unusual."

"I don't know what to say!" She folded her arms tightly across her bodice and set her toes to tapping. "Mr. Lassiter, I can assure you that you are terribly wrong about Clarissa. Whatever reason Mrs. Darlington has for returning to Boston it has nothing to do with your attitudes regarding marriage nor with Mr. Farnsworth's pending nuptials!"

The man's face reddened. "Er, you could be right. Excuse me if I offended you." He tipped his hat respectfully and strode past the Conestoga, stopping long enough to say Good morning to Clarissa, who was emerging from the wagon. She'd been crying.

Clarissa hurried to Abigail's side. "Thank you, for defending me. I heard everything. I appreciate your loyalty."

"Well, I couldn't have that man thinking that you would abandon your . . ." Her voice dropped as she read the message in her employer's eyes.

"My returning to Boston isn't only because of Mr. Farnsworth and Mr. Lassiter. I've been considering heading back ever since we left Independence."

Abigail recalled the woman's constant train of complaints. She should have guessed.

"Last night, I asked myself why I was putting up with the discomfort and inconvenience of the trail when I could be entertaining presidents and princes in my parlor back in Boston." Clarissa looked to Abigail for understanding.

Abigail frowned. "Before we left Boston you knew the trip would be rough at times."

Tears filled the dowager's eyes. "Yes, I know. I'm a foolish old woman. I admit it. I don't know why I thought Mr. Farnsworth was interested in me for more than my money." Clarissa cast about for words to say. "How I can be so astute in making money and so stupid in understanding men? Every man I know, including my dear departed husband, took advantage of me!" She sniffed into the handkerchief clutched in her fist.

"That's not completely true, you know," Abigail offered, fearful that she would receive a tongue-lashing for her impudence.

"What do you know about it?" the woman snapped.

"What about Winters? You sent him to Pennsylvania to purchase the most comfortable and elegant coach and the finest of Conestoga wagons. He endured blizzards and torrential rainstorms to prepare for your arrival in Independence. Anyone can see the man adores you."

A look of horror filled Clarissa's flushed face. "Abigail! Winters is hardly a suitable suitor; he's my butler! I can't believe that you, of all people, do not understand that. The idea—me and my butler! How Boston's society would laugh!"

Abigail couldn't hide her grin. "Do you really care what a bunch of dyspeptic old prunes thinks of your choice in men? He's a good man, and loyal, and he loves you. If you weren't so blind, you would have seen it for yourself."

Clarissa squeezed her eyes closed and shook her head several times. "Winters? In love with me? No, no, no!" She paced several feet away from Abigail, then back. "Winters?"

"You called, madam?" Abigail and Clarissa whirled about in surprise to see the topic of their conversation entering the campsite with Nell O'Grady in tow and an embarrassed army lieutenant following close behind. "I found Miss O'Grady, ma'am. It seems she up and married this young soldier last night."

"Married?" Clarissa's and Abigail's eyebrows shot upward in surprise.

"Yes, isn't it romantic?" Nell broke free of the butler's grasp and snuggled under the protective arm of the lieutenant. "You are looking at Mr. and Mrs. Benjamin Edward Young III. Benjy is a civil engineer with the United States Army. He's a surveyor." A cloud of uncertainty brushed across her brow. She turned to the uncomfortable lieutenant. "Sorry, muffin, but what is a surveyor?"

Before he could answer, she cast a quick glance toward Clarissa. "Of course, I'll be staying here at the fort with Benjy, Mrs. Darlington. I am sorry, but what could I do? It was love at first sight." The young woman giggled and blushed.

"Of all the—" Clarissa shot a disturbed glance toward Winters. She flailed her arms helplessly in the air. "Do something!"

"What would you have me do, madam?" The butler looked more than a little perturbed. "Kidnap Miss O'Grady and have the entire United States Army in pursuit?"

"Winters!" Clarissa gasped in surprise at the man's vehemence. "Whatever is the matter with you? You've never spoken to me in such . . . such impudent tones." The woman looked as if she might burst into tears at any moment.

The butler straightened his shoulders, adding a good four inches to his height. His silvery mane ruffled defiantly in the breeze. "Not insulting, madam, just honest. Not every problem in life can be solved by the flick of your wrist or your pocketbook."

"B-B-But . . ." Words failed the stunned socialite. Her right hand fluttered against the bodice of her pink-and-white dimity dress.

Suddenly, Winters seemed to remember his post. He bowed his head. "I'm sorry, madam. I should not have—"

"No!" A wicked grin teased at one corner of Clarissa's rosy lips. It was like she was seeing the man behind the butler's garb for the first time. "I never dreamed you had such fire in you."

Surprise flooded Winters's face. He straightened his shoulders once more and tried to reclaim his professional demeanor.

Confused, Abigail observed the unfolding drama. Less than an hour ago her world was safe, predictable, and, in no time at all, it had gone berserk. "What is going on here?" Even as she threw her hands into the air, she knew she was overreacting. "Have you all gone mad? I can't take much more of this!"

Abigail stormed into the Conestoga and closed the canvas flap behind her. Her mind was in turmoil. She fought back a wave of tears. *Doesn't anyone realize, as they callously arrange and rearrange their own lives, that the last thing I want to do is return to Boston?* She'd tasted freedom for the first time in her life, and she loved it. She trembled with emotion as she fell to her knees.

"It isn't fair, Lord. To be so close and have it snatched from me," she cried. "I don't want to go back to my sister's house, to not having a life of my own." She pounded her fist on the mattress as she had at the age of ten. "Please, please don't make me." Her tears moistened her embroidered sheet.

In the midst of her sobbing, the memory of a rainy English afternoon surfaced in her mind, an afternoon when Abigail was angry at her mother—for what, she didn't remember. As always, whenever the girl was upset, she ran to her bedroom, threw herself on the bed, and cried and kicked her feet. This afternoon her father, who seldom interfered in the raising of the two girls, entered her room. Abigail wasn't immediately aware he was there until he placed his hand on her heaving shoulder.

"Little one," he said, "I know you're angry with your mother and disappointed."

"But Papa, it's so unfair!" Abigail protested. "Can't you talk to her and change her mind?"

"Perhaps I could, sweetheart, but I'm not sure that would be the best thing for you in the long run." He sat down on the edge of the bed while Abigail turned over to face him. Lovingly, he stroked the side of her tear-stained face. "As a child, you are learning important lessons in trust and obedience every day, by submitting your will to that of your mama and papa. Someday Mama and I won't be around to tell you what to do. You will need to turn to your heavenly Father for guidance and wisdom. And if you don't learn how to submit your will to God's appointed caretakers as a child, you won't know how to obey your heavenly Father as an adult. And that can get you into all kinds of trouble as an adult."

Alone in the privacy of the luxuriously appointed Conestoga wagon, which had become her home for the past two weeks, Abigail suddenly felt foolish. She could remember being ten years old and spitting out her anger at her mother for some real or imagined insult. Hadn't she learned anything in the interim? Yes, she wanted to continue on to Oregon, but no, she didn't want to go in a way other than what God wanted.

Abigail sat up and blew her nose. She knew that if she returned to Chelsea she'd never again break free from her role as governess and cook for her sister's family. She knew that the greatest thrill of her life would be nothing more than joining a suffrage protest in the streets of Boston.

"Is that what You have for me?" Yet as she prayed the words of defiance, she knew God would never lead her wrongly. Back and forth, her emotions battled her logic, first one side winning, and then the other.

Almost without thinking, she opened her Bible to a text she'd underlined years ago as a child. She didn't have to read the words; she'd memorized them well. " 'In all thy ways acknowledge him and he shall direct thy paths.' "

Acknowledging Him when things were going her way had always been easy, but acknowledging her Lord when things weren't going to her liking? She knew that's what faith was all about. In her mind Abigail saw her father's gentle eyes looking at her with tender compassion. It was as if he were saying, "Trust the Father, child. Trust the Father."

Her heart softened; her belligerence melted. Tears of humble repentance replaced her tears of resentment as she fell to her knees and bowed her head. *Oh, dear Father, forgive my childish behavior. Will I ever really learn to trust You? You know I want to do Your will no matter what, but sometimes the stubborn little girl inside of me gets in the way.* She dabbed at her nose with her linen handkerchief. *I submit, Father, to You. Fill me with Your joy, despite my disappointment. Thank You for keeping me safe in Your hands. I promise to rejoice in this day no matter what. Amen.*

As she arose to her feet, she recited the psalm that had seen her through her worst storms, " 'This is the day which the LORD hath made; we will rejoice and be glad in it.' "

CHAPTER TEN

TOO MANY CHANGES

ABIGAIL YAWNED AND SLOWLY OPENED HER eyes. *Where am I?* She glanced about the wagon. The heat from the midday sun turned the canvas-topped wagon into a furnace. The growl in her stomach reminded her that several hours had passed since breakfast. After winning her spiritual battle, she'd fallen asleep on the plump, down-filled mattress she'd come to appreciate each night after miles of driving the carriage.

The aroma of meals cooking over open fires wafted into the wagon, meals being cooked over campfires other than her own. With Nell gone, Abigail realized meal planning and preparation would be her responsibility alone. She rose to her feet and straightened the wrinkles out of her green batiste dress. After brushing a bevy of stray tendrils from her forehead, she climbed out of the wagon into the deserted campsite.

Where to begin? She glanced about the area. The wood had been stacked and was ready to light. "Bless you, Winters," she mumbled to the air. Grabbing a couple of matches from the leather holder Clarissa kept nearby, Abigail crossed the short distance to the fire pit and knelt down to light the fire.

Would Clarissa and Winters return to the Conestoga in time for a noon meal? Would the Chambers children be hungry as well? What about Mr. Chambers? She had no idea what or how much food to prepare. *Oh well,* she thought, *I've dealt with that problem before at Rebecca's place.*

Two of the children who attended her nightly story hour walked by the Darlington campsite with their father. They called and waved to her.

She returned the greeting and then focused on lighting the campfire. When the fire didn't light after three matches, Abigail rose to her feet. *Who wants a hot meal on a scorching day like this anyway? Maybe a honey sandwich will suffice.*

Returning to the pantry area, she sliced a loaf of whole wheat bread Clarissa had bought from an Osage squaw, and then slathered a thick layer of honey on two of the slices. She'd barely licked a dab of honey from her fingers when she saw Evan Chambers and his children approaching.

"Miss Sherwood! Miss Sherwood!" Tyler ran to her. Abigail bent down to the little boy's height. "What is it, Tyler?"

"Guess what? We're going to Oregon! Isn't that great? We're going to Oregon! You are too!" The boy bounced from one foot to the other. "Tell her, Daddy. Tell her!"

Abigail glanced up at the grinning man and his two other equally delighted children. "What is this all about?"

"I'm sorry, I'm afraid Tyler couldn't rein in his excitement." The man eyed her honey sandwich. "*Mmm,* that looks good. Do you have an extra? The children are starving."

"Yes, yes, of course." She waved her hand in the air. "Now what is this all about?"

"Let's step over here." Evan gestured toward the front end of the Conestoga.

She handed the butter knife to Amy. "Help yourselves. I'll be right back."

"We just came from the fort's headquarters," Evan explained. "The general called a meeting of all those travelers intending to return to Independence. When the general learned that Mrs. Darlington was leaving the train, he offered to pay her to take his ailing wife to a doctor in Independence."

"And what, pray tell, does this have to do with me?" Abigail asked.

"Hold your horses, woman, I'm getting to that," Evan chuckled. "You're as impatient as my young son, Miss Sherwood."

Abigail folded her hands across her chest, tapping her fingers on her upper arms.

He laughed and continued, "Your employer said she'd be glad to help the general's wife if the general could find a way for her disappointed traveling companion, that's you, to continue on to Oregon."

Suddenly, the man had Abigail's full attention.

"This is what the general worked out. Since I need a nanny to care for the children and you need a ride west—"

Abigail's eyebrows shot up in surprise. An unmarried woman to travel alone with a widower and his three children? "Unacceptable! Totally unacceptable!"

"Whoa there!" Evan raised his hands in defense. "I'm not finished. You really are a testy one, Miss Sherwood."

She clicked her tongue in mild irritation. "Forgive me. Please go on. I'm listening."

"Perhaps I should reconsider . . ." he teased.

She leveled her most malevolent gaze at the man. "Mr. Chambers, are you always so odious or is this a special occasion?"

Evan chuckled aloud. "I like a woman with spunk. I think we're going to get along just fine."

She whistled her irritation through her teeth. "As of this moment, you and I are not doing anything together, Mr. Chambers."

"All right, perhaps I've teased enough, but I couldn't help it. You are so easy to bait."

"Bait? I don't understand." Her brow knitted with concern.

"Bait, you know, like a fish. You always jump at the bait." Evan Chambers chuckled at his perceived observation. "But, seriously, Miss Sherwood, I have no intention to compromise your reputation. It was Granny Parker who came up with the solution." A shock of blond hair popped out from under Evan's wide-brimmed hat when he pushed it to the back of his head. The grin on his face made him look ten years younger than he'd looked the previous day.

"You see, Granny's son, Perry, is turning back, too, but the feisty old lady has no intention of doing the same. So when she heard our predicament, she suggested she chaperone us." He blushed. "Er, you know, make the arrangement socially acceptable, in exchange for her son traveling with the Darlington entourage as far as St. Louis. You will care for my children by day and sleep in her wagon at night for obvious reasons." He cleared his throat before continuing, "Also, Granny has agreed to help you with the cooking and the other housekeeping chores. And in return,

I'll act as her protector as well as help her hired man with the driving and caring for her animals. She has two cows as well as her team of oxen."

Abigail was stunned. She struggled to process all the man had said. One minute she was graciously returning to Massachusetts, and the next following her dream to Oregon. A disturbing thought hit her.

"Excuse me, but how dare you, you and all the rest, include me in this outrageous plan without consulting me first!"

"That's what I'm doing right now. You weren't at the meeting, Miss Sherwood. We had to make immediate decisions." His face reddened. "I'm sorry. I'm sure I can undo—"

"No! Wait! I'm being foolish. Of course, I want to go. And I know I should be grateful." It was Abigail's turn to blush. Everything was moving too fast. "Please, give me time to absorb this." Her sister's fateful lawn party flashed though her mind. "The first and only time I've ever reacted on instinct is what got me where I am today." She laughed nervously.

Chambers scratched the back of his neck. "Well, miss, there's not much time to think about it, so I understand. The eastbound wagon train is breaking camp in the morning. And the general is waiting for your answer as we speak. The entire plan is hinged on your decision."

The trail of conditions seemed as convoluted as an English maze to the confused young woman. "What happens when we arrive in Oregon? I'm not independently wealthy, you know. Mrs. Darlington agreed to—" Abigail was miffed by her unladylike attitude, but the barbs kept coming unbidden from her mouth.

"Mrs. Darlington said that you have a sizeable sum coming to you for your services thus far, which she is ready to pay. And I will agree to build your cabin in the Willamette Valley before I build my own, if that is your desire. And Granny is more than eager to have you live with her for a while once we're west of the Cascades. She plans to settle in the Fort Vancouver area."

Abigail pinched the bridge of her nose to relieve a pain growing behind her eyes. "You seem to have an answer for everything."

"Not everything, Miss Sherwood. There is one detail I want to be sure you understand. You may ingratiate yourself with my children—that's fine. I would want you to love them and to have them love you in return, but understand, I've no intention of remarrying—not now, not ever. Our arrangement is temporary. I think it's important we establish this ground rule."

Abigail flushed uncomfortably. That the man would think she'd have designs on him embarrassed her. "Mr. Chambers, nothing pleases me more than to hear that. I do not see myself forming a romantic attachment with you or any other gentleman in the near future. With that understood, perhaps we can come to an agreement after all."

Detecting her ire, he fumbled over his words trying to redeem himself. "I didn't mean that you aren't a-a-a delightful and desirable—"

"Oh, please, Mr. Chambers, don't! I have a mirror. While I might be described as comely, I would not attach any more grandiose descriptions to my person. You have voiced your condition to this arrangement. Mine is that we take a vow of honesty with one another, no silly games. If you have something to say to me, say it, and I will do the same."

He pursed his lips thoughtfully. She glanced over his shoulder at nothing in particular but could feel him studying the determined set of her mouth and the petulant tilt of her chin. Returning his gaze, she arched one eyebrow. *Study me well, sir, for I won't be tapioca pudding for anyone.*

His gaze shifted to the children at the other end of the Conestoga, licking honey from their sticky fingers. "After I clean up my children's faces and hands, would you be so kind as to return with me to the general's office to sign an agreement to the arrangements we stipulated?"

"Allow me to fetch my bonnet, sir." She turned and climbed the steps into the Conestoga.

"Evan!" the man called, as she disappeared behind the canvas flap at the back of the wagon. "Call me Evan, and I will call you by your given name as well, if that's all right with you. There are many miles between Council Grove and the Willamette Valley."

Inside the wagon, Abigail dropped on to the foot of the closest mattress, which happened to be Clarissa's. *What are you doing?* she asked herself. *Do you know what you're doing?*

Finding her lightest weight sunbonnet, a pastel-blue cotton sprinkled with daisies, her favorite flower, she placed it on her head and tied the matching ribbons beneath her chin. A pesky fly buzzed her nose. Making a last-minute check in the mirror, she was surprised to discover color filling her cheeks. She smiled and giggled at her reflection. "Well, Miss Sherwood, it looks like you are truly heading for Oregon! Thank You, Jesus."

By the time Abigail emerged from the wagon, the children's faces and hands were clean. She tried not to show her surprise when she found that the mess they'd made of the cutting board was gone and the food was stowed in the food bin, safely away from ants.

From the moment Abigail fell into step beside Mr. Evan Chambers, the tempo of her life accelerated from confused to frantic. The next morning as she said Goodbye to a tearful Clarissa Darlington and Winters, now standing at the dowager's side instead of five steps behind her, Abigail realized nothing in her life would ever be the same.

Leaving Boston with Clarissa in all her luxury and finery had indeed been a giant step for Abigail, but to set out in the American wilderness with total strangers—an old woman, a widower, and his three children? Was she being a fool?

Throughout the night, she'd questioned her decision. She'd prayed in the darkness of the Conestoga, "Father God, I need to know that You are in this decision. In all my ways, I will acknowledge You, but I need Your peace." Soon after she said, "Amen," she fell asleep. In the morning, Abigail awakened, filled with an engulfing peace. She was certain that, as ridiculous as it may seem, she was following the will of God.

Before heading east, Clarissa slipped five extra gold double eagles into Abigail's dress pocket. "This is what I would have paid you if I'd continued on to Oregon. Since I was the one to wash out, I want to fulfill my promise. God be with you."

"Thank you." Tears filled Abigail's eyes as the wealthy dowager hugged her. "Give my love to Rebecca," Abigail said. "Tell her I'll write as soon as I get settled."

"I will." Clarissa drew Abigail's face close. "And thank you for helping me see Winters through new eyes. He is a delightful, funny man. Did you know that?"

Abigail shot a surprised look at the dour-faced butler as he waited by the carriage door to assist Clarissa on board. The general was inside the carriage, kissing his wife goodbye.

A surge of fear welled up inside Abigail as the entourage, led by the sleek and shiny black Darlington brougham, headed east. She watched until the caravan became a black dot on the horizon. She felt the wildest urge to run screaming after them. Instead, she turned to speak to the general and was surprised to find herself standing alone outside the fort. *Now what?* she thought. *Where do I go from here?*

The trunks containing her personal items had been delivered to Granny

Parker's wagon, a converted farm wagon like most of the other vehicles in the train. Gone were the extra niceties Clarissa had installed, including the porcelain water basin mounted on the wall of the wagon. When one removed the stopper in the bottom of the bowl, the water ran into a holding tank beneath the wagon to be disposed of at a later time.

The trunk containing her herbs and household utensils and her art supplies had been loaded onto the Chamberses' wagon, along with extra food supplies donated by Clarissa Darlington.

Being divided between the two households made Abigail feel unattached to either. " 'I am with you alway, even unto the ends of the world' " was the promise she claimed as she hunted for a familiar face.

The familiar face she found was that of Mr. Lassiter. "Well, now, I hear you're a part of the Chamberses' camp. Does that mean there is a more personal agreement between you and the grieving widower?"

She glared at the man. "I beg your pardon? What does that mean?"

"Please, if I am wrong, I apologize." The man touched the brim of his hat in respect. "But it would come as no surprise for Chambers to find a replacement for his late wife in more ways than the care and feeding of his brood."

"I resent your implication, Mr. Lassiter. I am disappointed. I thought you were much more of a gentleman than that."

"I'm sorry, I—"

"Yes, I will be caring for the Chambers children, but I am officially traveling with Granny Parker, not that I should need to explain any of my actions to you." With a huff, she headed for Granny's wagon.

The first thing I want to do is find out Granny's first name, Abigail told herself as she scuffed through the dust. *Either I call her by her given name or I'll call her Mrs. Parker. This "Granny" stuff is hardly a dignified title for such a nice lady.*

* * * * *

Two days later, Abigail and the children watched the wagons rolling southward leave Council Grove for Santa Fe and California. Granny, who insisted on being called Granny, and Abigail took time to inventory the supplies in both their wagons. They compiled a shopping list for Evan. Upon receiving it, the man scratched the back of his neck and clicked one side of his mouth. "Are you sure this is all you need, ladies?"

Abigail bristled at the sarcastic tone. Granny touched·her arm gently. "I'm sure we can add more if you're concerned about quantities, Evan." Evan and Granny were already on easy terms, while Abigail still stumbled over using the man's given name.

The man gave the older woman a gentle smirk. "Well, we wouldn't want to run out of—what is this? Pepper sauce—miles from the closest general store, now would we?"

Granny grunted. "You'll be glad for pepper sauce when we are dining on some gamey piece of prairie dog or some other wiry creature."

Evan rolled his eyes toward the sky while Abigail gagged at the thought. Abigail didn't understand either of them. Their dry wit often went beyond her comprehension, but there was no missing the element of respect between them. She smiled. If Granny were thirty years younger, the two would make a formidable couple.

The news that the "story lady" was staying with the wagon train spread through the campground. The children had missed their nightly sessions. So had their parents. The adults used the time the children were occupied to finish their preparations for the next leg of their journey.

Elections for company leader were conducted that evening during the story hour. While women couldn't vote, except for Granny since she had no man to represent her, the wives wanted to attend the meeting in order to influence their husbands' votes. Evan was considered by the company to be Abigail's employer; thus, he voted for her.

Mr. Englebert "Hawk" Lassiter was chosen to be the company's wagon master. Evan Chambers was voted to be his second in command. When Evan declined, Randall White received the most votes.

Mr. Lassiter introduced Sergeant Brumby, the army guide recommended by the fort's general. The men, along with Granny, chipped in equal shares toward the man's two hundred dollar fee.

By the time Abigail tucked the three Chambers children into their beds and kissed Tyler good night, it had been decided that the wagons would leave Council Grove at dawn. Abigail broke camp for the Chambers, then hurried to help Granny. She knew the men were checking the teams in the corral to be certain they were trail ready.

"I don't understand it," Granny fussed. "Why Evan wouldn't agree to be Mr. Lassiter's assistant, I can't figure."

"Maybe he was disappointed at not being chosen to be the head wagon master," Abigail suggested, though even as she said it, she knew Evan wasn't like that.

"Don't be ridiculous." Granny folded the canvas tarp she'd tacked to the side of her wagon each evening for shade. "You know Evan better than that, or at least, I hope you do."

Abigail, with hands planted on her hips, surveyed the vacant campground. Only the fire pit and the iron grate had been left standing for the morning coffee. "If you don't need me any longer, I'll check on the children before I turn in."

Granny nodded and climbed the short ladder into her wagon. "I'll be asleep when you return."

"I'll try not to awaken you," Abigail called over her shoulder, as she started for the Chamberses' wagon.

"Honey," the older woman replied, "you couldn't wake me tonight if you banged a Chinese gong next to my pillow. I'm exhausted."

Abigail had to admit that she, too, was exhausted, but she knew she wouldn't sleep until she was certain the children were safe and Evan had returned to the wagon. Tomorrow wouldn't be a problem since they'd arranged to have the Parker wagon follow the Chambers vehicle midway in the lineup. The only time their wagons would be separated would be when it was Granny's turn to be at the front of the line. And that wouldn't happen for several days.

One by one, the oil lanterns across the campgrounds flickered and went out until the only man-made lights shining were the dimly lit torches at the gates of the fort. The world was strangely quiet. Gone were the partiers, the gamblers, and the ladies of the night. Gone were the Indians selling beaded jewelry, deerskin trousers, and herbal potions. Only travelers heading for Oregon and the army personnel at the fort were left, and both groups would have a busy day on the morrow.

Silently, she slipped into the wagon. As her eyes adjusted to the darkness, she counted faces—one, two, three. Chip's feet had become uncovered. She tucked the blankets around them. She picked up Amy's rag doll from the floor and returned it to the child's arms. And she planted an extra kiss on Tyler's forehead. As she did, she warned herself about becoming too attached to another woman's children. *Someday they'll be gone.*

CHAPTER ELEVEN

ON THE OREGON TRAIL

NEWSPAPERS CALLED THE PLATTE RIVER THE "road to destiny." It snaked alongside the rutted trail, a river described by the army guides as "too thick to drink and too thin to plow." Abigail could see why as she bounced beside Evan on the wagon bench in the early morning light. The children had been sleeping when they pulled out of camp. So Abigail had little else to do but admire the scenery, if admire was the appropriate word.

The two- or three-mile-wide river was knee-deep in spots, but it was rumored to have swift currents and quicksand in unexpected places. When the children began to stir inside the wagon, Abigail climbed over the seat and into the wagon. She released the drawstrings on the canvas sides of the wagon and tied up the canvas to let the cooling breezes blow through the wagon. Then she gave each child a piece of buttered biscuit coated with the blueberry jam she'd preserved before leaving Chelsea. She also gave each of them a cup of lukewarm peppermint tea sweetened with honey.

She tapped Evan's shoulder and shouted, "Would you like a sandwich, Mr., er, Evan?" His given name stuck in her throat.

He shook his head and pointed to the overhead sun. "I'll wait. We'll be stopping for the noon meal in another hour or two."

She nodded and returned her attention to the children. Her skirts caught on the latch to one of the trunks. She yanked it free. Before leaving Council Grove, Abigail had packed her bouquet of crinolines in the bottom of her trunk. Moving about the wagon without them was much simpler, regardless of high fashion. *But then,* she mused, *what is high fashion out here in the American wilderness?*

"Tell us a story, Miss Sherwood," Amy begged. "I'm bored."

Abigail laughed. "How about I save my stories for the campfire tonight? Instead, let's see. Why don't I teach you how to draw?"

"Really? You'd teach us to do that?" Amy bounced on the edge of her seed-stuffed mattress, seed that would be used for next spring's wheat planting. Abigail missed the downy soft mattress she'd had in the Conestoga, but she vowed not to complain no matter how bruised her hips and thighs might become by the time they arrived in Oregon. *Imagine having callused hips,* she laughed to herself.

Taking four sharpened pencils from her trunk, she handed one to each of the children, along with a pad of paper. "Before we try to draw something, let me share a little secret with you." She set a spirit of camphor bottle at the foot of the bedding. "Before you draw one line, you need to study your subject—like this bottle."

"Study a bottle?" Chip frowned. "Why?"

"Everything in the world breaks down into squares, rectangles, triangles, trapezoids, ovals, and circles. Once you know the basic shape of your subject, it's easier to get everything else in proper proportion." She drew a vertical rectangle in the middle of her paper. "See? The main portion of the bottle is rectangular."

"But what about the bottle's neck, Miss Sherwood?" Amy asked.

"Good question. The curved sides form a trapezoid. See?" She sketched the geometric shape to the top of the rectangle. "There, add an oval, and you have a bottle."

Tyler wrinkled his nose at the sketch. "But that's messy, Miss Sherwood. Your pictures aren't messy."

"That's why you have these." She handed each of the children a large spongy eraser. "See?" She erased the unnecessary marks from the sheet and added details to the bottle's label.

"That's too easy and boring." Amy bounced on the edge of her bedding as the wagon hit a rut. "I want to draw people and animals."

"Me too!" Tyler's eyes shone with excitement. "I want to draw animals too."

"Horses. It's horses for me. Or maybe a rattlesnake if we see one," Chip added.

Abigail shivered at the mention of the slithery, ever-present creatures inhabiting the land over which they would pass. The travelers wore thick, knee-high boots to protect themselves from sudden strikes. Every day, someone had a story to tell of a recent encounter with one of the hated reptiles.

"All right, you want a horse? Let me show you how an artist sees a horse." Quickly, she broke down the profile of a horse's head into a rectangle, two triangles, a square, and an oval. Shaping and erasing, smoothing and darkening, a horse's profile emerged on her sheet of paper. Not just any horse, but the profile of Winnie, Granny's lead mare.

"Can I do that? Can I do that?" Amy bounced up and down with excitement.

"In time. But for today, we'll practice drawing bottles. Tomorrow we'll advance to rattlesnakes and horses." She teased a smile out of the disappointed girl. "Before too long, you'll be able to sketch just about anything you desire. You'll see."

By the time the wagon rolled to a stop for the noon break, each of the children had a "masterpiece" to show to their father. It was the first time since Sara took sick that Abigail had seen the man actively involved with and enjoying his children. He caught her gazing at him and winked. She blushed and returned her attention to the food preparation.

When the wagon master gave the signal and the wagons began to roll, Chip and Tyler joined their father on the driver's seat. Amy curled up with a book Abigail had lent her, while Abigail and Granny switched vehicles. Granny needed a break. She'd driven her own wagon all morning and was beat from the blistering sun and dust. Abigail appreciated the opportunity to relieve her boredom by driving for a while. The springless wagon jerked and lurched for hours across ruts and prairie dog holes, through coulees, and over mounds of sod.

It was late afternoon when Abigail noticed a billow of dark clouds gathering in the western sky. The air was filled with a disturbing energy. The closer the bank of clouds came, the darker the sky grew. Suddenly, a bolt of lightning shot between the earth and the clouds.

Deafening thunder clapped almost immediately. The horses bolted in fright. Abigail stood and shouted to the lead horse, "Whoa there!" The drivers of the other wagons were doing the same. Streaks of lightning filled the darkened sky, followed by thunder. Then the sky opened up. Massive drops of rain pelted Abigail's face, drenching her before she could bring the team under control.

Afraid to release the reins, she sat while the storm pummeled her. Ahead of her, she could see Granny and the kids quickly lowering the canvas sides and tightening the drawstrings at both ends of the wagon. Abigail managed, with one hand holding the reins, to tighten the drawstring on the front end of the wagon's canvas, thus keeping the worst of the rain out of the wagon.

Through the torrent, she saw Sergeant Brumby, their army guide, riding his pony from wagon to wagon. "Don't let go of your reins until we close the circle," he shouted.

Abigail could barely make out the lead wagon circling around with the others following. By the time the last wagon had closed the circle and it was safe to release the reins, she could barely open her stiff and frozen fingers. Her teeth chattered uncontrollably.

As she hiked up her soggy skirts to climb down from the wagon, Evan came running out of the blinding rain. "Here. Take my hands," he called.

"I can do it myself," she argued.

"Stop being foolish, and let me help you," he demanded.

"I am not fool—"

Disgusted, he snagged her left foot, causing her to lose her balance. Her arms flailed in the air.

"Grab hold of me," he shouted.

Without thinking, she obeyed by grabbing his head. The man's hat flew into the air as she crushed his startled face into her drenched bodice. What happened after that, she didn't know until she found herself facedown in a crater-size mud puddle, with Evan flat on his back beside her.

For an instant, neither moved despite the rain. The lightning and thunder had been so close and so loud that it had stunned her senses. So she couldn't believe her ears when she heard the man in the mud beside her laugh.

At first, it was a chuckle, but it quickly grew into full laughter and beyond into hilarity. She lifted herself to her hands and knees and stared at the crazed man. He pointed at her and laughed all the harder.

The storm eased, leaving steady rain behind as a reminder of its fury. Abigail struggled to her feet only to have Evan pause long enough to look at her again and burst into another round of insanity, as Abigail interpreted it.

"Mr. Chambers, you are insane!" She shouted above the sound of the rain. She turned to leave the giant puddle into which they'd fallen. As she tried to scale the slight incline, her foot slipped. She screamed, flailed her hands in the air trying to break her fall, and then landed back in the puddle, bottom first. By now, the man beside her was rolling in the mud with laughter.

"Mr. Chambers! Control yourself!"

He pointed at her face and attempted to speak, "You should see yourself. Mud!" With that, he returned to his former hilarity.

She touched her forehead with her hand and found a huge gob of mud stuck to the front of her hair. "And you think that is funny? Mud? If you think mud is so funny, here—" She splattered his face with a handful. "Laugh some more!"

Startled, Evan sputtered and cleared his eyes. Then grabbing a handful, he turned to splatter her face in return.

Abigail saw it coming. "You wouldn't dare." She scrambled to her feet and backed away from the man.

"Oh, wouldn't I?" He inched closer, both hands full of the brown, gooey soil.

"No, no, you wouldn't—" She struggled to get out of the puddle and away from him. "A gentleman would never—"

"True, but a lady would never have thrown the first mud pie either," he reminded, as he moved closer.

Still scrambling to escape the muddy pond in which she found herself, one foot again slipped. She fell to a sitting position, giving Evan the time he needed to loom over her, holding his mud clods directly above her.

"No, no. Don't! Please don't."

He paused for a moment. "All right, if you will apologize for calling me insane."

Abigail tightened her jaw. She did not want to apologize; besides, people were emerging from the other wagons and staring at their bizarre show.

Evan bent closer to her. The mud dripped between his fingers onto her nose and shoulder. "Come on. Say it. Say you're sorry for—"

"I'm sorry. I'm sorry!" she squealed, trying to scramble sideways.

Evan laughed and shook the mud from his hands into the puddle, rinsed his fingers in the surface water. Then he helped Abigail to her feet. "You really do look terribly funny."

"And you are less hilarious, I suppose?" She wiped the back of her hand across the tip of her nose.

"Here, let me help you."

She stood quietly as he slowly brushed away a glob of mud from her nose and forehead. "You have freckles," he muttered. "I never noticed before." His voice was husky and low.

Suddenly, as if he'd awakened from a daydream, he stepped back from her. "You need to get into some dry clothing before you take sick." After climbing out of the puddle, he lifted her out of it. Applause went up from the idle gawkers. Without further comment, he strode to his own wagon.

Abigail's mud-coated skirts clung to her legs as she waddled to the rear entrance of Granny Parker's wagon. After removing the ladder from inside the vehicle, she climbed aboard and closed the canvas flaps. Shivering from the cold, as well as from the unexpected encounter, Abigail shed her ruined dress. "This will never come clean," she admitted through chattering teeth. Once free of the soggy clothing, she dried herself with her Turkish towel and put on fresh clothing. *At least, the rain barrels are full again,* she mused as she tried to draw her boars' hairbrush through her tangled locks. Remembering the extra bar of lemon verbena soap Rebecca insisted she pack, Abigail smiled in eager anticipation. *Noontime or not, I am washing my hair!*

Granny marshaled the children to help prepare the food while Abigail filled a metal washbasin with fresh water and scrubbed the mud out of her tangled curls. She didn't even wait to heat the fresh rainwater. She didn't eat until her hair was wrapped in a fresh towel and her clothing scrubbed clean and hung out to dry, all but her unmentionables, of course. Those she hung on a rope inside the wagon. With the sun returning as quickly as it had left, she hoped the clothes would be dry before they stopped for the night.

When she finally emerged from the wagon with her moist hair combed and drawn back into a ponytail, Granny met her at the foot of the ladder with a bowl of lentil stew. She attacked the vegetables in the stew with a vengeance. It had been a long time since breakfast.

She was so busy filling the massive hole in her stomach she didn't hear Mr. Lassiter approach. "So, how are you doing after your morning mud bath, Miss Sherwood?"

She leveled a malevolent stare at the man.

He chuckled. "I understand the wealthy women of Europe pay outrageous fees for mud baths like yours. It does great things for a woman's complexion, so they say."

"That isn't funny!" she growled.

"Though I imagine they do so without the company of a man," he added, a twinkle filling his eyes.

Abigail closed her eyes and wagged her head. She would never live down the morning's fiasco. Recalling what her father always told her about meeting teasing with teasing, she grinned mischievously at the man, and then at the mud puddle less than ten feet behind him. Setting her empty bowl and spoon on a nearby rock, she sauntered toward him. "If you'd like to try it out, I'll be glad to oblige."

The man's eyes narrowed. "You wouldn't dare!"

A smile teased around the corners of her lips. "That's what the last man said."

Up flew the surprised man's hands in defense. "I take it all back, Miss Sherwood, and cry 'uncle.' I believe you would do it."

"Watch out for her, Lassiter. The woman is dangerous."

Abigail whirled about to see Evan leaning against the Parker wagon, downing a bowl of Granny's stew.

"I am dangerous?" Abigail gasped. "The whole thing was your fault."

"My fault?"

"Yes, your fault, laughing like a hyena. I've never seen . . ." She began to laugh. "If you could have seen yourself. And to think when I first met you at Serenity Inn, I thought you were a stick-in-the-mud."

Her analogy caused both men to hoot with laughter. Flustered, she clicked her tongue and strode over to the Chamberses' wagon to locate Granny and the children.

She was surprised to find no one around. Wondering where they could be, she rounded the end of the wagon and spotted them several yards from the wagon train, collecting buffalo chips for future campfires. The warm sun was quickly drying out the ground after the sudden morning shower. Grabbing her pad of paper from the wagon, she sketched the scene before her. When she paused to listen to a bee buzzing in the prairie blossoms nearby and the laughter of children in the distance, her heart swelled with joy.

" 'O Lord our Lord,' " she quoted from Psalm 8, " 'how excellent is thy name in all the earth! who hast set thy glory above the heavens. Out of the mouth of babes and sucklings hast thou ordained strength.' " As she added the finishing touches to her drawing, she gazed up into the cobalt-blue sky. " 'When I consider thy heavens, the work of thy fingers, . . . what is man, that thou art mindful of him?' "

She sensed someone approaching her. Before she could close her art pad and turn to see who it was, he spoke. "That's really good, you know."

She reddened and mumbled a "Thank you."

"My dear, you need to learn how to take a compliment," Evan added. "You are a gracious and talented woman, but I surmise that you don't see yourself that way."

Abigail was extremely uncomfortable with the subject of the conversation. "If you will please excuse me, Mr., er, Evan, I need to wash the luncheon dishes since Granny fixed the meal. Mr. Lassiter will be ringing the bell for us to break camp and head out any minute."

She turned to leave, but he gently grasped her upper arm. "You need to see yourself as others see you. Being honest with oneself is as important as not being prideful of one's abilities, don't you think?"

From a distance, they heard Tyler shout and run toward his father, dragging his partially filled gunnysack behind him. "Look, Daddy! Look at all the buffalo chips I found."

Evan knelt beside his son as the young boy showed off his findings. "That's good, son. Your chips will help keep us warm when the sun goes down tonight. You did a fine job." Evan paused to cast Abigail a significant look and then helped his young son drag the gunnysack around to the side of the wagon.

Flustered, Abigail brushed aside his words and set herself to the task of washing the soup bowls, dinnerware, and kettle. When she emptied the last of the lentil soup into a small bowl, she realized there wasn't enough of the delicious concoction to save. After glancing both ways to see who might be watching, she lifted the bowl ungraciously to her lips and drank the dregs. She was stowing the last of the noon-time supplies in to the wagon when the five-minute gong sounded.

Granny insisted on driving her own team and wagon during the afternoon. Abigail volunteered to drive the Chamberses' wagon, freeing Evan to give Tyler his promised ride with his father on the back of Betsy, the family's roan mare. Amy leaped at the chance to ride in the driver's seat with Abigail. As for Chip, he chose to walk alongside the trail with a few of his newly made friends, bringing down prairie dogs and other rodents with their slingshots. By instinct, Abigail couldn't help but warn him to be careful. And by the glare she received in return, she knew the lad didn't appreciate her mothering.

"Oh, don't worry about him," the little girl comforted. "He's still mad at God and the world for taking Mama. And he thinks you're trying to marry our dad." The way the child eyed her, Abigail wondered if Amy might also feel that way.

She shook the reins over the backs of the team, urging them to move a little faster. "Such an idea can't be further from my mind. Some women are meant to marry, and others are meant to remain single. I'm afraid I'm one of the latter. God and I have talked it over and have decided that it's all right."

The child seemed to relax after that. But she hadn't run out of questions. Amy wanted to know everything about Abigail's childhood, her sister, and her home in England. Without warning, Amy snapped her head around to face Abigail. "What about Mr. Hawk?"

"Mr. Hawk?" The question took Abigail by surprise.

"Mr. Hawk Lassiter. He likes you, you know."

Abigail clicked her tongue. "Amy, don't say things like that. It's not so."

"It is too!" the child defended, her body coiled to strike. "My daddy said it was so! And my daddy doesn't lie."

Abigail stared helplessly at the girl. "Your daddy told you this?"

"Uh-huh!" Amy's stubborn little chin quivered, but her eyes held their resolve.

"Are you sure you didn't misunderstand him? It's possible he was saying something totally different and you—"

"My daddy said," the girl interrupted, " 'old Hawk certainly has a thing for our Miss Sherwood. I hope we can keep her until we reach the Willamette Valley.' "

Abigail gasped, instantly trying to remember when, if ever, she'd given Evan cause to think such a preposterous idea. In the next instant, she wondered how many other people were thinking the same. "Amy," she grabbed hold of the girl's slim upper arm, "who did your daddy say this to?"

"Granny Parker."

Abigail threw her head back and closed her eyes. It was getting worse! "And what did Granny say?"

A pout formed on Amy's face. She looked as if she were ready to cry. "I don't want to talk about this any longer."

Abigail gave the child's arm a little shake. "Please try to remember."

The girl wagged her head emphatically, pulling her arm free of Abigail's grasp. "No! I don't want to." And she climbed back into the wagon.

CHAPTER TWELVE

NARCISSA'S CHILDREN

A BIGAIL COULD NEVER HAVE IMAGINED THE fortitude that would be necessary to be on the trail for weeks at a time. She'd felt the tedium and the discomfort of the long hours with the intense sun boring down on her shoulders like a blacksmith's bellows heating iron. She'd collected her share of buffalo chips. And the rattlesnakes! Evan called them "the hazards of the journey." Alone in the night Abigail wondered if that magical place of giant trees and rich, black soil, the place called the Willamette Valley, was more of a myth than a reality.

Her boredom lifted the day Sergeant Brumby spotted a herd of wild buffalo and the men set out to demonstrate their hunting prowess, while the women rested or caught up on their wifely chores. Abigail was grateful when the men returned unharmed though empty-handed, except for a few sacks of buffalo chips. Buffalo chips burned hotter and longer than either cow chips or wood. That night stories were told about the day's adventure. The next morning, the wagons again rolled westward, along with the tedious hours the journey entailed.

The day they crossed the shifting sands of the Platte River proved to be anything but boring. When one of the lead oxen hauling the Sever wagon lost her footing in a deep pothole and the youngest Sever child fell into the river, Hawk Lassiter dived into the muddy water and rescued the boy. It took most of the day to get all the wagons safely across. They set up camp early that day since many had to dry out after their crossing.

Traveling down into Ash Hollow didn't allow time for much tedium either. The trail, eroded by rains, dropped down the hillside. Granny and the two younger Chambers children watched the parade of wagons, their wheels locked with heavy chains, being lowered down the steep slope, one at a time. Amy waved to Abigail who was, along with every other able-bodied person, holding on to the chain to prevent the wagon from crashing to the bottom of the hill. That evening, after the story hour with the children, Abigail wasted no time in getting to bed.

In the morning, Granny gave her some ointment for her aching muscles. "It's made from aloe plants and peppermint," the older woman confided. "I use it for my lumbago all the time." Surprisingly, Abigail's back and neck did feel better after applying the magical balm.

A few days later, along the south banks of the North Platte River, a chill of excitement shot through Abigail when she spotted the famous Chimney Rock. The burning red clay and sandstone rock rose three hundred feet into the air. When the wagon train stopped for the noon break, she arranged to have Granny fix lunch while she sketched the magnificent landmark in her book.

She chose a large rock on which to sit, took out her charcoals, and set to work. *No one back home will ever believe this,* she thought, overcome with awe.

"Incredible, isn't it?"

She started at the unexpected voice coming from behind her. It was Hawk Lassiter. So intent on her subject, she hadn't heard him coming. If she had, she would have had to find a way to avoid the flamboyant company wagon master. Abigail wasn't accustomed to fleeing from men, and this man seemed to be everywhere. "I've never seen anything like it," she admitted.

She could feel him leaning over her shoulder and studying her sketch. "I just started."

"Share a piece of the rock?" He didn't wait for her reply but made himself comfortable on one of the outcroppings of its irregular surface.

Trying to appear unconcerned, she continued sketching. He'd been sitting beside her for less than ten minutes when Tyler ran up to her.

"My daddy says to tell you that lunch is ready." With the mention of his father, the small boy sent an accusing glance at Abigail and then glared at Hawk Lassiter. "Who's running the wagon train now, Mr. Lassiter?"

Hawk grinned and tousled the boy's hair. "How about you and me go check on the lead wagons, see if they're ready to roll?"

"Wow! Can I, Auntie Abigail? Can I?" The children had taken to calling her "Auntie" when Evan started using her given name.

"Only if you tell your father first," Abigail warned.

With that the little boy was off, dragging the rangy Englishman by the hand.

Deciding to put the finishing touches on her sketch later, Abigail closed her sketchbook and returned to the Chamberses' camp. Evan gave her an irritating smirk as she strode over to the campfire. She pretended not to notice.

"*Mmm*, that smells delicious, Granny." She sniffed the aromas coming from the large iron pot suspended over the hot coals.

The woman beamed with pleasure as Abigail dipped out a large bowlful. Granny's lentil mush, as the older woman called it, more than satisfied Abigail's hunger. A thick slice of oatmeal bread slathered with jam and a bowl of the thick gooey porridge would stick to her ribs all afternoon.

The silent interplay between Abigail and Evan continued whenever Hawk Lassiter was around. At other times, she and Evan had great discussions about everything from the day's problems to naming the constellations in the sky, another activity she'd not realized how much she missed sharing with her father.

The spring-green prairie grass had long since turned golden brown before the wagon train reached Fort Laramie. Regardless of the high cost of mailing a letter, Abigail, along with many others of her fellow travelers, wrote to loved ones back east to tell them of their adventures.

"You wouldn't believe the sunsets. They stretch from horizon to horizon," she wrote. "The electrical storm was an experience. Lightning crackled about us so close, it made my hair stand on end from the static. The thunder was so loud and so incessant it stunned the senses. Granny Parker, the woman traveling with me, says it was as

close to the 'eternal fires' (you know where) as she ever wants to be."
While Granny didn't mind saying the forbidden word, Abigail
couldn't bring herself to write it in a letter.

In the margins of the pages, she sketched scenes along the way,
including Chimney Rock and pictures of the Chambers children. She
placed it in an envelope and sealed it with melted wax just as Amy
asked her if she'd like to walk to the fort with her and her daddy.

Abigail and Evan strode along the dusty road side by side, accompanied by easy banter, while the children ran ahead. She stole a glance
at Evan as he talked about the danger of prairie fires started by electrical storms like some they'd experienced earlier. He was fast becoming
a good friend. Abigail had never had a male friend, except for her father.

"We've been lucky so far," Evan added. "I hope our luck contin-
ues."

"I don't believe in luck." She said it so matter-of-factly he looked
at her in surprise. "I believe God is the One who—"

"Come on. Do you think God has a hand in everything you do?"
he asked.

"Absolutely. But only because I ask Him to. He wouldn't interfere
if He weren't invited."

"I don't buy that."

"You do believe in God, don't you?" she asked.

"Sure, but as a Creator who set the world in motion with certain
laws of nature and then left everything to man's care. I don't see Him
mother henning us."

"Mother henning?"

Evan kicked at a stone with his boot. "Yeah, overseeing the tiny
details of our lives. For that matter, He's probably creating other
worlds as we speak."

"That's sad."

"Sad? Why?"

Abigail gave a slight shrug. "God was my father's best Friend. He
spent hours alone with Him every day. I think of Him as my best
Friend too. And like a good Friend, He's interested in me and what is
important to me."

Evan gave her a quirky smile and strode on in silence.

At the fort, Abigail posted her letter while Evan and the children bought a bag of gumdrops from the commissary.

In front of the commissary, a young lieutenant told the travelers about the Whitman massacre. Saddle-weary soldiers were only too happy to terrorize the tender-footed easterners with the four-year-old tale. Abigail had read the report in the Boston paper long before she joined the emigration westward, so it didn't come as a surprise. However, it did give her a moment of concern when she realized they'd be passing near the area where the murders occurred.

When it was time to head back to the campground, Evan and the children invited her to join them once more. On the way, a family of four from one of the other companies fell into step with them. The children ran on ahead, getting acquainted on their own terms while the adults strolled behind. Abigail smiled as the men struck up their own conversation separate from her and the other woman.

"Weren't the prices in that place horrible?" the woman exclaimed. "They're out to gouge the traveler!"

Abigail laughed good-naturedly. "I suppose it costs a pretty penny to transport supplies here from Missouri."

"Yes, I guess so," the woman nodded thoughtfully. "Oh, I'm sorry. I didn't introduce myself. My name is Suzanne Fletcher and that's my husband, Bill. We're from Kentucky." Suzanne continued, not waiting for Abigail's reply, "You have such a lovely family. I was watching you in the commissary. You and your husband look so happy together."

Abigail started in surprise. Before she could think of what to say, she felt Evan's arm slip around her waist. She shot a quick glance at his smiling face.

Her lower jaw dropped open when he said, "Thank you, Mrs. Fletcher. We're the Chambers, Evan and Abigail. We're from New England. Where are you folks heading?"

The shock of being introduced as Mrs. Chambers caused Abigail to stumble, but Evan's strong arm kept her from falling. She tried to pull away from his grasp, but he held her fast.

"We're thinking of settling down along the coast. They say it's great land for raising cranberries," Bill Fletcher volunteered. "How about you?"

"We've talked about settling in the southern part of Willamette Valley, haven't we, dear?" He glanced down at Abigail's shocked face. "Don't mind my wife. She's sometimes shy with strangers."

Bill Fletcher laughed. "That's one thing my Suzanne isn't. She turns every stranger into a friend. Why she was making friends with an Indian squaw back at the fort. Can you imagine?"

"I think that's very wise." Abigail slipped delicately from Evan's grasp. "From what the fort commander had to say about recent Indian uprisings, turning them into friends instead of foes could mean the difference between life and death for the pioneers settling in the area."

Suzanne gave her husband a broad I-told-you-so smile. "They seem like nice people. Do you really believe they do the treacherous things the commander claims?"

"Actually, yes." Evan pursed his lips thoughtfully. "When the white man first came west, the native tribes thought he was a god. But after being cheated, robbed, and mistreated, the Indians decided the white man was not a god as their elders had thought and that to survive, they'd have to fight back."

"But they're not all bad, just as all whites are not out to cheat and lie." Suzanne shook her head. "I can't accept that every red man, woman, and child is out to kill me."

"Well, dear," Bill Fletcher added, "let's hope we never need to test your theory."

While the two couples walked and talked, Abigail's mind kept returning to Evan's deception. Abigail had to tell these people the truth. They were nice people, and they deserved that much.

Taking courage, Abigail said, "There's something I need to—"

"Do," Evan interrupted, wrapping an arm around her shoulders. "She's so contentious. Before we went to the fort, she left some laundry drying on the wagon tongue. Go ahead, honey. I'm sure the Fletchers understand." He gave her a gentle push toward their campsite. "I'll be there soon."

The Fletchers waved surprised goodbyes to Abigail. Not knowing what else to do, Abigail left. But with every step, her anger grew. "How dare he do such a thing!" she sputtered. As she strode past the first of the Lassiter company campgrounds, Hawk Lassiter fell into step with her.

"Who did what?"

Her green eyes snapped with fire. She glared at the man. "Men!" She marched off, leaving the wagon master confused and stunned. Abigail was still stewing when she reached the Chamberses' wagon.

Granny saw her coming and poked her head out of the front of her own wagon. "So how was your outing?"

"Horrible! Absolutely horrible! Men!" Abigail stormed up the steps into the Chamberses' wagon and closed the canvas flap despite the warm temperatures.

"I should go right over to the Fletchers' camp and tell them the truth. That's what I should do." But even as she spoke, she knew she'd do no such thing. Frustrated, she took out her recipe book.

In whatever quiet moments Abigail could find, she illustrated recipes as well as drew pictures of her childhood home in England. This time when she put her pencil to the paper, Abigail realized she was too upset to work on her favorite project.

That evening, with all the talk of the Whitman massacre, the children wanted to hear about it at story time. Abigail wasn't sure talking about the gruesome event would do much for their sleep that night. After much coaxing, she relented.

"All right. Let's call our story 'Narcissa's Dream.' " She glanced beyond the children's eager faces to find the adults of the caravan drawing near to listen as well.

"Twenty-five-year-old Narcissa Prentiss stared at her reflection in the mirror as she brushed the snarls from her long auburn curls—"

"I have auburn curls," nine-year-old Lilly Anders squealed.

"No, you don't!" her brother argued. "Your hair is carrot red."

"Mama," the girl wailed.

The children sitting nearby told her to be quiet.

"Narcissa Prentiss was beautiful. She loved God with her whole heart. And more than anything else, Narcissa wanted to become a missionary to the American Indians, much like our Mr. Farnsworth." She gestured toward the quiet young man leaning against a wagon's wheels. His fiancée sat on a stool beside him.

"Narcissa's family laughed at her when she told them of her dream. Undaunted, she asked the American Board of Commissioners for Foreign Missions to send her to the Nez Percé tribe.

" 'Nonsense!' the mission board president said. 'We're not about to send an unmarried woman among the savages!' News of her outrageous request reached the ears of Marcus Whitman, a young man committed to taking the gospel of Jesus Christ to the western American Indians. Marcus visited the lovely Narcissa and fell madly in love."

A soft purr of approval swept through the crowd. Out of principle, a few of the older boys groaned.

"Immediately, Marcus proposed to her. Before Narcissa agreed to marry him, she made him promise to take her west. The happy couple presented their plan to the mission board. The board agreed to send them if they could convince another couple to go as well."

Abigail was so intent on her story she didn't see Evan join the ever-widening circle, nor did she notice Hawk standing on the outskirts of the crowd.

"Who would go?" Abigail threw her hands up in the air. "Every one of their friends refused. Finally, one couple accepted their offer. Henry Spalding and his fiancée, Eliza. Henry Spalding was a moody and difficult man who had previously courted Narcissa. When Spalding asked her to marry him, she refused.

"Hurt and angry, the rejected suitor asked Eliza, a shy and frail wren of a woman, to marry him. Both couples married and immediately headed west, along with a blustery handyman and preacher named William Gray. For four interminable months, they honeymooned along the trail, having to share one tent." Abigail noted a smirk on Mr. Farnsworth's face. She wondered what more he might know about the ill-fated couples. She'd have to ask him later.

The audience groaned when Abigail stopped for the night, leaving the Whitman party stranded in Independence, with Marcus hunting for a traders' caravan who would agree to take them to the Pacific Ocean.

"Mr. Chambers, may I see you for a moment?" Abigail called as the gathering broke up.

Pretending surprise, he pointed to himself. "Me?"

"Yes, you!"

"Is something wrong?"

Granny shot an approving glance over her shoulder as she corralled the three children toward the wagon. "Come on children. Tomorrow's another day," she urged.

On hearing the exchange between the two, Hawk Lassiter, who'd been making his way toward Abigail, paused and backed off into the shadow of the nearest wagon.

"Could we take a walk somewhere private?" she hissed.

Evan gave her a broad grin. "Sure enough." He reached for her arm; she folded it across her bodice. Silently, they strode away from the circle of wagons. "Aren't you afraid of rattlesnakes?" he asked, a smirk teasing the corners of his lips.

"Snakes aren't out at night!"

She saw Evan lift his eyebrows in disbelief. When they'd walked far enough that their conversation wouldn't be overheard, Abigail turned to face him. "Evan," she started, her voice halting and raspy. "Why did you lie to the Fletchers about you and me today? I don't appreciate falsehoods."

In the moonlight, Evan's hat shrouded his face. "Ma'am," he began, removing his hat and rolling the brim between his hands, "how would you have had me introduce you?"

"You could have told the truth!" The set of her chin and the defiance in her eyes dared him to challenge her.

"The truth? That you're a single woman traveling with me as my children's nanny?"

"But Granny—"

"By the time I would have finished explaining all the details of our arrangement, they would have forgotten our names. It just seemed easier to tell them what they expected to hear. I doubt we'll ever see them again. Besides, you should have seen the surprised look on your face. It was priceless."

"I would have preferred the truth as difficult as that may have been to explain." Abigail didn't know what else to say. She'd lived by a strict code of honesty that obviously differed from Evan's.

Tilting her face up toward his, he asked, "Was it so bad? Being Mrs. Chambers, I mean?"

Her eyes blinked in surprise. "Mr. Chambers, you leave me speechless."

His face broke out into a broad smile once more. "Good! You have to admit that's a rare and wondrous thing, you being speechless."

"Huh!" Her skirts swooshed about her ankles as she whirled away from him. Then slowly, she turned toward him once more. "I don't talk too much, do I?" she asked timidly.

He chuckled aloud, drawing her into his arms. At first she tensed at his sudden move. But the strong beat of his heart pounding against her ear weakened her resolve. In his arms, she alternately wanted him to release her or never let her go. Pushing Abigail's sunbonnet away from her face, he planted a kiss on the tip of her nose. "You are a delightful woman, Abigail Sherwood, an absolute delight."

Tenderly, he released her. His hands lingered on her upper arms and trailed the length of her arms to her hands and fingertips. All the while Evan stared into her upturned face, the shadows on his face concealing his expression.

Abigail struggled to assemble her thoughts above the pounding of her heart. She was experiencing foreign feelings. Her mind was a jumble of questions.

"This isn't right," she whispered, her voice throaty and low. "Your wife—"

At the mention of Sara, Evan released Abigail's hands. "You're right. I'm sorry. I have no right. Please forgive me." Abruptly, he turned and disappeared into the darkness.

CHAPTER THIRTEEN

MOONLIGHT ON THE PRAIRIE

COYOTES HOWLED THROUGHOUT THE NIGHT, like every night on the prairie. Abigail heard every blood-chilling cry. Although it was the wee hours of the morning, the summer heat was stifling. The temperature inside the covered wagon was easily fifteen degrees hotter than outside. Sweating through her nightgown, Abigail feverishly fanned the hot air with her leather portfolio. Her face glistened with perspiration.

The hours passed slowly as she tossed and turned on her narrow bedding. Again and again, the dazed woman reviewed her encounter with Evan Chambers. It wasn't that she didn't see him every day as she cared for his children, cooked his food, discussed topics of mutual interest, and shared his dreams for the future. She loved sitting with him and the children during church services each Sunday morning. Yet somehow, this encounter had been different.

She blushed as she recalled the tremor of delight she'd experienced when his hands touched her face and his lips brushed the tip of her nose. *Such silly things,* she thought. *Hardly worthy of note!*

Abigail remembered how, as a child, she would sneak a peek at her mother's French romance novels and, later, at her sister Rebecca's collection. They were always the same, beautiful heroines with fluttering hearts and throbbing pulses. She'd laughed at the author's description of clandestine meetings under the stars. She believed she knew the difference between reality and fiction—until now. Heaving a deep sigh, she rolled from her left side to her right.

"Abigail, are you ever going to go to sleep?" Granny growled from across the narrow wagon aisle.

The younger woman grimaced. "I'm sorry I'm so restless tonight," she whispered. "It must be something I ate."

Granny grunted and rolled over to face the canvas wall.

This is hopeless. Sitting up, Abigail swung her legs over the side of the mattress and slipped into her moccasin-style bedroom slippers. Granny grunted her approval when Abigail muttered, "I think I'll get myself a drink of water."

The young woman located her white cotton plissé robe at the foot of her sleeping area and put it on. When she raised the canvas flap at the rear of the wagon, a rush of fresh air blew across her face. She didn't need a lantern. The full moon provided all the light necessary. She climbed down the steps, made her way to the front of the wagon, and quickly located the water barrel and the long-handled wooden dipper.

The cool water trickled down her parched throat, bringing sweet relief. She sighed with pleasure and wiped the moisture from her upper lip.

"What are you doing up and about, Miss Sherwood?" a voice drawled from the shadows of the wagon behind her.

Startled, Abigail gave a yip. The wooden dipper splashed into the water bucket. Her hands flew protectively to her chest. She turned as Hawk Lassiter stepped out of the darkness. He cradled a Springfield rifle in his arms.

She gasped. "You frightened me. I didn't hear you coming."

"I'm sorry. Are you all right?"

Abigail gave an uncertain laugh. "Yes, I think so. But please don't ever do that again!"

Hawk Lassiter chuckled aloud. "I'll try not to. Everything else all right?"

"Yes, but why are you roaming the prairie at this hour? By the way, what time is it?" she asked.

"Somewhere about two in the morning I would say. And I'm 'roaming the prairie,' as you put it, because it is part of my job as company wagon master. We take turns patrolling the camp throughout the night. I don't like nasty surprises."

"But we're directly outside an army fort," Abigail said. She was surprised when a breeze swirled long strands of her hair into her face. She'd forgotten that her hair was cascading down her back instead of confined in its usual bun at the nape of her neck. From Hawk Lassiter's intense gaze, she knew the man was aware of her every move. Abigail hoped the darkness hid her chagrin. "There must be more than a hundred soldiers within shooting range."

The man shrugged and scratched the back of his neck. "I know. I guess I'm a little paranoid after talking with the camp commander this afternoon."

Knowing someone was awake and alert gave Abigail a warm, safe feeling. "Do you think we'll encounter hostile Indians?"

"Who knows? A couple of the military men I talked with said that for the most part, the local tribes were peaceful. But there are renegade Indians, young bucks wanting to prove their manhood who would like nothing better than to attack a company of wagons that might be straggling behind the main caravan." He gave a deep sigh. "I also talked with Mr. Farnsworth who's traveled the Oregon Trail more times than I. He's concerned."

"You know," Abigail began, "last night when I was telling the story about Narcissa Whitman, I sensed that he knew the Whitmans personally."

"He did. He stayed overnight at the mission on his first trip to the coast. I think he, like every other man who met her, was half in love with Mrs. Whitman."

Abigail smiled. "She did seem to have that effect on men, didn't she?"

Lassiter rubbed the back of his neck again. "So I've been told, ma'am."

"Well, I'd better try to get some sleep." Abigail yawned aloud. "It was nice talking with you. If you'll excuse me?" She turned to leave, only to find herself face-to-face with the second button of a familiar blue cotton shirt.

Evan's face was cold and hard. "Fancy meeting you here, Miss Sherwood. And you, too, Mr. Lassiter. A pleasurable night for a friendly tête-à-tête, isn't it?"

Abigail's hands flew to her face in horror. "Oh, no. It's not like that. I couldn't sleep and got up to get a drink and ran into Mr. Lassiter as he was walking his rounds."

Evan's gaze started at Abigail's feet and rose slowly to her blushing face. "You don't owe me any explanation, Miss Sherwood."

"What the lady says is true, Chambers, not that I would mind if it were otherwise." Hawk Lassiter grinned at Abigail. Then, as if a revolutionary new thought hit his brain, the wagon master narrowed his gaze. "I apologize if I've been claim jumping, Chambers. I had no idea—"

" 'Claim jumping'?" Abigail almost swallowed her tongue, but the two men barely noticed.

"No! It's not like that!" Evan hastened to assure the other man. "Miss Sherwood is free to enjoy the attentions of whatever man meets her fancy. Now, if you'll both excuse me?" Evan touched the brim of his hat and gave Abigail a slight bow.

"Of all the . . ." The flustered woman watched as he strode toward his wagon.

"I'm sorry." Lassiter leaned closer and whispered, "I had no idea that you and he—"

"There is no me and he!" The faulty grammar stopped her for a moment. "Or, whatever. There is only a me, Abigail Sherwood, and a he, Evan Chambers—two totally separate individuals—period! That's all."

Lassiter shook his head. "I'm not so sure about that."

Abigail planted her hands on her hips and glared. "Well, I am! Good night, Mr. Lassiter!"

The encounter did little to solve Abigail's sleep problem. She sensed, as she slid under her cotton sheet, that Granny was awake. "You heard, didn't you?" Abigail whispered.

"Yes."

"What is it that's making people crazy? A full moon or something?"

Granny chuckled and rolled over to face the confused young woman. "That could be one explanation."

"Maybe it's a phenomenon of the trail."

Granny laughed again. "That's an interesting possibility."

Abigail closed her eyes. "I've never seen the likes of it."

The older woman raised herself to one elbow. "Did your parents raise their own chickens?"

"Yes, but what does that have to do with anything?"

"And you had a rooster?"

"Yes. We called him Prince Albert, no disrespect to the queen, of course."

"What would have happened if another rooster wandered into Prince Albert's chicken yard?"

"Prince Albert would peck his eyes out." When she thought about what she'd said, color rose in Abigail's face. "Granny! It's not like that."

Granny gave a low chuckle, rolled over, and left Abigail to consider her words.

"It's not like that," Abigail protested. By the loud snore coming from the other bed, she realized Granny had fallen asleep. The young woman punched her pillow then curled into a ball. "It's not like that!"

The next morning was like any other morning as the wagons pulled out of Fort Laramie. It was Abigail's turn to drive Granny's wagon, and Amy decided to ride along with her. As for Granny, she was riding with Mrs. Peters, a very young mother-to-be, whose body was threatening to miscarry her first child.

At breakfast, Evan behaved as if nothing had happened between them. When Hawk Lassiter passed through the campsite, he, too, acted as if their encounter had been erased from his brain.

"We're right on schedule for Independence Rock," Lassiter volunteered when Evan offered him a mug of Granny's coffee. "Ever since some fur traders celebrated July 4 there in 1830, the westbound wagon trains aim to do the same."

"It's called 'the Great Register of the desert,'" Chip said. The boy was totally enamored with the wagon master, spending as much time as he could in the man's company. Abigail wondered how Evan felt about that.

"That's right, son," Lassiter saluted him with his coffee cup. "I was wondering if your dad could spare you today. I could use some company. It gets mighty lonely up there on the front wagon."

"Wow! Can I, Dad? Oh, please, can I?" The boy's eyes glistened with excitement.

Evan pursed his lips for a moment. "I guess it would be all right as long as you do your chores here in camp first."

"All right," Chip leaped to his feet, "I'll get busy right away!"

As Chip ran to find an empty gunnysack to fill with buffalo chips, Lassiter handed Evan the empty cup. "Are you sure you're comfortable with this?"

Evan glanced down at the two empty coffee cups in his hands. "Of course, why wouldn't I be? A boy can't have too many admirable men in his life."

"Why, thank you, Evan. What a nice compliment."

Evan set the coffee cups on a rock, and the two men shook hands. Miffed at their lack of attention to her, Abigail watched from the rear of the Chamberses' wagon, where she and Amy were straightening the bedding and packing the unused kitchen supplies for the day's journey.

"Unroll the canvas," she ordered sharply. "Tack it down. We're in for a dusty ride today, I think."

Amy scrambled across the bedding and did as she was told. "Where's Tyler?" she asked as she knotted the last free end of the canvas.

Abigail straightened. "Oh no, not again." The youngest Chambers had a knack of coming up missing on a regular basis. "You'd better go check with Granny. If he's not with her, check the Brewster camp. He could be with their son, Stephen."

The two climbed out of the wagon and ran in opposite directions, calling Tyler's name. Abigail found him playing in a pile of sand with two older boys she recognized from her story hour. "Tyler, the wagons are getting ready to leave. I need you back at camp."

"All right." He leaped to his feet and ran in the direction of his wagon.

"Sorry, Miss Sherwood." The other boys' mother came out from behind her wagon, wiping her hands on a dishtowel. "I should have sent him home sooner."

"That's all right, Mrs., er—"

The woman extended her hand to Abigail. "Julia, Julia Williams. These are my sons, Jason and Jeremy."

"It's nice to meet you. I don't mind having Tyler play with your boys as long as he tells me where he's going before he leaves our camp," Abigail explained. "Well, I've a basin of dishes to dry and put away before we break camp. It was nice meeting you, Julia, and your boys."

She strode quickly back to the camp, scrubbed the coffee cups, and returned them to the heavy oak footlocker where the kitchen utensils were stored. When the five-minute warning sounded, everything was in order, Amy and Abigail were sitting on the driver's seat of the wagon, and Tyler was standing behind the seat between them.

Another blast from the post horn of Lassiter's wagon boy and the wagons rolled forward for another long, sun-drenched day on the trail.

* * * * *

The days passed one after another with little change. After a week without any communication from either Hawk Lassiter or Evan Chambers, Abigail began to wonder if she'd imagined everything. With Granny caring for young Mrs. Peters, Abigail took over the meal preparation with relish, though she discovered cooking over a campfire and in a well-appointed kitchen had little in common.

Breakfasts proved to be her specialty. Apple pancakes made with dried apples from her sister's apple tree, mush funnel cakes, Dutch babies, oatmeal raisin hot cakes—Granny and the children raved about the food. Evan thanked her for each meal but seldom said more. If anyone had suggested that she was putting herself out, hoping to impress the man, Abigail would have laughed in derision.

On the days when Abigail didn't have to help drive and could walk beside the wagons, she enjoyed thinking up new possibilities to add spice to their limited cuisine. A dash of cinnamon here, a pinch of tarragon there could bring life to the most common foods.

While she no longer screamed and ran at the sight of rattlesnakes, she maintained a healthy respect for them, especially after one of the children in the company stepped into a nest of vipers and died from the venom. Yet, walking along the trail allowed her time for private thought. Since having taken over the kitchen chores, Abigail had little time to slip away from camp to sketch. Whenever she did, Amy usually accompanied her. The child had taken an interest in drawing and showed great potential.

Occasionally when it was necessary for the wagon train to ford a river or to stop for repairs, she found a quiet place away from the wagons to draw. She'd come to love the eerie sound the wind made through rock formations as well as the gentle whistle it made through the tall grass. Her sketchbooks filled quickly. She hoped to buy more when they arrived at Fort Bridger.

"Miss Abigail! Miss Abigail. Hi!" Tyler waved to her from the wagon. The little boy loved being with his father, whether bagging buffalo chips or riding next to him on the wooden bench while Evan drove the team.

"Hi, Tyler." Abigail waved back as she walked beside the Chamberses' wagon.

Evan smiled and waved at her as well. "Are you getting tired, Miss Abigail?" he asked.

"Not yet, but thanks for asking." If anyone had told Abigail that she'd be walking to Oregon, she would have scoffed, but walking was often more comfortable than riding in the wagon over the rutted trail all day long.

When the wagons stopped for the noon meal, Abigail sliced a loaf of soda bread she'd made the previous night and slathered the slices with honey. And as a special treat for the children, she sprinkled raisins on top. On Tyler's and Amy's bread, she arranged raisins in the shape of a smiling face.

Suddenly, Evan peered over her shoulder. She hadn't heard him approaching. "Hey, how come they get a raisin face on their bread and I don't?"

Surprised, she looked up at him, then laughed. With his lower lip protruding, he looked like Tyler after being disciplined. "If you'd like I can remove the raisins—"

"No, no, that won't be necessary. I'm just teasing, really." He gave her a wry grin. "Maybe next time though?"

She grinned, slapped a second slice of bread on top of the first and handed the sandwich to him. "I promise that the next time we have honey men for lunch, I'll make you one too."

He laughed and took a bite from his sandwich. "Lassiter said we'll begin fording the Platte in an hour or two. I'll drive the team across, of course."

Abigail nodded and added, "We'll have to keep an eye on Tyler. He's getting more and more adventurous. Yesterday I found him throwing rocks into the campfire's embers. Oh yes, I gave Amy permission to ride with Kathy Conner's family. It's nice that she's found a friend on the journey."

"Speaking of which, here they come." Evan pointed to the three children running toward them. "Why, would you look at that? Chip is finally hungry enough to leave old Lassiter's side long enough to eat." By the tone in his voice, Abigail knew Evan resented the attachment his oldest son had formed with the wagon master.

As the children ate their sandwiches and drank their portion of milk from Beulah, the family's Guernsey cow, who was still producing, they were abuzz with excitement. Just seven days until the Fourth of July and they'd reach Independence Rock, along with numerous other wagon trains. The tales told of holiday festivities promised to break the boredom of the trail.

For one or two days, depending on the wagon repairs needed, the camp on the Sweetwater River would be alive with gunfire, raucous drinking, and patriotic oratory. Then the wagon trains would race toward the mountains. Delays could find them stranded in an early snow, which could be disastrous.

The wagons crossed the Platte without incident, except for a broken axle on one of the company's wagons. On the other side, Hawk Lassiter, Evan, and several others helped make the necessary repairs while the first wagons in the train rolled toward Independence Rock. Abigail, with Tyler by her side, trudged upstream in the cool, refreshing water, with several other women from the train intent on washing clothes in the river.

The sun was a fiery orb burning relentlessly in the cloudless sky. With her skirts knotted at her waist, doing the Chamberses' wash, as well as Granny's and her own, Abigail tried to imagine how uncomfortable they would have been trudging the dusty trail across Nebraska instead of standing in the cooling water. It would feel so good to wear clean clothes again. Climbing into soiled, sweaty clothing each morning had been difficult for the fastidious young woman.

Abigail scrubbed at the stains on the children's clothing with the lye soap their mother had made before they left the East Coast. While the work was tiring, it felt good to loosen a layer or two of dust from her body. The women from the train chatted amiably with one another. While she'd never been comfortable socializing with her sister's friends, Abigail was enjoying the camaraderie that developed between the women on the trail. Rich or poor, educated or shop girl, they had so much in common.

"Miss Abigail." One of the younger mothers shyly edged over next to Abigail. "I haven't told you how much I enjoy your stories. I hurry with my evening chores so I won't miss anything. My husband too. Why, the other night, he helped me finish drying the cooking pots so we could go and listen together."

"How nice. Thank you. It gives me something to look forward to as well." Abigail blew a stray wisp of hair from her forehead.

"It's a big help not having to worry where little Jacob will be each evening after supper." The young mother splashed one hand idly in the water while she held her skirts above the water with the other. "You are so good with the children. You'll make a good mother some day."

Abigail blushed. "Uh, that's doubtful as I cannot imagine finding a man to marry."

"Really?" The woman's eyes widened. "But I understood that you and Mr. Chambers are to be married when we reach the Oregon border."

Abigail sputtered in surprise, "Where in the world did you hear that?"

"Everyone is saying so. A few people—in another company—even said you were already married. You make such a lovely couple."

Abigail coughed. "Everyone is wrong. When I reach Oregon City, I intend to apply for a school teaching job."

"Oh," the woman sounded deeply disappointed. "I was looking forward to your wedding."

Abigail chuckled, shrugging her shoulders. "Sorry." She glanced over the shoulder of the young woman to check on Tyler. He and several other children were splashing about in the muddy water, screeching and shouting.

With Amy traveling with her friend Kathy and Chip hounding Hawk's every step, Tyler was Abigail's only responsibility. Granny, who'd become the Lassiter train's midwife, was kept busy. Occasionally Abigail saw her long enough in the evening to find out how she was doing and whose baby was itching to be born next.

Three of the women on the train were hoping their children would be born at Independence Rock. As for Abigail, she'd seen the pain her sister, Rebecca, suffered with the birth of each of her children, and she decided that these women had to be out of their minds to want to give birth under such primitive conditions.

One of the women from the train shouted that the wagon had been repaired and it was time to move out. Abigail loaded the wet clothing into a large wicker basket and called Tyler. "Tyler? Where are you?"

At first, she didn't see him. Then she saw his head bob to the surface. He tried to shout, but took in water instead and sank once more. Dropping the basket, she dashed into the water, wading toward him. The other children were crying and pointing toward where Abigail had seen him disappear.

"Melissa!" someone shouted.

As she charged through the water, Abigail could hear a woman behind her scream, "Melissa! Where's Melissa?"

Suddenly, Abigail stepped into a hole and plunged beneath the water. As she struggled to reach the surface, she felt someone wrap his or her arms about her legs. Abigail stretched down and grabbed a handful of long hair and pulled the child up. Together their heads burst out of the water. The grateful mother grabbed her child.

Abigail looked about. "Tyler? Has anyone seen Tyler?"

One of the women shouted and pointed to a spot five feet away from where Abigail was treading water. "He came up over there."

Grateful for learning how to swim as a child in the pond behind her father's parsonage, Abigail jackknifed into the water. *Oh, dear God,* she prayed, as she flung her arms about in the thick, murky water, hoping to make contact with the child, *please help me find Tyler. I beg of You. Help me find—*

In the middle of her prayer, she bashed headfirst into the boy's back. She grabbed him about his middle. The boy hung limp in her arms as she kicked her way to the surface.

Immediately, someone took the child from her. Abigail gasped for air, then sank beneath the surface once again, causing her lungs to fill with the muddy water. She coughed, struggling to catch her breath, but only inhaled more of the river. Dots danced before her eyes. The reality that she might drown washed over her. For an instant, she relaxed, as if giving in to the thought.

She could see her mother's English flower garden and her father walking toward her. She saw the faces of Rebecca's children gathered around the dinner table laughing at some joke. She saw the smooth, tiny face of Rebecca's latest child, the one Abigail had never seen.

No! Life is too precious to give up without a fight. Kicking with all her might, she struggled to regain her footing, but the weight of her wet clothing dragged her down into the mud. It was as if a giant hand was pulling her to the bottom of the river. "I can't," she panted. "I can't—" She swallowed another mouthful of water and mud.

Suddenly, four strong hands grabbed hold of her arms and dragged her from the water. One of her rescuers swept her into his arms and carried her to the grassy shore. Hawk Lassiter lowered her to the ground. "Are you all right?" He leaned over her body, concern in his face.

When she tried to answer, she broke into a fit of coughing. "Tyler? Is Tyler all right?" she said between attacks. She thought she'd swallowed the entire river. Her rescuer pounded her on the back, encouraging her to cough up more of the water she swallowed.

During her diving expedition, her hair had come undone. It was a mass of mud and tangles. Hawk brushed it from her face with his free hand. When her coughing subsided, Abigail fell back against Hawk's arm. Then she again remembered Tyler. He'd been limp when she surfaced with him. "Tyler? Is he all right?"

"Tyler's fine. Evan is with him."

"Good." Her voice seemed to be far away, like it belonged to someone else. Then she heard a voice ask, "Tyler, is he all right?"

Hawk chuckled. "The boy's fine. He's fine."

"Oh, good. I tried so hard." And again she heard the babble of voices far away, and she was oh-so tired.

CHAPTER FOURTEEN

MORE THAN QUICKSAND

FEELING AS WEAK AS A SPRING CHICK, ABIGAIL WAS grateful when Hawk carried her to Granny's wagon and placed her on her bedding. Once Hawk left the wagon, Abigail tried to sit up only to have Granny push her back down. "Just where do you think you're going, young lady? Don't you know that you almost drowned in quicksand after you saved those kids?"

Quicksand? Abigail groaned. "So that's why I couldn't . . ."

Granny helped her out of her muddy clothing, brought a pan of water, and helped Abigail wash the soil from her hair. Sitting on the edge of her bedding in her camisole and bloomers, Abigail began to shake. Her teeth chattered. She'd never been so cold.

"Oh no," Granny pushed Abigail down onto her bedding and covered her with layers of blankets. "*You* are going into shock."

Abigail burrowed down in the warmth of the blankets, all the while protesting, "Granny, I'm all right. Let me up."

"You behave and lie still while I get you a cup of peppermint tea." The woman shook her finger in Abigail's face. "We can't have you going into shock."

"Shock? Shock? I'm-m-m . . ." The rest of her remark got lost in the chattering of her teeth.

A crowd had gathered outside the wagon. She could hear them asking about her condition. She wanted to call out, to assure them that she was perfectly fine, but when she tried to speak, her voice was barely above a whisper.

Abigail heard Hawk Lassiter telling them that the train would be moving out in twenty minutes.

"As of right now, Miss Sherwood is doing fine," he shouted over the commotion. "Granny Parker or I will keep you apprised of her condition should there be a change."

Abigail wasn't surprised when Hawk knocked on the side of the wagon and asked if he might speak with her. His face was drawn and concerned as he lifted the canvas and poked his head inside the wagon. Abigail tried to sit up to greet him.

"No, no, stay where you are." He climbed into the wagon and sat down opposite her. "Are you feeling any better? Granny said—"

"I'm fine, only a little chilled from the water," Abigail said through chattering teeth. She could see perspiration on his forehead and couldn't imagine he could be sweating on a frigid afternoon like this. He'd been in the water too. She could see watermarks on his pants. Somewhere outside the wagon, he'd shed his heavy military boots.

"Granny's fixing you some hot tea." He wiped sweat from his brow. He glanced around the confining space. "It sure gets hot in these wagons, doesn't it?"

Abigail laughed in spite of her shivering body. "I couldn't tell you." A new thought hit her. "The laundry! Did anyone remember the laundry basket?"

Hawk Lassiter laughed. "Oh, yeah, a group of ladies are draping it on the ropes outside Evan Chambers's wagon as we speak."

She sank back against her pillow in relief. "I'm so glad Tyler is all right. And the little girl? She's all right too?"

The man laughed aloud. "Last time I checked."

"Why are you laughing?" she asked.

"You need your rest. I'm getting out of here to let you sleep." He leaned forward and kissed her forehead.

As he did, the canvas at the back of the wagon was pulled open and Evan Chambers's surprised face appeared. In his hand, he held a white porcelain teacup. Regardless of her stupor, Abigail blushed uncomfortably.

Evan blanched at finding Hawk standing beside her bed but quickly resumed his composure. "Oh! Sorry! I see you're in good hands so I won't bother you." He stood on the lowest step of the ladder into the wagon. "I just wanted to thank you for saving my son."

Abigail smiled. "I'm so glad he's all right."

At first it appeared as if the father of the young boy would bolt from the scene, but instead he climbed into the wagon. The commanding presence of the two equally imposing men overwhelmed the small wagon, or so it seemed to Abigail.

Evan handed her Granny's cup of tea. "Granny asked me to bring you this tea while she sits with Tyler." He frowned when Hawk moved her in a sitting position to allow her to drink the hot liquid. When she finished, Hawk lowered her on to her pillow.

"Well, I guess I'd better be going," Hawk gripped the brim of his hat in two hands and rose to his feet. "Gotta get these wagons rolling, unless you're not up to traveling, Miss Sherwood."

"Don't be silly. We want to see Independence Rock by the fourth, don't we?" She gave him a slight grin.

"Yes, ma'am. The river crossing put us behind a bit, but we can still make the rock by the fourth." He grinned. "It is a tradition, you know."

"I would hate to be responsible for breaking tradition." She gave him a teasing grin. Abigail was surprised at her glib response while in the presence of the two men standing awkwardly beside her.

Hawk angled his way past Evan. "We'll roll in twenty minutes then. We're seven days out, barring any major breakdowns." He nodded respectfully at Evan.

"We'll be ready," Evan assured him. Turning back to Abigail, Evan added, "I've arranged for Granny to care for the children while you rest. Frank will drive my wagon, and I'll drive Granny's. That way, I'm here if you need anything, anything at all."

Abigail attempted to sit up. "I'll be fine. I really don't need to—"

Gently, he pressed her back against the pillow. "You'll rest like Granny ordered. We'll travel later than usual today to make up for lost time." With his hands resting on her shoulders, he paused and studied her face for several seconds. Abigail grew steadily uncomfortable. Clearing his throat, he said, "Thank you for saving my son's life. I owe you a debt that can never really be paid." Then he turned and left the wagon.

She watched the canvas flap fall into place, leaving her to think about all that had happened. Before long she heard the call for the wagons to move out and felt the jouncing from the creaking of the wheels as they began to roll over the deep ruts and potholes made by earlier wagon trains.

They'd been averaging eight to ten miles a day, a goodly distance for a fully loaded wagon train. While the members of the Lassiter company had had their share of broken axles and busted wheel rims, they'd encountered few of the other hindrances common to west-bound travelers and a minimum of deaths along the trail.

Before they'd left Council Grove, Granny had instructed the women on the importance of maintaining good hygiene on the train. She told them that drinking hot coffee would ward off cholera. And while members of several of the other companies had suffered and died from the dreaded disease, no one in their wagon train had succumbed. As a result, they'd lost little time along the trail.

Riding in a moving wagon was anything but pleasurable, which was why everyone but the drivers walked most of the way. By evening, Abigail decided she'd had all the rest her body could stand. She crawled out of the wagon, massaging her aching hipbones and imagining the size of the bruises she would have in the morning.

"What are you doing up?" Amy called to her from the fire pit. "Daddy said you should rest tonight. Besides, Granny is teaching me how to make soda biscuits and gravy."

"I am perfectly fine," Abigail protested as she staggered to steady her wobbly knees.

"Fine! Then sit on that rock over there while Granny and I serve you."

Abigail smiled at the eight-year-old's delightful confidence. From the looks of things, everything was under control. Having nothing else to do, Abigail grabbed her pencils and art portfolio out of the back of the wagon and walked toward an outcropping of rock a short distance from the camp. She would do some sketching.

Abigail's drawings of life around the camp had become popular with the travelers. Everyone wanted a drawing to send home to their family. She'd sketched for several minutes when the thought of Granny's soda biscuits and gravy caused her stomach to rumble. She slipped her pencils into their leather pouch and closed her portfolio cover.

As she rose to her feet, she saw a grinning Evan ambling toward her with a full platter of Southern biscuits with white gravy. "Thought we'd have to send out the dogs to find you, Miss Abigail." He spooned a mouthful of gravy-covered biscuit into his mouth. "You don't know what you're missing."

"*Mmm,* it certainly smells delicious. I'm hungry enough to eat all of yours and mine too."

"Hey, wait a minute." He cut off a piece of gravy-covered biscuit with his fork and offered it to her. "I'll let you have a taste, just a taste."

For a moment, she hesitated. There was something intriguingly intimate about sharing the same fork with a man. Throwing caution to the wind, she opened her mouth and accepted Evan's offering.

"Oops!" All but one droplet of the warm, satisfying food made it into her mouth. Before she could wipe away the glob of gravy, he touched the corner of her lips with the side of his index finger. "Here, let me."

She closed her eyes to savor the incredible gentleness of his touch, opening them to find Evan's eyes closed as well, and his lips less than an inch from hers. Startled, she gasped.

Evan's eyes flew open. He jerked away from her, his face flushed with color. "Forgive me, Miss Abigail. I don't know what came over me. I-I-I, if you'll excuse me." He shoved the platter of food into her hands and hustled away, his hands shoved deeply into his pants' pockets.

Bewildered, Abigail ambled back to the camp. Tyler greeted her, waving a piece of meat in the air. "Taste the jackrabbit, Miss Abigail. Chip and his friends killed them this afternoon with their slingshots. Aren't they yummy?"

Abigail nodded absently, turning to gaze in the direction in which Evan had disappeared. Without comment, Granny refilled Abigail's plate.

"Come sit by me," Amy called, patting the flat spot on the rock beside her. "You were so brave today. I was so scared. Were you scared?"

Abigail smiled and assured the child that she, too, had been frightened. "If God hadn't answered my prayer so fast, we both would have drowned."

"God answered your prayer? How could you talk to Him under the water?"

Abigail laughed. "Easy. You just think a prayer in your mind. You don't have to say it aloud."

"Really!" The girl's eyes twinkled with delight. "Can I try it too?"

Abigail gave the child a hug. "Of course you may. God would like that very much, Amy."

"Ummm, let's see," the girl frowned. "What will I pray for first? Maybe orange satin bows for my hair."

Abigail stifled a smile, nodding softly. "I think God likes when we pray for others—like when I prayed I'd find Tyler. But He'll listen if you pray for ribbons."

"Good." She stood up and took Abigail's empty platter from her hands.

Abigail watched the child march over to the wagon where Granny stood washing the dinner dishes. *What a delightful child Amy is,* she thought. *I couldn't imagine having a more perfect child of my own.* The idea of having children of her own came as a shock to her because with it came the memory of the near-encounter with the child's father.

Whatever had overcome Evan's reasoning to suppose that he . . . She touched where his finger had touched her lip. The pleasurable sensation sent a tingle through her.

When a fight broke out several wagons down from the Chamberses' camp, Abigail barely heard the shouting. It wasn't unusual for arguments to pop up, especially after an exhausting day on the trail. The men from the surrounding wagons rushed over to the trouble spot, while the women watched from afar.

Boredom combined with exhaustion triggered one of the three greatest dangers on the trail: snakebites, cholera, and friction among the travelers. From where Abigail sat, the third had been the greatest struggle thus far. And emotions ran higher the further west they traveled.

She'd seen husbands and wives abandon all sense of propriety to battle out their differences, regardless of how many of their neighbors were watching. A misunderstood remark or an imagined slight could trigger a genuine brawl between camps. Occasionally, Hawk Lassiter and the wagon's burly military guide had to break up the dispute.

As the shouting increased, so did the number of spectators. Yet Abigail stared into the dying embers, rehashing the day. A tap on her shoulder brought her back to reality. It was Hawk Lassiter.

"Miss Abigail, do you think you could begin the evening story hour soon? It would distract the crowd long enough for me to restore order down at the Montgomery wagon."

"Of course. I'll be glad to."

He helped her to her feet. As she strolled to the story hour podium, she heard Granny ring the triangle on the side of her wagon, the official call to story time. Abigail had barely stepped up on to the wooden platform when the first of the children arrived.

"Ya gonna tell us more about Narcissa?" a little girl asked.

"I sure am. Just sit right there. You get a front row seat tonight."

Within a few minutes, the crowd had wandered over to hear the next installment of the Narcissa Whitman story. Abigail was glad that the elusive Mr. Farnsworth had shared several more anecdotes with her about the first white woman to cross the North American continent. And, as always, she spotted him standing in the shadows of a nearby wagon, listening to her words.

The noise coming from the Montgomery wagon quickly subsided once the crowd was no longer there to egg on the skirmish. Instead, Abigail's smooth alto tones shared the adventures of Narcissa Whitman's travels.

When it was time to quit, Abigail left the beautiful Narcissa and her handsome husband camping in the Blue Mountains during a snowstorm. The children groaned and begged for more, but Abigail only laughed and promised to tell them more the following night.

As she stepped down from the podium, Hawk Lassiter touched her elbow. "Miss Abigail, would you care to take a stroll with me? I have several matters to discuss with you."

Abigail blinked in surprise. "Why, of course, Mr. Lassiter. I'd be glad to."

Firmly and possessively, he took hold of her arm and led her away from the camp. "Please, please call me Hawk."

"All right, I guess."

"Why do you find it so difficult?" he asked once they were out of hearing range of the camp.

"I suppose it's because I don't know you well enough to—"

Close to her ear, he whispered, "I'd like to change that."

"Mr. Lassiter, I hardly know—" She turned in surprise to find her face captured in his hands.

When she tried to speak, he brushed his finger across her lips. "No," he said, "let me finish."

She opened her mouth to speak again, and again he placed his finger on her lips. "I've been watching you for some time now, first on the riverboat, then with the children, especially the Chambers children. You are a brave and intelligent woman, a woman worthy of my love."

Abigail's eyebrows shot up. "Worthy? Of your love?" she gasped.

"That didn't come out right." He shook his head and took a deep breath. "Because of my royal lineage, I must choose my bride wisely."

"Bride?" She stared incredulously at the man standing in front of her. Her lower jaw rubbed against the ruffle on the collar of her calico dress. Despite the shadows hiding his expression, she could tell the man was sweating from discomfort.

"I'm sorry. This is coming out all wrong. No one would suspect I was once the president of Oxford University's debating team! What I'm trying to say is, since you have no one to whom I should go to ask for the privilege of courting you, I decided to come directly to you."

"Courting?"

"Yes. I want to court you. Is that such a strange idea?"

"I-I-I, er, a, well . . ." She searched for an answer. Did she want him to court her? She'd thought of him as marriage material for Clarissa Darlington, perhaps, but not for Abigail Sherwood. "Well, I-I-I don't know what to say."

"Don't say anything. Just promise me you'll think about it."

She nodded slowly. "All right, I'll think about it, and pray about it." *Will I ever pray about it,* she told herself.

To seal the promise, he planted a firm kiss on her lips, then stepped back.

"Forgive me, but what triggered this—this sudden burst of emotion?" she asked as she brushed the back of her hand lightly across her lips.

Slipping his arm around her waist, he started back to the camp. "The early bird gets the worm, Miss Abigail."

"Excuse me?"

"I wouldn't want you to confuse Evan Chambers's gratitude for love. There is a difference you know. The man recently lost his wife. It would be easy and natural for you or him to confuse love and gratitude."

She cast a surprised glance his way and then frowned. The man was serious. Abigail had never imagined in her wildest fantasies that she could be at the apex of a love triangle. It was ludicrous.

The camp was quiet by the time they returned to Granny Parker's wagon. At the tailgate, Hawk Lassiter released Abigail's arm, his fingers lingering on her hand. "You will consider what I asked?"

She looked up into his face, shadowed by the brim of his hat. "I promised I would."

Lifting her hand to his lips, he kissed her fingertips. "Till tomorrow then." He bowed and disappeared into the darkness.

The stunned young woman exhaled sharply. The bizarre evening had turned her world upside down. While she'd been harboring romantic thoughts about one man, a second man, one she'd never considered, wanted to court her.

Rather than enter the wagon and risk arousing Granny Parker's curiosity, Abigail ambled over to the campfire. She picked up a stick and idly stirred the dying embers. Cow chips and buffalo chips burned hot and long.

She found a seat on an overturned water bucket where she gazed into the red glow of the dying fire. From the east, she could hear the lowing of the train's cattle and the occasional whinny of a horse. Boston had never seemed so far away as it did that night.

Marriage. She'd always imagined that if she married, she'd marry for love. But what was love anyway? A kiss in the moonlight? Hands accidentally brushing against each other? Shared thoughts and dreams?

She recalled the times she and Evan had talked about the beautiful Willamette Valley. Was a shared dream a sign of love between two people? A mud fight? Abigail giggled aloud at the memory of the startled look on Evan's face when she threw the first mud pie at him.

Wait a minute. I'm supposed to be thinking about Hawk Lassiter, not Evan Chambers. She lifted her face toward the heavens, *Oh, dear God, I'm so confused. What am I supposed to do? Should I encourage Hawk Lassiter to court me? I don't love him, as nice a man as he is.* Her words startled her. *No, I don't love Hawk, but perhaps with time . . . He's a good man, and he says he loves me. No, he says he admires me. There is a difference.*

A cooling breeze reminded her that she'd left her shawl in the wagon. After her unexpected swim earlier that day, she'd better take no chances with catching a cold. She'd consider her quandary another day. Stirring the embers one more time, she dropped the stick, rose to her feet, and returned to the wagon.

CHAPTER FIFTEEN

THE COURTING

IT WAS EVIDENT TO THE ENTIRE CAMP THAT their company wagon master was courting the lady storyteller. Hawk Lassiter made his intentions known to everyone and anyone who would listen, including the object of his affections.

Gifts began arriving at the Parker wagon, bouquets of wildflowers, humorous rhymes, a Shakespearean sonnet over which Chip gagged and Amy swooned. When a bar of exquisite French lilac soap was delivered with a note from Hawk Lassiter, Amy announced, "What an insult! He must think you need a bath."

Abigail laughed at the girl's wrinkled nose. "We all need baths, if you ask me."

Not only did the three Chambers children resent Hawk Lassiter's intensified presence, but Granny Parker had her say about the man's frequent visits. And Abigail could read envy in the eyes of several other single women on the wagon train.

Hawk Lassiter did cut a commanding figure astride his black mare. The silver trappings on his saddle and reins glistened in the sunlight as he rode the length of the wagon train, checking for trouble spots and shouting orders.

It seemed to Abigail, and most likely to others as well, that Hawk Lassiter found it necessary to "check the perimeters" as he called it, more often since he declared his intentions toward the story lady. The only person who seemed unaware of Hawk's efforts to win Abigail's heart was Evan, the only one she wished would care.

Since the evening Hawk asked her for permission to court her, Abigail had spent long hours on her knees, praying for wisdom and equally long hours searching for God's guidance in His Word. Yet she'd found no answer.

In frustration, she cried aloud as she drove Granny's team, "Why, Father? Why aren't You answering my cries for help? I don't know what to do! I've never been so confused in my life!"

Suddenly, the lead right horse shied away from a coiled rattler. She flicked the reins, barely noticing the hated serpent. "You promised to give me peace, Father, a fruit of Your Spirit living in me, remember? So where is this peace? I surely don't feel it!" She felt trapped in an English garden, a maze where every pathway stopped at a dead end. Finally, she threw her hands in the air toward God. "I give up trying to figure this out. Teach me to trust You to make all things right."

Immediately, the promises she'd memorized as a little child entered her mind. *"My peace I give unto you. . . . Let not your heart be troubled, neither let it be afraid." "Be content with such things as ye have: for he hath said, I will never leave thee, nor forsake thee." "Be still, and know that I am God." "In all thy ways acknowledge him, and he shall direct thy paths." "He shall give thee the desires of thine heart."*

"How ya doing? Are you all right?" Hawk Lassiter rode by on his horse. He had Tyler seated in front of him on the saddle. Abigail's thoughts had been so intense she hadn't known Hawk was there until he called to her.

"Fine, just fine." She waved and smiled broadly. "Hold on tight," she called to Tyler. Abigail sighed, for she recognized Hawk's attempt to win her heart by winning Tyler's approval. *Abigail Sherwood! Of all the self-centered thinking. Believe it or not, the entire world does not focus on you and your interests. Just maybe, Hawk gave Tyler a ride to be nice. It could be as simple as that!* Even as she scolded herself, she knew better. *The man doesn't know when to stop!*

The Lassiter train arrived at Independence Rock on the afternoon of July 4. Several other wagon trains were already camped and celebrating the holiday. Abigail, Granny, and the children hiked to the Great Register of the desert to scratch their names into the granite monolith.

"Look!" Granny pointed to the name of a Parker who'd registered two years previous. "A George Parker. I wonder if that's my Earl's Uncle George." She read through the family names listed below. "Land sakes! I think it is. Imagine that!"

Like ants, the travelers climbed over the rock, seeking familiar names. It was like finding letters from long absent friends. Abigail found the signature of a William Sherwood, United States Cavalry. She knew he probably was no relation to her, but it warmed her heart to pretend he might be.

They would stay a day or two in the shade of Independence Rock. The campground by the banks of the Sweetwater River was a crowded, unsanitary transitory town like so many others along the Oregon Trail, complete with its own graveyard. Like waves on the ocean, the pioneers filled these campgrounds then abandoned them for the next way station. Abigail sighed. The rest would be welcome after weeks of crossing the hot dusty prairie.

While the men checked the wagons for repairs and women did the family laundry in the river, the children swam in the cooling waters during the day. Evenings were a time for boisterous celebrating and patriotic oratory.

Although Abigail had checked out the swimming area before letting Tyler enter the water, she didn't take her attention from him for any length of time.

"So, it's you and Mr. Lassiter, I hear." A blond woman she'd only seen at a distance cast a slanted eye at Abigail. "Will you be marrying the big man on the trail or after you reach Oregon?"

Abigail blushed. She hated being the center of attention, especially in matters of the heart. "I guess that remains to be seen."

The middle-aged woman placed a motherly hand on Abigail's arm. "Well, if you want my advice, I wouldn't leave a strapping young man like him dangling in the wind for too long."

Abigail tried to smile graciously, but she didn't feel a smidgen of grace toward the woman. The arrival of Evan to carry the basket of wet laundry back to the wagon saved Abigail from uttering a nasty reply.

"What is it with these people?" she asked Evan as they walked through the tall grass back to the camp. "Everyone is determined to marry me off! I wish they'd all mind their own business!"

She waited for Evan's reply. When none came, she glanced up at him. "Surely, you have some word of advice?"

He shrugged. A smile tweaked the corners of his mouth. "I'm just minding my own business."

"All right, I get the point. But I would appreciate your advice. You're the only one who hasn't had something to say about the attention Hawk Lassiter has been pouring on me. Surely you have an opinion."

"Yep."

"Well? What is it?" Her impatience flared. The man could be so obtuse!

"Don't let anyone rush you into doing something you're unsure about. When I courted Sara, her grandmother told her to winter and summer 'em before marrying 'em." He pursed his lips and scowled. "It was good advice. I think we were as happy as any couple deserves to be."

"What do you mean by that?"

"Sara was a sweet girl with a good heart. Her only flaw was she never learned to be content. Happiness was always ahead of her or behind her, never with her." He glanced quickly at Abigail. "Not that I fault her. She was a loving mother and a dutiful wife."

"Like heading west dutifully?" Abigail knew she was treading on dangerous ground, but she'd listened to Sara's griping, both at Serenity Inn and on the trail before she died. And Evan was right. Sara found it difficult to be happy. Abigail could detect the same disquieted nature in Amy.

"Yes, like heading west. Sara was all in favor of moving to Oregon while she was the center of attention back home in Maine. But once we were on the road, the glamour dimmed."

A wet pillowcase fell out of the basket on to the ground. Abigail picked it up and placed it on the top of the stack of wet clothing. "It's none of my business, really." She fumbled for the right words to say.

"I'm not being disloyal when I admit the truth about Sara, especially to you, the woman who so ably stepped in to care for her children." He picked up the pace. "I know that I owe you a debt of gratitude for so many things." Upon reaching the wagon, he set the basket of wet laundry down beside the wagon tongue, straightened, and cast her a sidelong glance. "But you, Abigail Sherwood, don't owe me any-thing!"

He turned away so abruptly that she didn't have time to respond. Hands on her hips, she stared after his disappearing figure. "What was that—"

"Well, hello there," a voice called. "I wondered where you were hiding." She turned to see a smiling Hawk Lassiter. "I was hoping you could attend the patriotic celebrations with me tonight. I'm sure Granny won't mind watching the Chamberses' children for a few hours."

She ignored the slight edge in the man's tone and draped a pair of socks over the tongue of the wagon. "Perhaps. I'll check with her. But first, I must finish hanging this stack of laundry to dry before I even think of anything else."

Hawk grinned at her, brushing a stray curl from her flushed cheek. "You are beautiful even when you're working. Imagine how gorgeous you will look strolling into Windsor Castle on my arm and wearing the Lassiter family jewels."

"Windsor Castle? In England?" Abigail had never before consid-ered the possibility of one day returning to her homeland as a bona fide member of the monarchy, no matter how removed from the ac-tual throne he might be. Her face must have revealed her astonish-ment.

"Of course, darling. Once I establish my presence in Oregon, I'll want to report back to my queen. I am first and foremost a British subject. Oh, Abigail, you'll be stunningly elegant wearing a Parisian-made gown of icy blue silk, with my grandmother's diamond necklace gracing your long, slender neck and the matching teardrop earrings attached to your delicate earlobes." He paused midstep and faced her. "Did you know that you have the most perfect earlobes for displaying my grandmother's diamonds? And your neck . . ." Taking his free hand, he ran his fingertips down the side of her cheek and neck.

Words failed Abigail. In all her fantasies she'd never imagined a man of title falling in love with her, the gawky, ugly duckling of her family.

As Hawk leaned forward to kiss her, Tyler came running to where they stood. "Miss Abigail! Miss Abigail! Look at the frog I caught. See? See?"

When Tyler opened the gunnysack, the frog leaped out of the bag and on to Abigail's sleeve. Startled, Abigail squealed and flailed her arms. The frightened frog leaped to the only stable place in the vicinity, the brim of Hawk's hat.

The man instinctively tossed the hat into the air, frog and all. The hat landed on a nearby wagon wheel. All the while Tyler shouted for them to catch his new pet. The frog disappeared under the wagon with Tyler close behind.

Obviously, the moment had passed. Abigail wasn't sure if Tyler's intrusion made her happy or sad.

As the boy scrambled to recapture his frog, Hawk gave her a wry grin. "Well, uh, I guess I'd better finish my camp inspection. Then tonight, do we have a date?"

Over his shoulder, Abigail spotted Evan rounding the corner of the wagon. Their eyes met for an instant. She could see a heavy sadness in his stormy gray-blue eyes. The man paused, whirled about, and disappeared from view.

Fighting the desire to run after him to explain, Abigail agreed to the date. By the time Hawk strode away, Evan was nowhere to be seen.

Exasperated, she yanked a dried pillowcase from the temporary clothesline strung between Granny's and the Chamberses' wagons. Holding the dry pillowcase in her hands, she held it up to her nose and sniffed. She enjoyed the sweetness of laundry freshly dried on the prairie. *If I could bottle the aroma and sell it to housewives back east, I'd be rich,* she thought.

As she gathered the family laundry from the line and lovingly folded each garment, Abigail wondered how many more times would she fold Tyler's brown canvas pants, Amy's yellow gingham Sunday-go-to-meeting dress, and Evan's sturdy broadcloth shirt that matched the shade of his eyes so perfectly. Would the next woman take care to smooth out the embroidered collar on Amy's favorite calico? Would there be a "next woman"?

Don't be ridiculous, she scolded herself. *Of course there will be another woman. Evan Chambers will not remain single once he settles in*

Oregon. Right now, some pretty little thing churning butter on her parents' back porch overlooking the Willamette River has no idea that the love of her life is heading her way even as she churns. The idea disturbed her. *It's the children, of course. I'll miss the children.*

To take her mind off such thoughts, she tried to imagine herself being presented to Queen Victoria and her court. Placing the last of the dried laundry in the basket, she gave a dramatic curtsy, then giggled.

"Practicing?"

Abigail whirled about in surprise to find Granny standing behind her, water bucket in hand.

"Thought you might like to walk with an old woman down to the river for a bucket of clean water. It's nearing suppertime. Chip's been sniffing around the pantry for a day-old soda biscuit."

Abigail recovered and reached for the bucket. "I'd love to walk with you. Here, let me carry that."

"On the way back I'll need your help. So, were you practicing?"

Abigail reddened, "Practicing what?"

Granny didn't mince her words, "Your curtsy for the queen?"

"Granny! That's silly. When would I ever meet a queen?"

"Not a queen, but *the* queen." The woman continued, "You will make a striking lady in the royal court."

"Granny! I am far from making up my mind regarding Mr. Lassiter's proposal. There are several factors to consider."

"Actually, my dear, there is only one factor. Do you love him?"

"I don't agree. First, I made a commitment to Evan regarding the children. Keeping my word is important to me."

Granny smiled. "That's admirable."

"And I would be amiss to leap into a marriage without being sure that I am acting out God's will for me." Abigail scowled. "My mind is in such a turmoil. A friend I made in Missouri before I left, her name is Serenity Cunard, warned me that there are seven men to every woman, but even with those odds, I never really expected to be faced with such a dilemma."

"What's the dilemma? You love him? You marry him. If you don't, you don't."

Granny had a way of simplifying everything. Abigail sighed. "It's not that easy."

"Of course it is. If you love him deep inside, you know it." She nodded, a secret smile spreading across her face. "When I married Earl, I hadn't a doubt in the world that he was the one and only man for me."

"And if God brought another man along?" Abigail teased.

The older woman shook her head emphatically. "Won't happen. Earl was the joy of my life."

"Is it possible to like and admire someone enough to marry him without—"

Granny looked completely surprised. "Without love? Honey, you marry anyone you want to for whatever reasons you might concoct, but a loveless marriage can be mighty lonely." She peered at Abigail over the rim of her glasses. "When troubles come, and they will, it's love, not like or admiration, that brings you through. Love, not tolerance, makes the difference."

Abigail felt as though she'd been soundly chastised by the time they reached the river's edge. Somehow she knew that had Serenity Cunard spoken, the message would have been the same. As she filled the bucket with the icy, cold water, Abigail remembered the endearing attentions the Cunards had exchanged with one another: his hand lingering on her shoulder, a pat on his back as she passed, a look, a silent kiss thrown across the room, the way they tenderly deferred to each other. It was the kind of marriage Abigail had only read about in books.

Though Granny continued sharing her nuggets of wisdom for marital bliss, Abigail was busy imagining herself and Hawk Lassiter sharing that kind of relationship.

Suddenly, Granny's voice broke through her reverie. "What does your young man think about God?"

"God?" Abigail jolted back to the present. She frowned. "Why, I don't know. I've never asked him."

Granny nodded sagely. "Mighty important information to know for the daughter of a preacher man."

CHAPTER SIXTEEN

MAKING DETOURS AND DECISIONS

O N JULY 6, WAGONS ROLLED WESTWARD ONCE more. Like a snake, the white-canvassed wagons wound their way, mile after mile, into the mountains. Since the Lassiter company had arrived at Independence Rock later than some of the other wagon trains, the company council decided to rest the animals an extra day before continuing on to South Pass and Soda Springs.

Abigail appreciated the relative silence that returned once the majority of travelers had left the camp. While the carnival atmosphere was fun for a short time, it grew tiresome after the second day.

Deciding they needed a ladies' day to relax, Abigail, Granny, and Amy packed a picnic lunch, took a change of clothing, and trekked upriver. They hoped to find an isolated spot where they could bathe one more time before the long, dry march across Sublette Cutoff.

Finding a secluded spot along the river, the three ladies shed their outer garments and slipped into the cool, refreshing water. Abigail was washing Amy's hair when she spotted three Indian braves watching them from a nearby cliff.

Furious, she shouted at them, "What kind of gentlemen are you, watching ladies bathe? Go on with you. Shoo!"

Granny, who'd been rinsing the soap from her own hair, spied the three braves just as they ducked behind a rock. She yipped and dived beneath the water. Amy did the same.

"Imagine, sitting there and watching us bathe!" Abigail sputtered. "Of all the poor manners—"

"They don't speak English," a voice called from the opposite shore. Abigail whipped about to see Evan standing with one leg propped up on a rock. A wicked grin was plastered across his face.

"You too?" Abigail screeched. "I would have thought better of you!"

"Daddy! Hi!" Amy squealed, frolicking in the water. "I'm getting my hair washed with perfumed soap."

"That's great, baby," he called. Returning his attention to Abigail, he added, "I'm not here to spy on you. I was bathing farther upstream when I heard you ladies laughing." He removed his hat and brushed his hand through his damp curls. "Tell me, do women always take baths wearing so many clothes?"

Abigail glanced down at the straps of her cotton plissé chemise. The water came up to her armpits. Indians or not, there wasn't much to see. "It's the principle of the thing. A true gentleman wouldn't come upon a lady bathing without warning her."

"Yes, ma'am. I'm sorry, ma'am." Evan hung his head in mock shame.

"Oh, you odious man!" Abigail skidded her hand along the top of the water, sending a spray toward shore. Evan jumped and laughed.

"Nice try." He waved, and then shouted, "Hey!" Pointing to the shore where the women had left their clothing, he asked, "Are those your dresses that the three Indians are taking?"

"What?" Abigail whirled about in time to see the flounce of her favorite calico disappear behind a rock. "Why didn't you stop them?" she shouted at Evan.

"From here?" He cocked his head toward his rifle. "And start a range war?"

Granny spun about in the water. "Tell me, young man, what are we suppose to do now? We certainly can't walk back into camp in our wet underclothing!"

"Daddy, do something!" Amy wailed.

"All right, all right. I'll run back to camp and get some blankets for you. Is that satisfactory?" He eyed Abigail as if daring her to complain.

"Well, what's keeping ya?" Granny sputtered. "Away with you. Imagine some Indian squaw wearing my favorite gingham!"

"Do you mean some little Indian girl will get to have my dress?" Amy's eyes were round with wonder. At each army fort along the trail, the child had seen the animal-skin clothing the Indian children wore. One night she confided to Abigail that she was glad she didn't have to wear the skin of deer or elk.

"Probably so," Abigail admitted.

The girl gave a pleased smile. "I'm glad. I hope she likes my dress as much as I did."

Granny's eyes softened. "It takes a child to put things into proper perspective, doesn't it?"

Abigail nodded.

Within minutes, Evan arrived with three wool blankets and a spare pair of shoes for each of them. He turned his back long enough to allow the three of them to get out of the river and to wrap up in the blankets.

When he received the all-clear sign, he lifted his daughter on to his shoulders. "Comfortable, honey?" he asked.

"Remember when you and Mommy would go for walks and you'd carry me like this?" the child asked from atop her enviable perch.

"Yes, honey." Evan dipped his head and looked away.

As Abigail turned to follow Evan down the trail toward camp, she remembered her portfolio. "Evan! My portfolio!" She pointed toward the opposite shore. He shook his head and shrugged. There wasn't much he could do.

Having planned to do some sketching while drying her hair in the sun, she'd left her art supplies with their clothing. And now they were gone. Hours of artwork that chronicled her journey from Boston. The faces of people she'd never see again. Gone. Even as she mourned her loss, Abigail was grateful that, at least, she hadn't lost her journal of Bessy's recipes as well.

That evening the thieving Indians were the topic of conversation. Abigail was surprised to hear the diverse opinions about Native American people that were held by the travelers, everything from tolerance and Christian love to "the only good Indian is a dead Indian." *What will these people think when I get to the part in Narcissa's story where she was massacred?* Abigail wondered.

That night, after the evening story time, Hawk smoothly maneuvered her away from the others. "I thought a walk in the moonlight would be a pleasant diversion while we're rested from our trek. To-morrow morning we break camp and begin climbing to the Great Divide—a torturous part of the journey, to say the least."

"How romantic, Mr. Lassiter." Abigail chuckled. "Taking a stroll in the moonlight before we're too exhausted to do so. You could turn a girl's head with sweet talk like that."

"Really? I was beginning to think nothing could turn my woman's head." He drew her protectively to his side. "It might be wise if you and the other women didn't stray too far from the wagons without letting someone know. Sergeant Brumby, our guide, has reported seeing several Indian camps in the foothills. Your braves probably came from one of them."

Abigail shuddered, remembering the tales of white women taken captive for slaves, or worse yet, to become squaws for the braves. Determined not to dwell on such thoughts, she asked, "Tell me about the Great Divide, as you call it. It's at South Pass, right?"

"Yep. It's said that you can stand at one point and if you spill a cup of water on your left, the water will eventually end up in the Atlantic Ocean, and if you spill a cup of water on your right, it will eventually end up in the Pacific Ocean, theoretically of course."

"That's amazing. I wonder who made the discovery?"

"Some trapper, I suppose."

As they approached the Chamberses' wagon, Evan strode toward them. "Glad to see you back, Miss Abigail." He scowled at them both. "Tyler has eaten something he shouldn't have and has been upchucking for the last half hour."

"Oh, no, the poor baby. Is he in your wagon?" Abigail didn't wait for an answer; she rushed toward the wagon.

"Yes, Granny's with him. I sent Amy to sleep in Granny's wagon and I don't know hide nor hair where Chip could be." It was obvious the boy's father was distraught. "I need to go looking for him." Evan shifted his gaze to Hawk. "I'm sure he's in camp somewhere. He knows better than—"

"I'll go with you." Hawk sprinted toward the corral. "Let me get my horse."

Abigail left the men to solve the problem of the missing boy. She knew how quickly rumors of cholera could start through the camp, so she wanted to check out the youngest Chambers boy herself.

Inside the wagon she found Granny coaxing the boy to sip her peppermint-chamomile tea. She'd filled a leather canteen with the hot liquid. "This should last him until morning," she advised the younger woman. "If you need me, I'll stay."

"Nonsense," Abigail scolded. "You need to get your rest. I've been noticing how your rheumatism has been acting up since we reached the mountains."

Granny started to protest, but Abigail wouldn't have it. "It will be a big help if you keep Amy tonight. If Tyler's coming down with something, it wouldn't do to have his sister contract it as well."

Granny nodded. "You're right. I've filled a bucket with water, and here's a washrag to cool his head. Better keep the chamber pot handy too," she warned. "This child gets little warning."

When Granny disappeared out of the wagon, Abigail smiled down at the big blue eyes peering out from beneath a muslin sheet. "I'm sorry," Tyler mumbled, a tear streaking down his flushed cheek.

"Oh, honey, it's not your fault you got sick." She sat beside his tiny body. "Can you tell me where you hurt the most?"

"My stomach and my head," he groaned.

"When did you start feeling sick?"

"During your story tonight. I didn't tell anyone because I didn't want to miss the story," he shyly admitted. "Daddy's real upset, isn't he?"

"Not at you, honey. At Chip. He's worried about you, but he's not angry with you."

His forehead knitted into a frown. "Are you sure?"

"Very sure." She touched her lips to the child's fevered brow, then wrung out the Turkish cloth and placed it on Tyler's forehead. "That feel better?"

"Mmm." The tiny smile on his face was a sweet reward. Abigail remembered many times she'd seen the same grateful smile on the faces of her sister's children when they'd been sick. Poor Rebecca flew into a tizzy whenever one of her babies was ill, leaving the ever-practical Abigail to care for the child and her sister.

As she sat by Tyler, Abigail wondered how her sister was doing. Had the new baby arrived? Was it a boy or girl? How were the older children getting along with their new nanny?

"Miss Abigail?" Suddenly, Tyler shot upright. "I'm going to be—"

Before the next word came from his mouth, the peppermint-chamomile tea he'd been drinking at Granny's insistence spewed forth all over her, the bedding, and himself. "I'm sorry," he wailed. "I tried to—"

She leaped for the chamber pot and set it on his lap. "Here, you might not be finished."

The boy was sobbing. She caressed his shoulders and back, cooing reassurances in his ear. "Don't you worry. I'll have this cleaned up in a flash." She grabbed the clean rag Granny had laid at the foot of the mattress and sopped up the liquid. "Aren't you glad you weren't eating greens and grits? *Yech!*"

The boy laughed in spite of his tears.

"Or, what if you'd eaten, um," she thought for a moment, "gingerbread and sarsaparilla soda?"

"*Euugh!*" he grimaced.

She collected the soiled cloths and stood up. "Are you feeling better?"

He nodded and handed her the porcelain chamber pot. She slid it against the side of the wagon.

"Well enough for me to leave you alone while I rinse out these cloths?"

"Uh-huh. My stomach's feeling lots better."

She brushed a shock of damp hair from his forehead. "Good. I'll be right back. Just call me if you need me."

She lifted the canvas at the end of the wagon and inhaled the clean, fresh night air. It took no time at all to scrub the soiled cloths clean and hang them along the side of the wagon to dry.

Stretching to remove an annoying stitch in her back, Abigail closed her eyes and yawned. It had been a long day. With any luck Tyler would sleep through the night.

She sighed, whirled about to return to the wagon, and slammed into Chip Chambers. The alcohol on the boy's breath hit her with more force than did his body. "Chip!" She gasped in surprise. "Your father and Mr. Lassiter are looking for you."

"Likely story!" The boy snarled. "All those two can see is you, the marvelous Miss Abigail Sherwood. You're all anyone on the train talks about— not the danger of snakes or Indians, but the incredible Miss Sherwood."

"Chip, I—"

Out of the shadows came a giant hand which grabbed the slight boy by the nape of his neck. The hand was followed by a furious Evan Chambers. "Apologize to the lady, son!"

"Oh yes, sir!" he snarled. "Wouldn't want to insult the next Mrs. Chambers, would I?"

His father gave him a shake, but the boy glared at Abigail anyway. "Or is it to be Mrs. Lassiter today? You can't fool me. You're having a great time making my dad and Mr. Lassiter dance to your silly tunes."

When Evan bought his hand back to slap the boy's face, Abigail stepped in and cried, "No! Don't." The father's hand caught her on the shoulder, sending her sprawling in the dirt. Instantly, Evan released his son and helped the stunned woman to her feet. "Oh, Miss Abigail, I am so sorry. I-I-I don't know what to say. Are you all right?"

Abigail rubbed her hip. "I think so. I couldn't let you hit—" She stopped midsentence, realizing she'd overstepped her authority.

"How I discipline my son is my business, *Miss* Abigail."

Her side ached, but her heart ached more as she stared at the stranger before her. She hated being caught between two people. Gathering her skirts in her hands, she rushed into the wagon.

"What happened?" Tyler asked.

"Nothing! Go to sleep."

The boy cowered under the sheets. "I'm sorry."

Regretting her cross words, Abigail kissed the boy's forehead and adjusted the sheet over him. "No, you did nothing wrong. I did, and I'm sorry. Will you forgive me?"

"Uh-huh." One of the things she loved best about little children was their capacity to forgive. She turned down the wick in the oil lantern and stretched out, fully dressed on what was usually Amy's bed. Chip's anger disturbed her. Did he truly believe that the two men he most admired were fighting over her? *How ridiculous!*

Outside the wagon, Chip and his father shouted at each other until a male voice from another wagon told them to pipe down. The last words Abigail heard brought tears to her eyes. "You want Miss Abigail to fill Mom's shoes. Well, she never can!"

As Abigail closed her eyes, she recalled a sermon her father gave one Easter morning about Jesus calling the little children. At the end of the service, her father called all the children in the sanctuary to the front and gave each of them a white lily and then admonished them to treasure the delicate innocence of childhood. "Remember, the kingdom of heaven is made up of children just like you." In a strange way, her father was one of those people who never lost the beauty of childhood.

She rolled to face the canvas wall. A tear trickled down her cheek. "Oh, Papa, I miss you so much. If only you could tell me what to do. No matter which way I turn, I hurt someone." For the first time since leaving Council Grove, she wondered if continuing on to Oregon had been the wisest decision.

Tyler slept most of the night, as did Abigail. Both were awakened by the sounds of their neighbors breaking camp for the day's journey through the desolate South Pass and across the dry, barren Sublette Cutoff. It was a section of the journey Abigail had been dreading. How this stretch of road could be drier than the areas they'd come through she couldn't imagine.

Granny brought a bowl of oatmeal to each of them in the wagon and insisted they both relax since she knew they'd been up most of the night.

"Actually, we—" Abigail began.

"Nonsense." Granny placed the tray of food on the foot of Tyler's bedding. "Amy and I have everything under control. Here's some fresh clothing for you." The woman paused, then added, "By the by, pay no attention to young Chip. He'll come around."

"But where did he get the idea—"

Granny's face softened. "Why, child, surely you must see—"

"See what?"

Granny patted Abigail's cheek tenderly. "You, my dear, are going to have to choose between those two men soon."

The older woman's words hung in the air as Abigail ate her breakfast and helped Tyler finish his. When the child rolled over to go back to sleep, Abigail washed as best she could and slipped into fresh clothing.

The morning heat was already climbing. The cooler temperatures at the higher altitudes would be welcome. Before she began brushing her hair, Abigail rolled up the sides of the canvas to allow the breezes to blow through as well as to catch glimpses of the changing terrain.

Sitting cross-legged on a mattress, Abigail began the tedious chore of brushing her hair one hundred times, as she had done every day since her twelfth birthday. She'd barely completed seventy strokes when Evan drew back the canvas separating the wagon's living area from the driver's seat. He gasped at the sight of her honey brown locks cascading down around her shoulders. For a moment, he didn't speak, silently watching the color rise in her cheeks.

"Yes?" She couldn't believe that he'd sit and stare at her.

Clearing his throat, he asked, "Ready to roll, Miss Abigail?"

Her stomach churned despite the fake smile pasted on her face. "Absolutely." Unconsciously, she flipped her hair behind her shoulders and heard his breath catch in his throat. The canvas panel fell between them, blocking any further conversation.

CHAPTER SEVENTEEN

IN THE HANDS OF GOD

O N THE WAY UP THE MOUNTAIN PASS, ABIGAIL ignored her loosened hair. The wind whipped it about her shoulders. She didn't care. The other sojourners were too caught up in their own little worlds to notice.

The sweeping sagebrush plain sloped imperceptibly upward. In the distance, she saw a herd of pronghorn antelope. Overhead, soaring hawks and feathery clouds cast shadows on the weary travelers.

It was the Chamberses' turn to be the last wagon in the day's order, making the journey altogether pleasant. Abigail rested her chin on her arms as she stared out the side of the wagon, enjoying the breezes that ruffled her hair around her shoulders and down her back. She'd pull it back and braid it later. But for the moment, she felt as free as a child again.

She glanced at the sleeping Tyler and sighed with relief. His face was no longer flushed and the cooling breezes were helping him rest better. She returned her attention to the passing landscape.

The famed mountain pass, nestled between two little hills, grew larger as the long stream of white-canvassed wagons inched closer. As they ascended the rocky pass, the wagon train suddenly came to a halt. Abigail craned her neck to determine what caused the holdup.

"A broken spoke on the Farnsworth wagon," Sergeant Brumby announced as he rode by on his palomino mare. "They'll have it changed in no time."

Satisfied with his explanation, Abigail pulled back the canvas flap between the wagon and the driver. "Tyler's sleeping, and I think I'm going to join him for a while."

Evan nodded. "Think I'll go see if they need my help." He tied the reins to the brake handle and hopped down from the wagon.

Abigail stretched out on the mattress and closed her eyes. The sweet sensation of the mystical world between sleep and wakefulness washed over her.

"Miss Abigail? Miss Abigail?" Tyler's voice broke into her stupor. "Miss Abigail, I gotta go!"

She rolled over to face him. "Use the chamber pot, honey."

"No, please. Will you take me out there?" He pointed toward a large outcropping of rock, the perfect blind for preserving the traveler's occasional need for privacy. Trying to be sensitive to the boy's feelings, Abigail eyed the wagon where the men were busy changing the broken wheel.

"All right. Come on. They're still working, but we have to hurry. We don't want to keep the wagon train waiting."

The boy hopped down from the wagon with surprising agility considering how ill he'd been the day before. Not waiting for Abigail, he galloped across the rocky terrain and disappeared behind the first large bolder.

For her own privacy, Abigail veered toward a massive boulder on the left. Then the unexpected happened. A rock shifted beneath her boot. Her left ankle turned, causing her to lose her balance. As she fell, she hit her head against the granite boulder with a sickening crash. And her world went black.

* * * * *

The first thing she felt when she awakened was cold—cold from the dew-laden earth and the crisp dawn air. Shivering, she lay on the grass wondering where she was. The blinding pain in her head throbbed with the rhythm of a military drummer. Was she at Fort Laramie for morning reveille? Or Fort Kearny? She shook her head in an attempt to clear her mind. She groaned from the excruciating pain the movement produced. Her mouth tasted like she'd swallowed a dried prickly pear.

The image of a boy came into her mind—Tyler. Tyler? Her eyes flew open. Where was Tyler? All too clearly she remembered her fall. How long had she been lying there? She had to get to the boy. He needed her.

She tried to lift one hand to her forehead but couldn't separate her hands. Why were her hands lashed together with a leather cord? She stared at her hands, not comprehending her situation. When she tried to move her legs, she discovered her ankles were also tied together, like a calf roped for branding.

Her head flopped back against the ground, and she lost consciousness again. When she awoke a second time, Abigail found herself astride a mule, her face nuzzled in the creature's bristly mane. The animal moved in a leisurely fashion, with no haste.

She lifted her head enough to see an Indian brave leading her mule. He wore a tan deerskin shirt and trousers. They were part of a line of pack animals. Reluctant to reveal that she was no longer unconscious, Abigail moved her head imperceptibly and spotted a group of women as well as several small children walking beside the pack train.

How did I get here? And where is Tyler? Is he strapped to the back of one of the other animals? Her heart beat wildly at the thought.

But then a worse thought entered her mind. *Where is the wagon train? What if it left without us?* Her palms dripped with sweat. Her heart thumped uncontrollably. All caution evaporated as she lifted her head, hoping to spot the wagons and the young boy.

A flurry of unintelligible words came from a nearby woman. The brave leading her mule stopped and spoke to her. She recoiled from the gruffness in his voice. Whatever he said caused the entire caravan to stop. Carefully, he lifted her from the back of the mule and sat her on a small boulder.

"Sit." His expression remained hard and inscrutable.

She blinked. "Do you speak English?"

"Some." He pointed to himself. "Running Elk."

Abigail smiled. "And I am Abigail Sherwood."

His expression didn't flicker.

"Perhaps you can help me . . ." She started to rise to her feet. He pushed her back.

"You sit."

"Please, tell me—when you found me, there was a boy, a little boy." She gestured with her hands, forgetting they were still bound.

"No boy. Just you."

"But there had to be. A little boy, four years old. He was—"

"No boy. Just you." With that he turned, said something to one of the women, and strode to where the rest of the men waited. An older woman strolled over to Abigail and handed her a leather water bag.

Grateful, Abigail gulped the precious liquid, splashing it on her clothes and face. But she didn't care. The older woman snatched the bag from her with a frown and, Abigail suspected, a sound scolding.

The leather thong binding her hands cut into her flesh. Figuring it was worth asking, she lifted her hands to the woman. "Please, can you remove this? I promise not to run away."

The woman uttered a guttural sounding phrase and pointed toward Running Elk. When she looked in the direction the woman pointed, Abigail was surprised to see that Running Elk was the only adult male left in the group. Where had the others gone?

The old woman left Abigail to rejoin the other women who sat in a ring, chatting in an Indian dialect and frequently laughing in Abigail's direction. Abigail studied the knots used on the leather thong that restrained her ankles. She realized she could undo them with her eyes closed if need be. *I could escape. Come night, I could escape. But where to?* She tried to ignore her rising panic. She didn't know where she was or how she might go about finding her wagon train.

To take her mind off her discomfort, she watched the small children playing games together. One of the women called to the children. Abigail gasped when she saw the woman wore Granny's calico dress and held Amy's dress while she beckoned to one of the little girls. A second woman wore Abigail's gown, while a third proudly wore Granny's camisole and crinolines. Abigail giggled aloud. *Wouldn't Granny be scandalized to see this?*

A gray-haired woman, her hair tightly wound in a bun at the nape of her neck, withdrew a leather-bound portfolio from her pack. Abigail recognized the portfolio immediately.

The woman called to the Indian children. They gathered around to see the sketches in the book. When an eagle soared overhead, the woman pointed to one in the sketchbook, then to the bird in the sky.

The children laughed with glee. Then, as if possessing a magical wand, the older woman took a pencil from the pouch and made a mark on the paper. A loud *"ooh"* passed through her audience.

Abigail's mind raced. This could be her method of rescue. Her art could save her. "I know how to use that!" she called.

Everyone turned, uncomprehending looks on their faces.

"Let me show you." She tried to stand up. The world spun before her. She sat down with a thud.

The woman who'd given her a drink rushed to Abigail, scolding her for trying to stand and fussing over her like a grandmother.

"I am the artist who drew those pictures," Abigail tried to explain.

"Pictures?" The woman said.

"Yes. Yes. I drew the picture of the eagle." She pointed to the black dot in the sky, and then moved her hand as if sketching on a sheet of paper.

The woman watched her intently for several seconds. Slowly a light of understanding lit behind the woman's dark eyes. Her interest piqued, she called to the squaw holding Abigail's sketchbook and pencils. The woman's announcement set off a flurry of gibberish, or so it sounded to Abigail.

Soon Abigail found herself surrounded by Indian women and children, their eyes bright and their mouths strangely silent. The squaw who claimed the portfolio reverently handed the sketchpad and pencil case to Abigail.

Abigail ran one hand over the familiar drawings of Amy, Tyler, Chip, Evan, and Granny. The sketches blurred before her eyes as she wondered if she'd ever find them again. She felt an unfamiliar tug on her heart as her fingertips lingered on a profile sketch of Evan. *Such a good man, so understanding,* she thought.

The older woman, who'd obviously been assigned to be her caregiver, spoke sharply and pointed to the pencil. Abigail lifted her tied hands. "I need my hands freed."

The woman understood her immediately. Whipping out a sharp knife from the folds of her garment, she severed the cord. Abigail rubbed her wrists and flexed her fingers to restore circulation.

Finding an empty sheet of paper, she sketched a picture of the little girl wearing Amy's dress. As the artist caught the pixy tilt of the girl's chin and the sparkling laughter in the child's eyes, the women leaning over Abigail's shoulder gasped in amazement. Abigail showed the little girl the sketch. The child giggled and hid her face behind Granny's full skirts, which her mother wore.

Without a word, Abigail sketched each of the women who wore the white women's garb. If she ever did rejoin the wagon train, she'd want to share these images with the others.

Running Elk, who had been standing at a safe distance from the gaggle of women and children, appeared to be disinterested and aloof. But when Abigail sketched him astride a shiny black stallion, he couldn't resist a peek.

Taking the portfolio from Abigail, he studied the sketch for several seconds, and then returned it to her. Immediately, she tore the sheet from its binding and handed it to him. "Here, keep it. It's yours." She began sketching the faces of the children gathered about her.

Reverently, he held the picture in his hands. "What magic you have in your fingers?" he asked.

"No magic. Drawing is a skill like—" she spotted the cache of arrows slung on his back, "hitting a target with one of your arrows. It takes practice."

He continued staring at the sketch. "No, not the same. Only ancient holy men can make images of people. They paint them on walls of caves to tell the people's story."

Abigail squinted up at the tall, lean Indian brave. "Where did you learn to speak English so well?"

The expression on his face remained unchanged. "At the age of seven, I was captured by a neighboring tribe and sold to a mountain man who spoke English and French fluently. He was determined to return me to my tribe, which he did four years later."

A wry smile spread across Abigail's face. "Then what was all that stuff about magic and holy men?"

"My people are simple. Their faith and their rituals are as well. If it can't be explained, it must be either black magic or God."

Abigail chuckled aloud. "That's not much different from what my people believe."

One corner of Running Elk's mouth twitched. "Probably so. But you are gifted."

"Thank you." She added the finishing touches to a picture of a small boy resting his head on what appeared to be his grandmother's knee. "Am I your captive?"

Abigail watched the muscles in his jaw flex several times before he spoke. "You were unconscious when I found you. Your wagon train had left you behind."

"My head, I fell." She grimaced when she touched the back of her head. Then she remembered the boy. "But, Tyler. He was with me."

The Indian brave gestured with his hands. "No boy. Boy your son?"

Abigail reddened at the idea. When she held him on her lap and comforted him, she fanaticized about being his mother. "No. His mother died on the trail. I'm not married."

The brave nodded.

"What is to happen to me?" She exchanged her dull pencil for a sharper one and continued sketching. After filling one page with faces, she moved on to the next, occasionally sketching either the grazing mules or the face of a mountain lion or prairie dog for variety.

"We are joining our brothers for the annual buffalo hunt. On our way, we will leave you at Fort Bridger."

She lifted her skirts revealing her restricted ankles. "Is this necessary? I won't run away."

Running Elk grunted, knelt down, and removed the leather thong. She gratefully smiled up at him. "That feels much better."

Carefully, she separated the portraits and gave them to the delighted subjects only to have more eager faces press in, wanting to be immortalized by her pencil.

The sound of thundering hooves announced the return of the men and dinner. All interest in the artist and her magic pencil vanished with the arrival of freshly killed meat. The women instantly went to work cleaning a variety of wild game and building a cooking fire. The children ran to carry out their assigned tasks while the victorious hunters rested on blankets of animal skins.

Although the meat was nearly raw, Abigail relished every bite. After the meal, from what Abigail could guess, the hunters told exaggerated tales of their afternoon kills while the women and children responded with appropriate enthusiasm.

When the last tale had been told and the glow of evening silhouetted the mountains to the west, the warriors smoked their pipes and stared into the fire. Running Elk took a moment to stride across the clearing to where the tribal council sat.

Abigail watched as the young brave spoke with the chief, gesturing with his hands. Occasionally, the leaders glanced past him to Abigail, and then back at Running Elk. After a short dialogue, Running Elk walked to where she sat with the women and children.

With the dignity of an English prince, he said, "The council would like for you to . . ."

"Sketch them?"

The Indian brave nodded, a breath of a smile tugging at the corners of his lips.

Abigail chuckled aloud and started sketching. She began with the man she assumed was their chief, an old man with graying hair and leatherlike skin. The women of the tribe moved in to watch as the carefully placed pencil marks began to take shape.

With her customary artistic flair, she sketched a rough outline of his chiseled face, taking time to detail the elegance of his abundant headdress before adding the interesting crags and wrinkles to his cheeks and jaw. When she sketched in a four-inch scar that ran along the side of the man's face, the women uttered an approving grunt.

"A battle trophy from the Sioux," Running Elk explained.

Abigail meticulously added the faces of the other council members to the scene. Each face told a story of wisdom, bravery, and pride. When she finished the page, she handed it to Running Elk.

The man shook his head. "The chief wants you to present it to him."

Abigail's breath caught in her throat. A rumble of disapproval passed through the gathering of women behind her when Running Elk helped the captured woman to her feet. One glance from Chief Red Fox silenced their displeasure.

Running Elk escorted her to the chief. When the brave spoke, he did so in English, and then repeated it in his native dialect. "Father, this is Abigail. She has a gift for you."

Abigail shot a surprised glance at Running Elk. "He's your father?"

Running Elk glared at her. "Hush, woman," he hissed. "Give Chief Red Fox the paper."

Flustered, Abigail nodded. Her hand shook as she placed the sketch in the chief's hands. Immediately, the other council members pressed in to see their own faces as portrayed by the artist's hand.

As the chief studied the artwork, a quirky smile crept across his face. He pointed to his likeness, laughed aloud, and uttered something in his dialect. The council members grunted in agreement.

"He likes the scar," Running Elk whispered out of the side of his mouth.

Abigail covered her mouth with her hand to hide her smile. *People are people,* she thought, *whether riverboat gamblers or Indian chiefs.* The chief liked her sketch so well that he ordered her to make one of him and his four sons as well. She did so by firelight.

When the chief saw the results, he ordered the women of the tribe to dance for Abigail. After the women and young girls danced, the men and boys took their turn. Abigail raced to get the colorful rituals down on paper.

By the time her protector suggested she rest for the night, Abigail's fingers ached, but her heart was full and her panic was gone. Running Elk turned her over to an older woman for care. "This is my mother, Little Flower," he explained.

Little Flower was anything but little and certainly not delicate like a flower either. However, the older woman's demeanor had changed since their first encounter. The woman's cold, brisk expression had been replaced by a shy, coy smile.

Abigail turned to Running Elk. "Chief Red Fox's wife?"

Running Elk shook his head. "Not in the way you think. My father has four wives, one for each son." He thrust his chin with pride, avoiding her gaze. "Do not be surprised if in the morning, he asks you to become his fifth."

Abigail gasped, "Me?"

"Your sons would be honored in the tribe for the magic in their fingers they would inherit from you."

"You can't mean it. I couldn't marry your father."

"Why not? You have no man of your own."

Abigail licked her parched lips and blurted out a statement that surprised her. "No, but my heart belongs to someone else." *Where did that come from?* she wondered.

A frown spread across the young man's face. "That is too bad, I think, for your young man."

Abigail blinked in surprise. "I don't understand."

"My father won't accept No."

A skitter of fear traversed her spine. She shuddered.

Running Elk uttered a few words to his mother and walked to the opposite side of the campfire, where the braves were bedding down for the night.

Little Flower rushed to Abigail and thrust a deerskin shift at her. "No!" Abigail pushed the animal skin back at the astonished woman. "I will wear what I have on."

One call from Little Flower and the other women descended on Abigail, surrounding her. They removed her calico dress and slips despite Abigail's kicking and screaming. After they slipped the supple deerskin garment over their prisoner's head, Little Flower secured Abigail's ankles and wrists once more. The other women scooped up handfuls of dirt, mixed it with water to make mud, then covered Abigail's pale complexioned face with it. Tears streamed down the frightened captive's face as Running Elk's mother braided the white woman's hair. "Please, please, don't do this," Abigail cried.

When the women finished, the chief's wife urged Abigail to lie down on a brightly colored blanket that had been laid out for her. After lashing the end of the leather rope to her own ankle, Little Flower spread out on another blanket beside her prisoner and prepared to sleep.

Within five minutes, Abigail heard the Indian woman's gentle snoring, but for her, sleep wouldn't come. Throughout the night, every movement Abigail made disturbed the older woman's sleep. Escape would be impossible.

Before she heard of the chief's desire to make her his bride, she'd had no reason to flee. Perhaps Running Elk was wrong; perhaps her own sense of direction was wrong. The whole thing was too incredible to believe— her, the daughter of an English clergyman being taken as a wife by an Indian chief. The chief was an old man, revered by the others. Surely, near the end of his days on this earth, he wouldn't want a fifth wife.

The more Abigail thought about it, the more ludicrous Running Elk's warning seemed. The Indians would take her to Fort Bridger and turn her over to the army. In time, she would find her way to Oregon. Her mind froze. *To what? To Evan Chambers?* By that time he'd think she was dead. *To Hawk Lassiter?* He'd probably be dining with the queen of England by then. Despite Hawk's declaration of love, Abigail knew there would be a newer, younger woman by his side in a short time.

Granny? No. Boston? Abigail shook her head at the thought of returning to her sister's home. She couldn't imagine ever being content attending her sister's afternoon teas and evening dinner parties after all she'd experienced.

She recalled her remark, "My heart belongs to . . ." *To whom?* She resisted the urge to explore that thought and stared into the night sky, vibrantly alive with stars. Neither in England nor in Massachusetts had she seen so many.

A star flashed across the sky and disappeared, and then another fell. Her nephew would love to see the shooting stars. *Maybe someday,* she thought, *I could pay for him to visit me in Oregon. This brought an unexpected thought to mind. Oregon? I might not make it out of the Rockies, let alone Oregon.*

The Indian woman lying on the ground beside her grunted.

"Oops! Sorry Little Flower." It had been hours since she'd moved. Her former headache had returned, preventing her from falling asleep. Counting stars was an impossible task, so she began reciting Bible promises: Psalm 23, Psalm 91, James 1, Ecclesiastes 3, Isaiah 58. Scripture after Scripture came to mind.

As she stared up at the stars, she remembered hearing her father quote Habakkuk 3 during a crop failure in their little parish. " 'Although the fig tree shall not blossom, neither shall fruit be in the vines; the labour of the olive shall fail, and the fields shall yield no meat; the flock shall be cut off from the fold, and there shall be no herd in the stalls: Yet, I will rejoice in the Lord. I will joy in the God of my salvation.' "

Tears welled up in Abigail's eyes as she prayed, *I will take joy in the God of my salvation. You, Father, are my salvation. I have no other hope. I know You hold my future in Your hands, therefore I will rejoice!*

It wasn't until the first rosy glow of light softened the eastern sky that she realized that her fear had left her, and she had no anxiety over what the new day might bring. Both her mind and her body were saturated with a healing balm of peace.

"Lo, I am with you always." Thank You, Father. Abigail closed her eyes and slept.

CHAPTER EIGHTEEN

THE PAINFUL TRUTH

BIGAIL SIGHED WITH PLEASURE AT THE sight of the tall ever-greens towering over her head, the deep blue river gurgling nearby, and the puffy white clouds floating on the horizon. Instinctively, she knew she was in the beautiful Willamette River valley, the place she and Evan had discussed so many times since leaving Council Grove. She glanced down and discovered she wore a white, diaphanous cotton batiste gown, woven so fine that the skirts rippled in the gentle breeze coming off the river. The wide, satin baby-blue ribbon tied about her waist fluttered in the breeze as well.

Her hair cascaded down over her shoulders and on to the embroidered bodice of the dress. On her head she wore a halo of daisies and blue satin ribbons. The ends of the ribbons were woven through the locks of her hair. Accustomed to wearing a practical calico or muslin, Abigail sighed with pleasure. For the first time in her life, she felt lovely and desirable.

A voice called to her from a distance. Like a flower turns toward the sun, Abigail turned in the direction of the voice, expecting to see the face of—

Suddenly, someone grabbed her shoulder and shook her awake. Abigail's eyes flew open. She found herself staring into the face of an agitated Little Flower. The Indian woman dragged the groggy Abigail to her feet, pushing her roughly and scolding her in her native dialect.

This time Abigail would not have the luxury of riding on the back

178

of a mule. The woman removed the leather thong from around Abigail's feet, tied the thong to the one around Abigail's wrists and urged her forward.

"My portfolio," Abigail gasped, glancing toward the leather-bound book she'd used for a pillow the previous night.

The Indian woman grunted, picked up the treasured artwork, and stuffed it in the pack she carried on her back. Where the previous day's pace had been leisurely and slow, this morning's was fast and determined. Abigail stumbled forward in an effort to obey. The sun had barely appeared over the horizon when the captive realized the Indian procession was heading north instead of south toward Fort Bridger.

She had studied the hand-drawn maps Hawk Lassiter had shown her. Roughly sketched trails were drawn on sheets of parchment he wore under his shirt. Fort Bridger was south of South Pass and the Sublette Cutoff, where the last of the California-bound wagons left the Oregon Trail for the Great Salt Lake and the mountains of California.

Like a house being swept of cobwebs, Abigail's brain cleared. Running Elk and his tribe were definitely heading north toward Montana and the British-held territory beyond. And from what she could remember, she knew nothing was identified on the map beyond the Missouri River source. The realization that she might never rejoin her wagon train, that she might never again see Granny and the children, and that Evan or Hawk might never be able to find her sent a chill of fear through her body. Before it had been speculation—now she faced reality. She shuddered and stumbled forward.

The stories she'd heard of European women being made slaves or the squaws of Indian men flooded her mind. How had they coped with the enforced servitude, so foreign from their own culture? How would she cope? Could she survive a servitude that might be accompanied by cruel torture?

For much of the years since Narcissa Whitman and her husband had headed west, the treaties the prairie tribes made with the United States government had maintained peace, but she'd also heard the soldiers at Fort Laramie telling how the Indians were getting uncomfortable with the unending train of white people moving across their lands and killing their game.

The more Abigail recalled what she'd heard, the more her insides rumbled with fear. "Lord," she whispered, not wanting her captors to hear her praying, "what shall I do? Try to escape?" The idea rattled around in her brain for many miles.

She studied the mountainous terrain. Without supplies, especially water, no one could survive alone and on foot. She caught a glimpse of her feet shod in the soft leather suede, and then gazed at the wall of rock towering over her to her left. How long could the moccasins hold up against those sharp rocks? And to where would she run? South to Fort Bridger? That's the direction Running Elk would search first. And how could she outdistance and outsmart a band of Indian braves who'd spent their lives in these mountains?

Abigail remembered the Bible story about the time Abraham sent Hagar, his second wife, and Ishmael, his firstborn son, out in to the desert and God preserved them. Is that what God wanted her to do? She eyed the spires of rock. Above her head, three buzzards circled, lazily dipping into the rocks and rising into the sky to circle once more. She wondered about the dead carcass hidden by the rocky crags.

Will that be my end, dying alone in the mountains without food or water? Abigail took a deep breath and decided fleeing into the desert or into the mountains would not be a wise move. As she plodded alongside the animal train with Little Flower nipping at her heels, Abigail forced her mind to recall pleasant memories of her life: cooking in the kitchen with Bessy; the parish house in England, and sketching sheep in the field behind the village; the aroma of leather and paper in her father's library; sitting on his lap in the giant leather wing-backed chair next to the fireplace and hearing him tell her the stories of the Bible; crossing the Atlantic with her mother; playing in the autumn leaves with Rebecca's children; and tasting the pleasures of the riverboats' cuisine.

Umm. Her stomach growled. She hadn't eaten since the previous night. Would they feed her? Forcing hunger from her mind, Abigail returned to what she'd begun thinking of as her "litany of joy."

An abandoned shack peeking out from among the rocks to her left brought to mind Serenity Inn outside Independence, Missouri, and Serenity.

Abigail remembered the woman's story of losing her mother and her home and thinking her father was dead. She remembered the texts

Serenity quoted that gave her courage as she watched her home being engulfed in flames.

The captive woman began mouthing the familiar verses. " 'He that dwelleth in the secret place of the most High shall abide under the shadow of the Almighty.' " Abigail gazed into the cloudless sky. It would be another scorcher of a day.

" 'I will say of the LORD, He is my refuge and my fortress: my God; in him will I trust.' " She glanced up at the rocks towering to her left. She'd thought of them as a danger, not a fortress.

" 'Thou shalt not be afraid for the terror by night; nor for the arrow that flieth by day.' " Abigail remembered the quiver of arrows lashed to Running Elk's back and smiled.

" 'There shalt no evil befall thee, neither shall any plague come nigh thy dwelling.' " Her smile broadened. *God's promises have seen me this far,* she reasoned, *why would He quit now?* A note of confidence entered her voice as she began quoting the familiar promise aloud. " 'Because he hath set his love upon me, therefore will I deliver him.' " She gazed at the rocky cliff with a new appreciation. " 'I will set him on high, because he hath known my name.' "

Up ahead, she heard a shout and the animals slowed to a stop, as did the women and children. A second command and Little Flower removed the thong from Abigail and handed her a canteen of water.

The water soothed her parched throat. She closed her eyes and savored the refreshing liquid on her tongue. Little Flower opened her pack, withdrew a small slab of dried meat, and handed it to her prisoner. Abigail snatched it from the woman's hands and wolfed it down like a starving animal. Ashamed of herself, she paused long enough to say, "Thank you," to the Indian woman.

From a rock crevice to her left came the hoot of an owl. A second came from somewhere behind her. Running Elk rushed to his mother and barked an order. The woman cast a frightened look at Abigail and grabbed her by the arm. A woman standing nearby grabbed Abigail's other arm, and together they dragged her into the rocks at the side of the trail. They'd barely dropped behind the lowest outcropping when Little Flower hissed something and pushed Abigail to her knees behind the largest of the rocks. The second woman clamped her hand over Abigail's mouth.

Stunned, Abigail struggled but the women held her firmly in place. Able to catch a glimpse of the rest of the Indians and pack animals, she was surprised to see them resume walking as if nothing had happened. The thunder of horses' hooves shook the ground. Abigail's heart leaped for joy. The U.S. cavalry had come to her rescue.

Frantically, she tried to stand up to let the soldiers know where she was, but the two women pressed her face into the rock, scraping the skin from her nose. Abigail whimpered in pain, but the two women held her fast.

An army officer and Chief Red Fox talked while the soldiers searched the caravan. Hope rose in Abigail's heart when a soldier found Abigail's and Granny's clothing in one of the horse's packs. But whatever the chief said satisfied the officer in charge, for the soldier returned the clothing to the pack and moved on.

Abigail wanted to shout, "Look up here. Here I am!" But she couldn't. The woman's sweaty hand remained firmly plastered over the captive's mouth.

Abigail's knees ached. The blood from her skinned nose dribbled along the side of her face to her mouth. Hot tears stung her cheeks. To be so close to rescue and so helpless. Abigail's bravado wilted.

Oh, dear God, she silently whimpered. *I know Your promises are true, but are You, dear Father, a match for Running Elk and his father?* As the words touched the tip of her silenced tongue, Abigail knew otherwise. She'd traveled too many miles, through too many troubles, and across too many mountains to lose faith now. She vowed she would continue to acknowledge her heavenly Father, regardless of her fate.

If You can part the waters of the Red Sea to save Your people, if You can bring down the walls of Jericho with a blast of trumpets, if You can save a captive from a den of lions, You can handle Red Fox and a thousand like him.

Even as she prayed, she watched Running Elk gesture toward the east. The soldiers remounted their horses and rode off in the direction the brave had pointed. Abigail collapsed against the rock in defeat as the soldiers disappeared beyond the cloud of dust stirred by their horses' hooves.

An owl hoot from the rocks, a reply from Running Elk, and the two squaws lifted Abigail to her feet. When the woman's hand fell away from Abigail's mouth, the prisoner moistened her lips with relief. A jab between her shoulder blades by one of the women urged Abigail down the side of the cliff.

Below, the procession was once again heading north. The three women would need to run to catch up. Abigail was intent on satisfying the women's desire for speed when she heard the familiar owl hoot from the rocks above her. It was followed by a second.

She and her guards whirled about to locate the source of the signal. Suddenly, Running Elk shouted from the rear of the pack train. Immediately, Little Flower grabbed for Abigail's arm.

"No!" Abigail twisted free from the surprised woman's grasp and snatched the leather art portfolio from the woman's pack. Before Little Flower could recover, Abigail darted out of her, reach. The two Indian women screeched excitedly and ran after Abigail.

Fleeing toward the south along the rocky hillside, Abigail ran, not knowing where or to whom she was running. She just knew she had to run. Her female captors followed after her, shouting and shaking their fists in the air. From the valley, Running Elk joined the chase. On her right, farther up the mountain, Abigail saw two Indian braves leap from behind boulders and bound down the side of the cliff toward her.

Abigail felt her lungs would burst. *"They shall run, and not be weary; they shall walk, and not faint."* She laughed aloud at the promise that popped into her head. She was grateful for the freedom of movement the deerskin dress afforded her. She sprinted over rocks and around sagebrush, giving no thought to the possibility of rattlesnakes or lizards. Tired or not, she determined to run as long as her body would cooperate.

Her lungs ached. She scraped her knees and ankles on the rough rocks, yet she ran. Tears blurred her vision, but she ran and ran and ran.

Suddenly, she heard her name echoing down the slope of the rocky cliff. She looked up in surprise to see two horsemen coming toward her, riding dangerously hard for the condition of the terrain. The brims of their hats assured her they were not her enemies. They'd come to rescue her. She shot a quick glance over her shoulder and discovered she ran alone. Her captors had disappeared into the rocks.

Abigail ran toward the advancing horsemen, clutching her treasured portfolio to her chest. As her rescuers drew closer, she recognized them. Evan and Hawk! When they were fifty feet or so from her, Evan leaped from his moving steed and ran to meet her.

Abigail's heart soared. With tears flowing, she charged into his open arms, causing him to lose his balance. They staggered but continued to cling to each other. The portfolio dropped to the ground as she buried her face in his neck.

"Evan," she panted. "I can't . . . believe . . . it's you! I thought I'd never see you again," she said between gasps for air. "Tyler? Did you find Tyler? Is he all right? How did you know where to find me? When the Indians headed north instead of south toward Fort Bridger, I knew I was in trouble. I thought about escaping in the night, but—"

Placing his leather-gloved hands on each side of her tear-stained face, Evan kissed her soundly.

She pulled back in surprise, bringing a blush to Evan's face. "It's the only way I could think of to get you to stop talking," he said. "Are you all right? Did they hurt you?"

Hawk Lassiter rode to where they stood and dismounted. The lazy grin on his face didn't match the sadness Abigail saw in his eyes. Her gaze returned to Evan's flushed face. She could feel the color rise in her neck.

"Tyler is fine. He's with Granny. But are you all right?" Evan asked again, his voice raspy with emotion.

"Yes, I-I-I think so," she answered in halting tones.

"I am so glad!" Timidly, he touched her face with his gloved hand. "We were so worried. If Hawk hadn't suggested we hang back behind the cavalry, we would never have found you."

At the mention of Hawk Lassiter, the two stepped apart. Abigail looked shyly at Hawk, her emotions still alive from being in Evan's arms. "Thank you, Hawk, for saving me. How can I ever thank the two of you enough?"

The man smiled and placed a kiss on her muddy cheek. "My pleasure, ma'am."

"We didn't miss either of you until we stopped to eat," Evan explained. "While a couple of men rode to the Fort, Doc, Hawk, and I retraced our tracks. That's when we found Tyler."

"The little tyke came running out of the rocks, screaming something about you being kidnapped by Indians. We couldn't believe it," Hawk added. "Doc checked out the boy. And except for being mighty thirsty, he was fine. It's amazing that he hid so well the Indians didn't see him. Anyway, Doc took him back to the wagon train. The cavalry caught up with us on the other side of this mountain pass."

Evan drenched his kerchief with water and dabbed at the streaks of mud on Abigail's face. While the woman's mind told her to remove the mud herself, a strange lassitude held her captive to his touch.

The two men insisted she rest for a few minutes before beginning the long ride to Fort Bridger. After a light meal of beef jerky and lukewarm water, they climbed the mountain where they'd tethered a horse for Abigail to ride. Exhausted, she mounted the sorrel horse for the long ride south toward Fort Bridger where the wagon train was camped.

Abigail's welcome involved her telling and retelling the story of her capture and rescue to the entire Lassiter company. She learned that it was Sergeant Brumby who had discovered the direction the Indians had gone. Evan and Hawk set out immediately, while Brumby reported the kidnapping to the commander at Fort Bridger. Knowing the Indians wouldn't release their prize willingly, the two men separated from the cavalry, hoping the Indians would do exactly what they did.

Later when Abigail was alone with Granny in her wagon, Granny had lots to say.

"I thought those two men would go wild when Sergeant Brumby found Tyler hiding behind a rock. The boy told them he'd seen the Indians take you away."

Abigail dabbed a moistened washcloth on her nose, as Granny continued, "In all my born days, I've never seen two men act more like children. Land sakes, if Sergeant Brumby hadn't been here to ride herd, I don't know what might have happened."

Abigail grimaced as Granny applied an ointment to her abrasions.

"Woman, you need to acknowledge the corn."

"Acknowledge the corn?"

"Tell them which man you love. You're killing them. They both love you, you know."

Abigail's breath caught in her throat. "I don't know what to say or do." She knew what Granny said was true. She'd seen it in both men's eyes. But how could she choose? At the very thought, she had the urge to break into wild laughter. She felt daffier than the heroines in her sister's French novels. Two men loved her? Did she, could she, love both? If so, how should she choose between them?

She pictured the laughing face of Hawk Lassiter and recalled his tantalizing promise of taking her to meet Queen Victoria. Hawk was offering her the possibility of returning to her homeland. She'd be able to visit the little parsonage where she'd grown up and her father's grave. She toyed with the idea of being a real English lady. Or would she be a duchess? She wasn't sure.

"Are you listening to me? I'll empty the soiled water and wring out the washcloth, if you'll hand me the cloth." Granny stood over her with her hands on her hips.

"Huh? Oh . . . uh . . . so sorry."

Granny heaved a huge sigh. "It's all right. I'm glad you're safe. So are the children. You saw how excited they were. Why, Tyler clung to you as if he expected you to disappear in a whiff of smoke."

Abigail nodded. Her eyes misted at the thought of the serious little towhead who told her that he prayed for her the whole time she was gone. "And God answered my prayer, just like you said He would, huh?" The child's eyes twinkled with assurance.

The glitter of the royal palace dimmed when contrasted with Tyler's beaming smile. And then there was Amy, at one moment a child, and the next mothering Abigail. Her thoughts drifted to Chip, the boy-man with a chip on his shoulder and pain in his heart. Even he had seemed pleased to have her back safely.

Her family. The thought warmed her heart and turned her thoughts toward the one who held the family together—Evan, the man with the warmest, gentlest eyes and most understanding smile. Abigail wouldn't describe Hawk as understanding or gentle. Exciting? Yes. Understanding? No. She and Evan had shared a thousand miles of laughter, of tears, of frustrations, of fear, and most of all, of dreams.

Abigail drifted into a peaceful sleep. The dream she'd had on the Indian trail returned. She wore the same gossamer white gown. A myriad of satin ribbons tumbled freely among her long brown tresses as she reclined on a bed of pine needles beneath the tallest trees she'd ever imagined and beside the deepest, bluest river she'd ever seen.

When she heard someone call her name, instinctively she knew it was the voice of—*Who?* Her eyelids fluttered open. She found herself inside the white canvas-covered wagon. She sighed and draped her arm over her forehead. Someone had called her name. She was sure of it.

Voices rose from outside the wagon. She recognized them instantly. Hawk Lassiter and Evan Chambers were discussing her and her future. She sat up on the edge of her bedding and froze.

Evan was speaking. "I've decided to bow out. Three's a crowd. I've no right to her. And you have been courting her for some time."

"No, no." Hawk Lassiter's tone became insistent. "I saw the look on her face when she ran to you today. She loves you. You must know that. And I love her too much to stand in the way of her happiness."

"No, you misread her feelings. She was relieved to be rescued, that's all. You can offer her so much more than I can. A position in the British court compared to raising another woman's children—hardly an even trade, I fear."

Abigail pressed her ear against the canvas so as not to miss a word. How dare they treat her like she was a side of buffalo to be traded!

Hawk's voice grew raspy, "You must be blind, man. Don't you see . . ."

Furious to be discussed so openly, Abigail wrapped her robe about her and stormed out of the wagon, bare feet and all. She whipped around the end of the wagon. "How dare you discuss me like I am a prized heifer for you to parade before your aristocrats, Mr. Lassiter, or a nanny to raise your motherless children, Mr. Chambers!"

The men stared at her in surprise. She charged forward, unexpectedly stepping on a prickly puncture vine. She squealed and hopped on one foot, while trying to maintain her dignity. "How can two supposedly intelligent men be so insensitive?" Tears of humiliation sprang into her eyes. Abigail had never been so angry or so mortified in her life.

"I will not have you or anyone else determining my fate." Abigail shook a finger in Hawk's face, moving within a hairsbreadth of accosting his nose with her fingernail. "Here, you take her; no, you take her; no, I insist! Believe it or not, if and when I choose a husband, I won't sit idly by and twiddle my thumbs while two yahoos toss a coin! As for you, Mr. Lassiter, you can take your royal palace and your title. I don't need it. I'm the daughter of the King of the universe. That's royal enough for my blood!"

She whirled about to face the stunned Evan. Her cheeks flamed with anger. "And as for you, Mr. Chambers, why would I want to saddle myself with another woman's children? I wouldn't, if I loved them any less than I would my own." She didn't break to breathe.

"Believe it or not, Mr. Chambers, I'm not such a dolt or so desperate to marry either for a man's children or for a title to the British throne." Her fury forced the two men to step back in self-defense.

She snapped her fingers in the air. "If and when I marry, it will be for love and love alone! The man I marry will need to woo me with tenderness and love. Now, if you gentlemen, with accent on the word *gentlemen,* will excuse me, I'm going to try to go back to sleep!"

A loud round of applause and cheering came from the nearby wagons. Everyone had been listening to the conversation. Humiliated, Abigail fled into the wagon and threw herself face down on her mattress.

CHAPTER NINETEEN

THE COLOR OF REGRET

BIGAIL HAD NEVER BEEN SO HUMILIATED IN her life, and she'd inflicted the pain upon herself. Whatever caused her to leave the security of her wagon to scold her two rescuers, she didn't know.

"Of all the stupid, idiotic behavior!" She vented her rage by pummeling her fists into her pillow. "How could I be so stupid? No man would want me anyway, after seeing my lack of restraint." The memory of the battles she'd fought against Ralph caused her to cringe. When she left Chelsea, she'd claimed victory over her fiery temper. She thought she was finally the calm and self-controlled creature she'd always wanted to be.

She'd have to keep working at her temper and try to forgive herself. Just when she'd almost regained her equilibrium, she remembered her horseback ride in Indian dress and was embarrassed all over again. Talk about humiliation. To mount the creature, she'd had to hike her skirts, revealing her ankles and much of her calves. Her face reddened at the thought.

Where had the proper young English lady gone, the one who could make Russian tea cakes that would melt in one's mouth or Scottish shortbread cookies light enough to charm an English count? What kind of hooligan had she become since leaving Independence, Missouri? Had she abandoned all semblance of propriety?

When she rode into the camp after being rescued, the children were fascinated with the soft deerskin dress she wore. They had all kinds of questions to ask about her capture and her time among the Indians. The adults had questions as well.

As for Abigail, she was too tired and too relieved to be back with the wagon train to remember that the garment didn't cover her arms or her lower legs adequately until she reached the privacy of Granny Parker's wagon. Now, remembering, she was mortified. How would she ever face anyone again?

Abigail didn't think she could handle any more humiliation. For a fleeting minute, she considered sequestering herself in the wagon until they reached Oregon. She laughed aloud at the impossibility of such a plan. Like it or not, one way or another, she would have to face the other members of the wagon train, including Evan Chambers and Hawk Lassiter. And she would do so with a determined smile on her face.

The next morning, Abigail prepared herself for the worst, but no one mentioned either the Indian garb or the altercation in the night.

Quickly, she fell back into the routine of life on the trail. Most days Evan made himself scarce, leaving Abigail to drive the wagon and Amy to ride with her. Chip ran with his friends as usual while Tyler rode on the back of his father's horse or with Granny.

Days passed. Except for her nightmares, Abigail didn't allow herself to think about her frightening ordeal. The journey over the mountains had been rough. Abigail noticed Evan watching her as she moved about the camp or when she was spending time with the two younger children. She regretted her harsh words and would take them back in an instant if she could figure a way to do so while maintaining a modicum of dignity.

Occasionally, Evan's and Abigail's eyes met across the campfire or during the weekly worship services, but they quickly looked away. At one point, Chip's misbehavior forced the two of them to discuss the boy's behavior and punishment. They did so by keeping things between them as impersonal as possible.

Sergeant Brumby had caught four boys, including Chip, drinking with a couple of the teamsters in the middle of the night. The boys would be punished, and the owner of the whiskey and the second teamster were expelled from the wagon train since alcohol was strictly forbidden on the trail.

For punishment, Chip would ride in the wagon either with Granny or Abigail for the rest of journey. And at night he would not be allowed to leave his father's side.

"One way or another, he needs to be curbed in," Evan growled as he ran frustrated fingers through his tangled hair. "I've been too easy on him since his mother died."

"The boy is old enough to be responsible for his own choices, good or bad," Abigail reminded. When she reached out to touch his forearm for comfort, he flinched. Startled, she withdrew her hand quickly. "I'm not your enemy, Evan."

"I know." Turning on his heel, he strode away.

Abigail found Chip sulking in the back of his father's wagon. She climbed into the wagon and sat on the bedding across from him. "Chip? May I help?"

"Huh? How could you help?"

"I don't know. You could tell me what you're thinking."

"I wish my mother were here," he mumbled.

"I'm sure you do, but she's not. Will you let me help?"

The boy's eyes flashed with anger. "You are not my mother, Miss Abigail, and you never will be, so stop trying!"

His vehemence left her speechless.

"You may have sweet-talked Amy and hornswoggled my little brother and my father into forgetting my mother, but you will never take her place. I don't care how hard you try."

Abigail bit her lower lip. The boy was filled with so much pain. "Chip, I know I can never take your mother's place. I don't want to. A body can have only one mother in a lifetime. That's the way God planned it. But a body has several friends in one lifetime." She shrugged and grinned sheepishly at the miserable young man. "I'd sure like to be one of your friends, if you'd let me." She knew she was showing her feelings, and that the boy could, with one word, break her heart.

Chip averted his eyes. His arms remained crossed, his face suffused with anger. When the horn sounded for the train to move out, Abigail climbed out of the wagon and into the driver's seat. Raising the canvas separating them, she called, "You're welcome to join me on the driver's bench if you like." Not waiting for his reply, she turned around, breathed a quick prayer and shook the reins. As the wagon lurched forward, Chip silently climbed through the opening of the wagon and onto the seat beside her.

They'd ridden side by side for several minutes when she handed the reins to the boy. "Would you like to drive for a while? I'll bet you can handle the team even though they can be skittish."

Chip looked surprised. A grin spread across his face. "Sure."

"Help yourself." She switched seats with the boy, and leaned back to enjoy the milestone that had been accomplished. Once she was certain Chip could handle the team, she allowed herself the luxury of dabbling in a little reverie. She thought about her decision not to marry Hawk Lassiter. In little more than a week, he was courting the Webster's eldest daughter, a cuddly blonde of seventeen. Although the man was fifteen years older than the sprightly teen, she was happy for them both.

However, Abigail was surprised at how little the news bothered her. She'd expected Hawk to court another young woman, knowing the man's charm, wit, and his sudden, unexplained desire to marry. When she came upon the couple taking an evening stroll, Abigail greeted them both warmly, feeling a mild sense of relief, with only a twinge of regret.

She'd done the right thing, although she admired the celebrated and charming son of British royalty. She laughed when she thought of Clarissa Darlington and her fight to snag Hawk for her second husband. Abigail wondered if Winters could handle the capricious woman and the change in their relationship.

Near Soda Springs, at a rock formation more impressive than Chimney Rock, the wagon train stopped to rest for Sunday. After the morning services, the pioneers hiked to the springs that reportedly sounded like a steamboat coming down the river. The men in the train found the water from a second spring more enticing. It tasted like beer, but without the alcohol kick.

Abigail couldn't resist tasting the natural spring water. She grimaced and spit out the foul-tasting brew. Wiping the bitter taste from her lips, she looked up and caught Evan grinning at her. She withered him with one glare. Turning to Granny, she asked, "How anyone can stomach drinking that stuff, I'll never know."

Granny nodded in agreement.

From Soda Springs, the wagon train crossed the Portneuf River and descended to Fort Hall, an isolated fur-trading center and supply point for trappers on the Snake River.

For days they traveled along the Snake River, which crossed a wide prairie leading to another exhausting climb up another mountain range. As the trail grew harder and the parched travelers wondered if they could endure going any farther, Mr. Farnsworth encouraged them with visions of clear, rapidly flowing mountain streams and a protective umbrella of century-old shade trees once they reached the river Boise.

What the travelers didn't know was, the few days of easy travel along the river Boise would be followed with the treacherous crossing of Burnt River Canyon and the Blue Mountains.

At the end of each day, Abigail wondered about the limit to her own fortitude. Her back and shoulders ached from wrestling the team of horses for twelve hours. And at night around the campfire, as she told the children's story, she saw exhaustion in the faces of her audience, child and adult alike.

While their train had not suffered many deaths, several young children succumbed to the rigors of the journey. As she gazed out at her attentive audience, her heart ached for the missing faces, the ones who hadn't made it.

Every day they came across roughly hewn wooden crosses marking the graves of earlier pioneers, those less fortunate who never saw their dreams fulfilled. Abigail's interest in recording the sights she saw along the way dwindled with her energy.

The Oregon Trail ended at The Dalles. As the wagons rolled down the muddy main street of the thriving community on the Columbia River, her heart rejoiced. While her fellow travelers cheered and shouted, Abigail opened her mouth and sang the words to "Old Hundredth."

"Praise God from whom all blessings flow." She was simultaneously laughing and crying. Amy, on the wagon seat beside her, laughed and waved to the people strolling along the boarded walkway in front of the shops. Abigail hadn't seen so many shops since leaving Council Grove. A desire to go shopping suddenly surfaced within her.

The wagon train circled outside town in a large field, along with three other companies. Abigail waved to a little redheaded mother of twin boys that she'd met at Independence Rock. The lively, innocent glow of youth she'd admired in the woman's face had faded. The redhead appeared gaunt, and her arms were empty. One look in the woman's eyes revealed heartache. Without asking, Abigail knew that her infant sons occupied two of those little graves along the trail.

As the wagon in front of her slowed to a stop, Abigail hauled in the reins and pressed her foot against the brake. The team responded to her commands. She'd barely tied the reins to the brake handle when Evan arrived, offering to help her down from the wagon. As her feet touched the ground, he cried, "We're here!" His eyes glowed with happiness. "We made it—you and I—we made it!" He grabbed her about the waist and hugged her so tightly she feared she'd never breathe again. All around them, the members of the Lassiter train poured out of their wagons, adults and children alike, shouting and dancing with abandon. One old man, a loner on the trail, grabbed Granny and whirled her across the grass, laughing and waltzing to the music of their success.

Being so close to Evan, Abigail felt the accelerated beat of his heart. She saw his racing pulse throbbing in his neck. It was a moment she'd imagined many times since her fateful speech but had come to fear might never occur.

"Evan, I'm sorry—" she began.

"No, don't." He touched her lips with his finger. "We can talk about it later. But now . . ." He pulled back and took her hands in his. "I suggest that the women of the Chambers party go shopping in town this afternoon."

Her mouth fell open in amazement. "How did you—"

He ignored her question. "Chip, Tyler, and I have agreed to set up camp and make a kettle of lentil stew."

"You cook?" She cast him an incredulous glance. "Will the stew be edible?"

"Absolutely." He laughed. It was the first laugh she'd heard from him since crossing the mountains. "Sara used to say I made the best lentil stew east of the Mississippi. And now that we're west of the Mississippi, a long way west, I'd like to extend my reputation to include the entire continent."

"All right. I'll trust you, if for no other reason than I am dying to go shopping!"

His grin stole her heart away. "So go. Find Granny and Amy. And have fun."

Obediently, Abigail searched for Granny and the child. But her heart was in turmoil. *One little touch from him,* she admitted, *and I go all weak-kneed.*

"Isn't it exciting, Miss Abigail?" Amy danced up and down with glee. "Daddy gave Granny some money to buy me a new Sunday-go-to-meeting dress to replace the one the Indians stole."

Abigail laughed at the child's excitement. "I need to put on a fresh bonnet."

The child's face fell for an instant. "Is it all right if we start for town, and you catch up with us?"

Abigail started toward the rear of Granny's wagon where her clothes were kept. "I think that would be a good idea."

She fetched her best calico poke bonnet from the trunk and secured the ties beneath her chin. Catching a glimpse of her suntanned face and streaks of sun-bleached hair reflected in the small mirror Granny kept at the head of her mattress, Abigail barely recognized herself as the proper young woman who'd left Boston six months earlier.

She ran to catch up with the cluster of women heading for town. Most other women from the Lassiter company had shared the same idea upon arriving in The Dalles.

As Abigail expected, Granny was in the center of the action. The older woman had become every woman's second mother on the trail. The women in the Lassiter company could count on Granny to know the cure for colds, cramps, and croup. She could ease birth pains and relieve backaches, keeping the patient laughing while she did so. Granny could scold, bully, or soothe the wounded spirit when needed, while directing her patient to the heavenly Source of peace.

The shops were few and shabby like a frontier town would be expected to have, but it didn't matter. The women's eyes danced with eagerness as they peeled off in different directions at the eastern end of town, each intent on purchasing whatever her purse allowed.

"There! Look, Granny." Amy spotted a sign for a ladies' dress shop at the end of the first block. "May I run ahead and see what they have?"

"Sure, honey," Granny said.

"She's so excited." Abigail watched the little girl skip along the wooden sidewalk, her braids synchronized with her gait. Abigail lifted her skirts to step up onto the wooden sidewalk, then offered her arm to Granny.

"Think she's excited?" Granny took hold of Abigail's arm and stepped up as well. "I never dreamed I would miss shopping as much as I did. If I could, I'd buy out the town."

"I know what you mean." Abigail laughed, falling into step beside the older woman. "The first thing I want to do is find a general store that carries lemon drops, licorice sticks, and giant dill pickles."

Granny paused to gaze up and down the street. "I think I like this town. I could be happy here."

But Abigail hadn't heard the woman's remarks. Ahead of them, in the dress shop window, the young woman couldn't believe her eyes. She saw the gown that had been in her dreams, flowing white gossamer lawn with a baby-blue satin sash. It was more beautiful than she'd imagined.

Vertical rows of delicate tucks edged with fine lace filled the bodice from the waist to the daintily crocheted edging around the high neck. Embroidered daisies decorated the full caps of the mutton sleeves. The same white daisies began at the waist and cascaded in swirls to the embroidered hem. Abigail touched the window with her gloved hand like a child in front of a candy store. She wondered if the vision would disappear if she glanced away.

"Come on," Granny said. "Are you coming inside?"

Abigail couldn't speak but continued to stare.

The older woman followed her gaze and found the dress. "It is a beautiful frock, isn't it?"

"Yes, it is." Abigail had never been so taken with a garment before. All the party dresses her mother had insisted she wear never struck her like this one.

"Try it on," Granny urged.

Abigail shook her head. "Where would I wear a dress like this? White is too impractical."

The two women entered the shop and found Amy looking at a bolt of yellow batiste. "This is it, Granny. I want a dress from this." The child darted across the small shop to a rack of ribbons. "With an orange sash."

Abigail missed the entire exchange. She was admiring the gown in the window from every angle.

"Do you like it?" The seamstress removed the gown from the dress form and held it out for Abigail to touch. "I made it for a young woman who changed her mind about marrying her fiancé. She was to wear it to her engagement party. Alas, the fickle young miss was tall and willowy like you. Few women can carry off the dress's length well."

Abigail removed her glove to caress the delicate fabric with her fingers.

Gently, the seamstress placed the garment in Abigail's arms. "Try it on."

Amy danced with delight at the sight of the gown. "Oh, yes, Miss Abigail, try it on."

The seamstress led Abigail to a small room behind a brocade satin curtain where she helped Abigail remove her homespun dress and slips. The supple silk lining slid down over Abigail's shoulders and hips and was quickly followed by the dress itself. The seamstress chattered as she fastened the long row of pearl buttons up the back of the garment, then tied the light-blue satin ribbon about Abigail's narrow waist. "I knew this dress was made for you and you alone."

The seamstress stepped back to admire her creation. She gasped with delight. "You look ravishing."

From beyond the curtain, Amy called, her voice filled with excitement. "Come out, Miss Abigail. I want to see you too."

The shop owner held the curtain back and allowed Abigail to step out into the shop where her fans eagerly awaited. Both Granny and the child *ooh*ed at the sight of the statuesque Abigail and the gently flowing gown of white.

"It's beautiful!" Amy cooed. "You're beautiful, Miss Abigail. I wish my daddy could see you in that dress. He'd ask you to marry him for sure."

Abigail paled at the child's audacity.

"Amy!" Granny scolded. "You shouldn't say things like that."

"But it's true." A petulant frown formed on the girl's lips. She folded her arms and stuck out her lower lip. "Everyone knows he wants to. Seeing Miss Abigail in this dress would give him the courage to do it."

Abigail gasped, then fled behind the curtain with the seamstress following. The embarrassed young woman tore at the tiny pearl buttons fastened at the back of her neck. "Don't bother. I can do this myself!"

The woman fluttered about the room frantically trying to help Abigail shed the dress. "It's no bother, miss."

"Please!" Abigail snapped. "I wish to be alone. I can do this myself."

The seamstress fled the dressing room.

Tears welled up in Abigail's eyes as she paced the small room, fumbling with the stubborn buttons. Beyond the curtain she could hear the whispered voices of Granny, Amy, and the seamstress.

Abigail stopped pacing when she heard Amy say from the other side of the curtain, "I'm sorry, Miss Abigail. I didn't want to hurt you."

Abigail's shoulders slumped in surrender. "I know you didn't, sweetie." Slowly, she untied the sash and finished unfastening the buttons. The dress fell to the floor about her feet.

"Are you mad at me?" Amy called through the curtain.

"No, of course not. But promise me you won't say anything like that again." She could imagine the child's saddened face. Amy lived to please.

"All right. I promise."

Abigail put on her homespun clothing and stepped out from behind the curtain where Granny and the seamstress had begun measuring Amy for her new yellow dress.

"If you will excuse me, I have some shopping I need to do." Abigail escaped from the dress shop as quickly as possible. Out on the sidewalk, she knew her face was still crimson from Amy's remark. Abigail rushed past fellow shoppers in an effort to outrun her own thoughts that had been so similar to Amy's.

At the corner, she stepped off the wooden sidewalk into the pathway of an oncoming buggy.

The driver of the farm wagon swerved, shook his fist at her, and sped around the corner.

Gathering her breath, she was relieved to enter the bustling mercantile shop. The familiar sights and smells of the general store brought memories of faraway places. Her face lit at the sight of a jar of lemon drops on the counter. After buying a quarter pound of the sweets and two dill pickles from the pickle barrel, she browsed through the store until she spotted a shelf of books in a back corner of the store.

She'd read every book she'd packed, as well as Granny's supply and the books of every other member of the Lassiter company. Her favorite had been one of Hawk Lassiter's—a volume of Shakespeare's poetry. When she'd ended their courtship, she'd reluctantly returned the treasured book. And now she'd found one like it.

She picked up the gray leather-bound book and reverently stroked the gold-embossed lettering on the cover. She opened to the index and searched for her favorite sonnet.

Her lips barely moved as she read the familiar words of love. "Let me not to the marriage of true minds admit impediments."

The memory of a night she'd recited the sonnet to Evan eased gently through her mind. Being avid readers, they'd been sitting beside the dying coals of the evening's fire, discussing their favorite authors. While he appreciated American writers such as James Fenimore Cooper and Edgar Allan Poe, she admired English authors such as Jane Austen, William Shakespeare, and the Scotsman poet, Robert Burns.

"Meringue. Purely meringue." Evan called her beloved Jane Austen's *Pride and Prejudice* into the discussion. "Tell me, which was it, pride or prejudice?"

"Both," she explained, "that was the hero and the heroine's problem. They had too much of both."

He'd shaken his head and grimaced. "Very unrealistic. Two mature adults would discuss their feelings honestly, I would think, not bumble about in suppositions and innuendos."

She'd argued with him to no avail. And now, older and somewhat wiser, she had to admit to a naïveté both in herself and in Jane Austen's writing. For hadn't she and Evan behaved in much the same way?

Their discussion had become heated when Evan teased her about Robert Burns's penchant for writing about mice and lice. That's when she switched to the familiar Shakespearean sonnet after which Evan had to admit it was indeed beautiful. Memories she would pack away like outgrown clothing and old dreams.

Gently, she closed the book, sniffed the fine leather binding, and returned the volume to the shelf. Someday she hoped she would again be able to enjoy the sonnets without thinking of Evan Chambers.

CHAPTER TWENTY

WHAT'S IN A NAME?

O N THE RETURN TRIP TO CAMP, GRANNY confessed that she was serious about staying in the small town on the edge of the wilderness. "The Dalles is a friendly, charming town, and quite cosmopolitan, you know."

The idea that Granny would suddenly be out of her life frightened Abigail. She'd come to lean on the older woman's wisdom and her presence. "What would you do here?" Abigail asked.

"I talked with the local apothecary. He's eager to retire. You know my interest in herbs and healing. Well, here's my chance."

Abigail tried to hide her emotions. "I hope you'll pray about this before deciding."

"I've been praying for months to know where God wants me to be, and when I first saw the town, I knew."

Abigail swallowed hard, biting back tears.

Amy wasn't so subtle. "But, Granny, what will we do without you? We love you."

The older woman patted the girl on the head. "Don't you worry, darling. God has a perfect plan for you too." Lifting her eyes to meet Abigail's, the woman added, "And for you, too, dear one."

Abigail knew the woman was right, but she didn't like the thought that perhaps Granny would no longer be an active part of that plan.

When the three ladies arrived back at the Chamberses' camp with their arms filled with packages of all sizes, the aroma of frying fish accosted their senses. Three homemade poles were propped against the wagon. Nearby Evan was demonstrating to Chip and Tyler how to tie a fishing lure. In the frying pan on the fire grate, two large fish sizzled, filling the air with the delicious aroma of hot grease and cooking flesh. The promised pot of lentil stew rested on three large rocks to one side of the fire.

"Mmm," Amy sniffed the air appreciatively. "That smells yummy."

Evan looked up and smiled. "Hoped you gals would wander home soon."

Tyler hopped to his feet and ran to Abigail. "I caught a fish, a big fish." He exaggerated the size with his hands.

Abigail laughed. "Really?"

The boy's excitement grew with the tale. "And Chip caught the other. The fish Daddy caught was too small to keep. He had to throw it back."

"That's too bad." Abigail cast a look of mock sympathy at Evan.

The man arched one eyebrow. "And you could do better?"

"I didn't say that." She dropped her packages near the food cabinet. "Though I was known to be quite the fisherman in my youth."

"You, a fisherman? Who baited your hook?" Evan threw back his head and laughed at his own humor.

"I'll have you know I baited my own hook. My father would take me fishing early Monday mornings until my mother decided digging for worms was too earthy for her younger daughter. The dirt did terrible things to one's cuticles." Dramatically, she inspected her nails as if they'd been manicured in a ladies' salon.

"Forgive me, fair lady." Evan gave her a deep bow. "Obviously you are a woman of many talents."

Abigail laughed and sniffed the air. "And you, kind sir, are as well. When do we eat?"

Evan gave her a mock look of disgust and turned to Chip. "See, son, they only appreciate us for our cooking skills!"

Abigail laughed and proceeded to store the foodstuffs she'd purchased in the large wooden chest they used as a pantry. *Tonight,* she thought, *would be a good time to bring out Mama's linen tablecloth and napkins.*

Being a carpenter of sorts, Evan had built a fold-up table and fold-up campstools before leaving Independence. They'd enjoyed the comfort of dining at a table while most of their fellow travelers made do with wooden boxes as tables and large rocks as places to sit while eating.

"All right. I want all of you to shoo out of here for five minutes. I have a surprise," Abigail announced.

"But my fish will burn," Evan protested as he slowly rose to his feet.

"I'll take care of your fish. I promise. Obey!" She pushed him gently by his shoulders.

Tyler and Amy laughed at the idea of someone ordering their father to obey.

"Go behind the wagon and no peeking! If I catch you peeking, there'll be no dessert for you. That includes you, too, Granny." Abigail waited until they were out of sight and flew into action.

After spreading the white Irish linen cloth on the well-oiled tabletop, she set the table with her mother's dinnerware that she'd brought from England. She ran her fingers lovingly over the delicate blue of the English Abbey pattern and recalled family meals in the rural parsonage. As a last touch, she unpacked a pair of crystal candleholders she'd stored in the stocking drawer of her clothing trunk. Abigail lit two candles and placed them in the middle of the table.

Finding a pewter platter in the dish supply, she placed the fish on the platter, added a pinch of paprika for color, and served up steaming bowls of hot lentil stew.

People from neighboring wagons walked by, staring at the finery, but she ignored them. She placed Granny's bread and the freshly churned butter on plates and set them on the table.

She frowned. She needed a centerpiece—flowers. Out of the corner of her eye she spotted daisies growing close by in a field. *Perfect!* she thought, snatching the flowers up by the handful and placing them in a blue enameled pitcher.

When she was certain the table was set to perfection, she called the family to dinner. The looks on their faces and the *oohs* and *aahs* they uttered when they saw the elegantly appointed table were all the thanks Abigail needed for her efforts.

With the flair of a New York dandy, Evan extended his elbow toward Abigail. "Madam, may I escort you to the dinner table?"

The meal proved as delicious as the aromas predicted and the setting indicated. The fish was cooked to perfection—a rare admission from the culinary expert. Abigail had to admit that Evan had used a delicate hand with his herbs and spices—a dash of black pepper, dried onion, rosemary, and salt.

In record time they finished off the fish and lentil stew, as well as a loaf of cranberry bread Granny had bought in town. The freshly churned butter Abigail purchased made her taste buds sing. The butter was so creamy the children didn't ask for a layer of jam. Abigail couldn't help but notice that Chip didn't beg to be excused earlier than the rest of the family.

After savoring the last mouthful of fish on his plate, Evan sat back and closed his eyes. "*Mmm,* these are the good times."

Granny nodded in agreement.

Evan shot a quirky grin at Abigail. "You and I make a formidable team, Miss Abigail."

She nodded gracefully to the man seated at the opposite end of the table, trying not to read more into his remark than he intended. "And now, for dessert. Amy would you clear the table while I dish out the dessert? Be careful with the china. It's very special."

The children's eyes lit with excitement. It had been a long time since they'd enjoyed a real dessert. Amy immediately leaped to her feet and gathered the soiled dinner plates while Abigail walked to the pantry.

Abigail removed the creamy frosted cake from the bakery box and placed it on one of her treasured plates. Putting an ivory-handled cake server on the edge of the plate and carrying seven dessert plates in her other hand, she returned to the table and placed the dessert before Evan.

"*Mmm,* this looks good. What kind of cake is it?"

"Carrot cake." She hid her smile when the children groaned and Evan looked at her in surprise.

Recovering, he mumbled, "I like carrots, but—"

Granny grimaced. "Cake made from carrots?"

"That's right." She smiled broadly as she sliced the loaf-shaped dessert. "It's a local specialty, though I had it once in a tea room in Boston. Try it. It's good."

Tyler shook his head and curled his lip. "I don't think so."

Abigail shrugged and placed the first slice on a plate and handed it to Granny. Granny, in an effort to behave graciously, accepted the plate and set it on the table in front of her. Evan did the same.

When Amy took her place at the table and Abigail sat at the end of the table, Abigail cut off a piece of cake with her fork and placed the tasty morsel in her mouth. She closed her eyes with pleasure. The creamy frosting melted in her mouth. The dessert was as good as she'd remembered. When she opened her eyes, she was surprised to see everyone watching her intently, their empty forks suspended in their hands. "Try it," she urged. "It really is good, you know."

Evan was the first to take a bite. Granny and the children watched to see any adverse expression that might come on his face. He chewed the morsel of food without response and then suddenly grabbed his throat, rolled his eyes back in his head, gave a wrenching groan, and dropped his head on the edge of the table, face forward.

The children gasped in horror. Chip looked at Granny. "Do something!"

Before the older woman could respond, Evan sat up, pointed at the children and laughed. "Gotcha!" he said. Eyeing the horrified expression on Abigail's face, he laughed. "Got you, too, didn't I?"

"You-you-you-you—"

"You loved it, didn't you? Admit it. And I love this cake." He eyed Tyler's slice of cake greedily. "And if you don't eat your piece, I'll make the sacrifice and eat it for you."

"Oh, no, you won't. You can't fool me." The little boy stuffed a forkful of cake in his mouth. His eyes widened in surprise. Immediately, he stuffed his mouth full of a second and a third bite.

Evan tapped the child's arm gently. "Manners, son, manners."

"Manners?" Abigail raised her eyebrows toward Evan.

He bowed his head respectfully. "I know. And I'm sorry, but I gotcha, didn't I?"

She had to admit he'd fooled her completely. By this time Granny and the other two children were wolfing down their servings of carrot cake and looking around for more. As Abigail gazed at the faces around the table and listened to their exchanges, her heart ached. She knew their days together were limited. They'd been through so much as a group, and it was soon to end.

After her last bite of cake, Granny stood and announced that she and the children would fetch the water for washing the dishes. "Come on, kids, let's fill the buckets."

Chip started to protest, but one look from Granny and he changed his mind. Amy and Tyler eagerly ran to the wagon, grabbed two empty buckets and followed Granny from the clearing.

Evan gazed down the length of the table at Abigail, who'd begun stacking the soiled dessert plates. "It looks like it's just you and me." He stood and gathered the soiled dinner napkins. His fingers brushed across her hand.

Abigail lowered her eyes, ordering herself not to blush. While he acted as if the contact were nothing to him, her heart did a somersault.

In a low voice, he said, "You and I need to talk. We've some important decisions to make about our next move, but we need to include Granny as well." He circled the table collecting the dessert forks.

Abigail saddened. "Perhaps . . . perhaps not."

"What do you mean?"

"Granny's talking about settling in The Dalles."

"The Dalles? But it was her dream to live in the Willamette Valley," he protested, taking the stack of dessert plates from her hands.

"Your dream and my dream." Abigail's voice quivered as she gathered the soiled tablecloth into a bundle and headed toward the wagon. "But not necessarily hers, I guess."

"Wow!" Evan fell into step beside her. "That changes everything, doesn't it?"

She gave him a sideways glance, uncertain of his meaning.

The frown on his brow deepened. "Abby, we can hardly travel together unchaperoned."

Abby? She looked at him with wonder. *He called me Abby.* No one ever called her Abby except her father.

"Don't you agree?"

"Huh? Sorry, I guess I . . . what did you call me?"

"Abigail." His curious gaze told her he'd not been aware he'd used the nickname.

"No, you didn't."

"What are you talking about?"

She set the dishes on the wooden shelf where she washed the daily dishes and turned to face him. "You called me 'Abby.' "

Color rose up his neck and into his face. "Isn't that your name?"

Her eyes grew soft and wistful. She averted her gaze for a moment. "No one has ever called me Abby, except my father. Abby was his pet name for me."

"Oh, I'm sorry—"

She lifted her gaze to meet his. "No, it's all right. I like it."

"You do?" His gray-blue eyes darkened to a mysterious indigo. A strange smile formed on his lips. "I've been thinking of you as Abby for months now."

"You've been thinking of me?"

The tenderness in his eyes took her breath away. "More than I ever imagined possible."

She gulped back the tears blurring her vision. "I don't know what to say."

Like the brush of a butterfly wing, he caressed the side of her face. "Say you've been thinking about me as well."

She lifted her eyes to meet his. "I have, Evan, I truly have."

He ran the backs of his fingers along the contour of her face until he reached her chin where he drew lazy circles as he spoke. "I've missed you so much these last few weeks when the driving was so hard, not being able to talk with you, laugh with you, or just be with you."

Her throat constricted. She was totally unaware of anyone else's presence. "Me too."

She held her breath as he dipped his head forward, slowly closing the gap between their lips. She closed her eyes in anticipation.

"Daddy! Look what I found." At the sound of Tyler's voice, she and Evan sprang apart. The child came running around the end of the wagon with a small brown lizard cupped in his hands. "Can I keep him, Daddy? Can I?"

Evan exchanged a frustrated look with Abigail and turned to admire his son's latest find.

The boy held out his hands toward his father. "His name is Skitters, Daddy, because he skitters across rocks. Isn't that a good name?"

Evan knelt on one knee before Tyler. "It certainly is, son. But how are you going to keep Skitters from skittering away?"

The child thought for a moment, and then his eyes brightened. "I can make a box for him, one with holes in the sides so he can breathe."

"That's a good idea, but wouldn't Skitters miss his family if you took him away from his home?"

The boy's eyes grew sad as he studied the creature for several seconds. "You mean like Mommy missed Grandma and Grandpa?"

Abigail walked to the other side of the wagon. The boy's question probed an area of her heart she didn't want to disturb. Grabbing an empty bucket, she headed toward the well. On the way, she passed Granny and the two other children.

"Hey, where ya going?" Granny asked. "We have more than enough water to do the dishes."

Abigail waved a distracted hand toward the woman.

Granny grabbed her arm. "Are you all right?"

The young woman shook her head. "I can't talk right now."

"What happened?" Amy asked. Again Abigail shook her head, sniffed, and walked away. As she did, she scolded herself. *Abigail, my girl, you can't always run away from your problems. Sooner or later, you will have to face them.*

The trail led her to a quiet place along the banks of the mighty Columbia River. The cooler evenings along the river were a relief from the heat she'd endured along the trail. Abigail found a large rock beside the fast-flowing river, sat down, and trailed her fingers in the water.

She stared across the water to a small island of trees and scrub brush. Though the current was swift, she could tell by the waterline that the river was at a low point. When the rains came, the river would become even more treacherous.

The tiny island looked so enticing, a sanctuary from the pain in her heart. Suddenly, she had the urge to go wading. She abandoned her bonnet, removed her boots and stockings, and dipped her toes in the water. She inched her way into the deeper water. Before long she'd hiked her skirts to her knees and was wading knee-deep. The refreshing water loosened her emotions. She threw back her head and laughed aloud.

Slowly she inched out into the current, lifting her skirts higher and higher. *Tomorrow afternoon,* she vowed, *Granny and I are going to hunt for a secluded bathing spot—with no Running Elk around to steal our clothing.*

She paused to appreciate the dramatic colors of the sunset in the west. *You kept Your promise, Lord. You saw me all the way to Oregon. But I never dreamed how much confusion would come with the success.*

"You're not planning to go any farther are you?"

Abigail whirled about to find Evan standing in the water behind her. *"Aaigh!"* She screamed, throwing her hands wildly in the air, releasing her skirts into the river. Evan lifted his arms to defend himself.

She pawed at the wet garments, trying to gather them together in her arms. "What are you doing here? You should be ashamed, sneaking up on a body like that."

He stepped away from her, in an effort to regain his footing. "I didn't sneak up on you. I called to you from the shore, and I guess you didn't hear me."

"You're right. I didn't hear you."

"Obviously not."

"You think this is funny?" She held yards of wet, soggy fabric in her hands.

Evan could only grin.

"How about this?" Using one hand to secure the bundle of soggy garments, she used the other to send a splash of water into Evan's startled face, which was all he needed.

"Oh, so you want to play?"

Realizing what he was about to do, she turned to escape, but it was too late. The weight of her waterlogged clothing inhibited movement. Before she could run more than a few feet, he grabbed her by the waist and lifted her kicking and screaming into the air before plunging her beneath the surface of the water.

If he thought a dousing would tame her, he'd underestimated Abigail's spirit. Instead of surfacing immediately, she turned and yanked his legs out from under him. While he struggled to regain his footing, she raced toward shore. He caught up with her in ankle-deep water. Catching her by the waist, he whirled her around and kissed her with an urgency that stole her breath and weakened her knees.

"What a lion of a woman I've fallen in love with," he whispered in her ear. He drew her tightly against his pounding chest and covered her neck with kisses.

If she'd felt weakened by his touch in the past, she was totally bereft in the strength of his arms. He pressed his lips against hers a second time, and a third, and a fourth. With great reluctance, he groaned, "Please don't ever run away from me again."

Confused, breathless, and bewildered by the delicious waves of emotion erupting inside of her, Abigail abandoned herself to his kisses.

A rustling on the shore broke through their passionate embrace. Thinking they had an audience, the couple broke apart to see a doe and young fawn delicately make their way to the river's edge for a drink of water.

Evan let out a heavy sigh and drew Abigail against him until her head rested on his shoulder. "*Oooh,* you are one remarkable lady. Did you hear me tell you that I love you?"

"Uh-huh." Abigail timidly kissed his neck. "Are you sure?"

He groaned with pleasure. "More sure than I've ever been in my life."

"But your wife—"

"My deceased wife," he corrected. "Sara was a good wife and I did love her, but I love you in a totally different way. I've learned that in the last few months."

Abigail closed her eyes and listened to the rhythm of his heartbeat as he spoke.

"God gave me time to make peace with Sara and with Him, in fact. So many nights I wandered out on the prairie and later in the mountains, seeking answers from the God I knew you loved. I knew I had to find Him before I could come to you."

"I didn't know . . ."

"I know. That's how I wanted it. I knew how important your God is to you. I knew that anything less on my part would damage our love for each other. And in the process, I found Him to be my God too. Does all this make sense?"

She nodded, her head still resting on his chest. He tipped her chin up to meet his gaze. "My only worry was not knowing if you loved me as much as I loved you. I found a Bible in Sara's trunk and began reading it on the trail. There are some incredible things in the book of Psalms."

"Yes, there are," Abigail admitted.

"And the Song of Solomon! What a beautiful love story."

Recalling the first few verses of the book, Abigail blushed.

"It's an allegory, isn't it?" he asked.

"Uh, my dad used to think it was a picture of how God wants us to love Him, first as our King, then as a Friend, and most of all, as a Lover." Her breath grew shallow as her heartbeat accelerated.

Evan cleared his throat and changed the subject. "Speaking of lovers, I have to ask this question, Abigail. I want to be fair to you. While you were worried that I might not have emotionally laid my wife to rest, have I given you enough time to recover from your romance with Hawk Lassiter?"

She stared at him incredulously. "Hawk Lassiter? Oh, Evan, you don't know me very well, do you? I never loved Hawk. I was flattered by his attention. He was my first suitor. But you—" She stood on her toes to kiss his lips. Except for her father, she'd never before kissed a man. Standing ankle-deep in the Columbia River, she kissed him a second time.

As she leaned back to gaze into his eyes, he asked, "Dare I hope that you love me as much as I love you?"

"Hope? Would I be standing in the middle of an ice-cold river in Oregon, kissing you if I didn't love you?" A gentle laughter echoed from her heart. "I've loved you since the night you kissed the tip of my nose in the moonlight. Remember?"

"Remember? Of course I remember. How could I ever forget?"

Abigail suddenly scowled. "The children, what will they think about all this?"

"They've been after me for weeks to tell you I love you. Even Chip. I had to threaten Amy to keep her quiet on the subject."

As the sun disappeared beyond the horizon, the river canyon darkened. A breeze came up on the river. Abigail trembled.

"Are you cold? I'd better get you home," he whispered.

Home—that sounded so nice to the young woman. Somehow she knew home would be wherever Evan was. Arm in arm, the couple reluctantly stumbled out of the river, their clothing saturated with water and their hearts saturated with love.

A full moon rose in the east as they sat beside each other to dry their feet as best they could and put on their boots. Turning her back, she wrung as much water as possible out of her skirts, valiantly trying to smooth them around her legs and ankles.

When she stood, she found Even gazing at her. "Dear God! You are so beautiful in the moonlight. Thank You. Thank You, dear Father, for bringing her to me."

Abigail smiled shyly, tipping her head to one side. Her heart threatened to burst with happiness. She remembered the promise in Psalms where God delights in giving His children the desires of their hearts.

He leaned toward her as if to kiss her and then suddenly straightened. "If you keep looking at me like that, I'll have to kiss you."

Her smile broadened; her lips parted.

"No, please. I've got to get you back to camp before I compromise your reputation, if it isn't already." He cast a disparaging look at their wet garments and held out his hand. "May I have the honor, Miss Sherwood?"

Giving him her best curtsy, Abigail placed her hand in his, picked up the bucket that held her stockings, and allowed him to escort her back to the wagon.

No one said a word to them about their wet clothing; no one asked why they were gone so long. No one needed to. As Granny said later, "We could see the change in both of you, in your eyes. You weren't fooling anyone."

CHAPTER TWENTY-ONE

ON GOSSAMER WINGS

BIGAIL AWOKE THE NEXT MORNING AS RESTED as if she'd slept on a cloud. She stretched and yawned. Her eyes fluttered open; a smile filled her face. She could have been sleeping on sheets of satin and a mattress of down, instead of muslin and wheat seeds for the way she felt.

Had she dreamed Evan's declaration of love or had he told her? She sat up and spied her wrinkled dress and slip crumpled on the floor at the end of her bed. Her stockings lay in the bottom of the empty water bucket at the end of her bedding. It was true. She hugged herself. It hadn't been a dream. Evan had told her he loved her.

Abigail hadn't heard Granny enter the wagon to sleep or leave the following morning. And by the temperatures building under the canvas roof, Abigail suspected the sun was already high in the eastern sky.

Reluctantly, Abigail slipped out of bed, opened her trunk, and dressed in a lightweight chemise and her lightest weight cotton dress. That the delicate lavender frock with the white eyelet ruffle around the hem of the skirt made her eyes look dark and mysterious, and her complexion a rosy pink, had nothing to do with her choice.

Idly she fingered the tiny embroidered purple-and-white violets edging the oval neckline and thought of Evan. Eager to see her beloved again, she brushed the snarls from her hair, gathered her front locks at the nape of her neck, and secured them with a lavender grosgrain ribbon. As a final touch, she loosed several tendrils around the sides of her face, curling them with her fingers.

One look in Granny's mirror brought a smile to her lips. *I'm almost pretty,* she thought, feeling decidedly naughty for harboring such a vain thought.

When she left the wagon, she found the campground abandoned. This wasn't how she'd planned to make her grand appearance. Near the Webster wagon, she spotted fourteen-year-old Jordan, one of the Webster boys, carrying a bucket of water from the river. She called to him and asked where everyone was.

He pointed toward town. "They're having a meeting with the river people."

"The river people?"

"Yeah, the guys who run the rafts through the gorge to Portland."

She'd heard about the treacherous ending to the two-thousand-mile trail across the continent—running the rapids of the Columbia Gorge. A pioneer could either run the rapids on rafts through the dangerous Columbia Gorge or take the Barlow Trail over the Cascades into Oregon City. This trail was so steep that ropes had to be tied to the wagons and wrapped around tree trunks in order to lower the vehicle down the side of the mountain.

She suspected this was what Evan wanted to talk about the previous night, which option to choose. Abigail smiled and blushed at the memory of the kisses he rained on her neck and face.

If Evan was at the meeting in town, that was where she wanted to be as well. Returning to Granny's wagon, she grabbed her white eyelet sunbonnet and tied the ribbons about her neck, leaving the hat to drape down her back. She slipped her fingers into a pair of white crocheted gloves her mother had made for her several years ago.

As Abigail was about to leave the wagon, the image of the white lawn dress popped into her mind. She had the extra money Mrs. Darlington had so generously given her. Clarissa would approve of her spending a little on herself. She slipped a twenty dollar gold piece into her left glove and another into her right.

Abigail's skirts whipped about her ankles as she set off for town, humming a tune she recalled from her childhood. She strolled past wooded evergreens growing on each side of the rutted road, her arms swinging at her sides, and her voice singing at full volume. "I'll give to you a paper of pins and that's the way our love begins, if you will . . ."

Upon reaching town, she met Granny and Amy exiting the town bakery, their arms filled with packages. "I had to have more of that carrot cake," Granny explained. "Who would think anyone could improve upon the taste of the Creator's carrots?"

"Granny! Don't be sacrilegious." Abigail laughed in spite of herself.

"Sacrilegious? The good Lord did make carrots, did He not?" Granny acted indignant at Abigail's suggestion.

"Yes, but—"

The older woman's eyes twinkled with delight. "But what? A little sugar, a cup of cream, and a few pecans and carrots become almost palatable."

"Carrots are good for you," Amy defended. "They make your eyes strong. That's what Mama used to say."

"And she was right!" Granny shrugged. "How many rabbits have you seen wearing spectacles?"

"Granny!" Amy clicked her tongue. "Rabbits don't wear eyeglasses."

"Exactly my point!" The old woman primly wagged her head from side to side in victory and started across the street toward the mercantile. "Come child, you and I have things to do."

Amy ran to catch up with her.

"See you later, Abigail dear," Granny called.

Abigail stood alone on the boardwalk, watching the two of them walk away. She was miffed that they didn't invite her to come along. "Amy, have you by any chance seen your father this morning?" she called.

The child giggled. "Not since breakfast."

What was that all about? Abigail watched until they disappeared inside the mercantile. Shrugging her shoulders, she headed up the block toward the dress shop and the dreamy white gown in the window. Except the dress wasn't in the window. It was gone! Instead a mint-green taffeta frock hung on the wooden dress form.

The bell over the door clanged as Abigail hurried into the shop. The chances of the garment being sold overnight were slim. Most likely the seamstress had merely changed her window display.

As the door slammed behind Abigail, the seamstress stepped out from behind the curtain. "Hello again."

"Hello." Abigail gestured toward the window. "The white dress?"

"Sold it this morning."

"No!" Abigail wailed. Tears sprang into her eyes.

"I'm afraid so. I'm sorry." The seamstress looked genuinely sad but then brightened as if to console the disappointed young woman. "I understand that some lucky bride will wear it on her wedding day."

Abigail's high spirits plummeted to the toes of her boots, along with her heart.

Attempting to ease her customer's disappointment, the clerk added, "I have a little blue organdy number. It may be too short for you, but I could add a couple of ruffles to the hem, a gusset or two in the bodice, and a—"

Abigail shook her head. "No. No thank you. I had my heart set on the white one." She turned to leave.

"Wait! I have an extra bolt of the white lawn. I could make another dress by the end of next week, without the embroidered daisies, of course."

Abigail shook her head again and left the shop. *Don't be silly. There will be other dresses,* she told herself. Hoping to spot Granny and Amy, or anyone she might know, she paused to look up and down the busy street. Shoppers were rushing by in carriages, on foot, and on horseback, intent on their missions. There were no familiar faces.

After a stop in the bakery for a small bag of gingersnaps, Abigail ambled along the boardwalk nibbling on her cookies. She had nothing to do and nowhere to go. She ignored the two grizzled old men who stopped playing checkers on a bench outside Ed's Watering Hole to watch her stroll by. Their unwelcomed attention caused her to increase her pace.

The warm afternoon breeze stirred the long tresses cascading down her back, reminding her of her folly of not pinning up her hair into a wad like a proper lady. At her age!

Disgusted with herself, Abigail whirled about and set out toward camp. She would correct her error in judgment before anyone else, especially Evan, saw her. *Who do you think you are,* she scolded, her face hardening into a scowl, *an empty-headed lass of fourteen?*

At the end of the block, Abigail stepped off the boardwalk into the street as a two-horse brougham whipped around the corner. Two strong hands snatched her from the horses' path. She stumbled against her rescuer, her bag of gingersnaps landing in the dirt.

Shaking from the close encounter, Abigail turned to thank the portly middle-aged man who'd rescued her from injury. Wagging his finger in her face, she noted that the man was better dressed than most of the men she'd seen since leaving the East Coast. He wore a steel-gray morning coat with matching trousers, a gray suede hat with a small red feather tucked under a black grosgrain ribbon, a pearl-gray brocade vest, and a black cravat tie held in place by a silver stud.

"You should watch where you're going, miss. Those horses would have trampled you to death at worse, and at best, maimed you for life!"

Abigail floundered for an excuse. She'd been feeling sorry for herself for losing the dress. "I-I-I'm sorry, sir. I wasn't paying attention."

Being the same height as she, the man glared at her, eye to eye. "That's an understatement."

Her dander rose at the man's sarcastic tone.

"Is there a problem here, sir?" It was Evan.

Tears of relief fought with a relieved smile spreading across her face. Before she could speak, her rescuer asked, "Is this your woman? If so, you'd best take better care of her. She stepped out in front of a racing carriage."

"Of all the—" she sputtered.

Evan ignored her protests. "I have been remiss, sir. Thank you for saving my dear one from tragedy. I promise to take the very best care of her in the future."

"Good!" The man tipped his hat toward Abigail, stepped off the boardwalk, and strutted across the street.

"Who was that man?" Evan asked, taking her hand and placing it in the crook of his arm.

"What are you doing?"

"Taking better care of you like I promised." Evan chuckled at her discomfort. "Who was that man?"

"I really don't know. But he acts like he owns the place."

"*Tsk! Tsk!* Such ingratitude for saving your life." Evan started across the street.

Abigail gave a huff and allowed him to direct her down the street. They'd walked a block when Abigail asked, "Where are we going?"

"Up the street a ways. I have a surprise for you." When they arrived at the west end of town, he stopped and put his hands over her eyes.

"What are you doing?"

"*Ssh!* Remember the little New England churches with the graceful spires that you love so much?" He inched her forward and turned her to her left. "Look."

When he removed his hands from her eyes, she gasped with delight. "It's beautiful."

At the end of the cross street was a tiny, white clapboard church, complete with forest green shutters and a slender spire. "Oh, Evan." Her hands flew to her lips in an attitude of prayer. "It's beautiful."

Tears brimmed in her eyes as she gazed on the building surrounded on three sides by dark green forest. "I didn't realize how much I missed the East."

"Come on, let's go inside."

"Can we?" She glanced at him over her shoulder.

"Sure, why not?" He grabbed her hand and ran toward the building.

Catching his spirit, she laughed and sprinted ahead of him, up the steps of the chapel, with him a footstep behind. "Beat you!"

When she reached for the iron door handle, he placed his hand over hers. He opened the door and urged her to enter the tiny foyer.

There was a closed door off each side of the narthex. Straight ahead, through the set of swinging doors, Abigail guessed, was the sanctuary. Evan opened one of the sanctuary doors to allow her to enter before him.

Her light, playful mood disappeared as she stepped inside the sacred place. She gazed at the sanctuary's whitewashed walls, the rough-hewn benches, and the wide-planked floor. Bare, paned windows lined the walls, four on each side of the chapel.

A pump organ, an upright piano with a revolving stool, a hand-carved lectern, and four straight-backed chairs were the only furniture on the platform. No stained glass, no marble carving, no fine linen or velvet draperies. This was a place where humble people came to worship God.

"Isn't it beautiful?" she whispered, sensing Evan standing directly behind her.

"Yes, you are," he whispered in her ear. His breath tickled her neck.

"Evan, I'm talking about the chapel. Isn't it beautiful?"

"And I'm talking about you." Gently, he turned her around to face him. When she protested, he touched her lips with his index finger and tugged on the ribbons to her bonnet. The bonnet fell to the floor. Her breath caught as he twirled a tendril around his pinkie finger.

"Evan." Her voice was raspy with emotion. "This isn't the appropriate time or the place—"

" 'Let me not to the marriage of true minds admit impediments,' " he began. " 'Love is not love which alters when it alteration finds, or bends with the—' I forget the rest." He retrieved a leather-bound book of Shakespearean sonnets from his jacket pocket and placed it gently in her hands. She stared at the treasured volume in awe. Slowly, she opened the book to the title page and read the inscription.

"To Abby, my beloved, on the day of our engagement. From the man who loves her more than life itself, Evan." She gazed at him through a film of tears.

" 'Shall I compare thee to a summer's day? Thou art more lovely and more temperate: rough winter winds do . . .' " The gray-blue in his eyes deepened as he quoted the famous poem of love. "Can you think of a more appropriate time or place for me to ask you to become my bride?"

Her breath stopped. The inscription written in the front cover blurred before her eyes. She opened her lips to speak, but no words came.

"Well?" His question and his precious love gift had caught her by surprise.

"I-I don't know what to say."

"Is that a polite way of saying No? Did I . . . presume . . . too much from last night at the river?" His question came out painfully slow.

"No!" she wailed, throwing herself into his arms. "Evan, I do love you so much, but I'm scared. I never imagined myself as the marrying kind."

His eyelids closed partway, concealing his disappointment. Slowly, he extricated himself from her grasp. "Take all the time you need." She held her breath as she watched him retreat down the aisle.

As his left hand pushed against the swinging door, Abigail whispered, "Wait! I will marry you."

Evan froze.

Her voice was stronger the second time. "I've thought about it, and I will marry you."

He glanced over his shoulder. "Did I hear you right?"

She took a deep breath and whispered, "Yes."

He cocked his head to one side, intently studying her face. "Are you sure?"

She nibbled on her lower lip and nodded. "Uh-huh."

Static electricity more powerful than the lightning of a prairie thunderstorm charged the atmosphere between them.

She'd had months to determine her love for him. She'd seen him at the best of times and at the worst of times. She knew more about this man and his dreams than anyone else on earth, and she suspected that might include his deceased wife.

During the lull in their relationship, she'd waited on the Lord. She'd avoided leaning on her own understanding. Abigail's heart and her head were in complete agreement. She loved this tender, compassionate man. The pain in his eyes tore at her heart.

A cry of anguish burst from Abigail. "Yes, Evan. I will marry you anytime, anywhere."

She ran into his surprised arms, burying her face in his neck. His arms tightened around her until she could hardly breathe. "Darling," he breathed into her ear. "I would marry you this instant except we're no longer alone."

"What?" She opened her eyes in time to see the doors to the sanctuary swing open and the three Chambers children burst in, with Granny in tow. "What are you doing here?"

"Waiting for you to accept his proposal. What took you so long, woman? The children and I've known your answer for weeks." Granny strode past the couple to the front of the church. "I think this will do just fine."

"What will do just fine?" Abigail stared from the children to Granny and back again.

"For a wedding. I think we can fit most of your friends from the wagon train in here."

Before Abigail could react, Amy tapped her gently on the shoulder. "May I be your flower girl? Miss Simons, that's the lady at the dress shop, said she'd work all night if she had to, to finish my new dress in time."

"Whoa. Wait a minute." Shooting a questioning gaze at Chip, Abigail asked, "And you, Chip, our marriage is all right with you?"

"Sure. I've gotten used to you. If any woman is going to come into our lives and mess things up, I'd want her to be my friend." Chip cast her a wry smile, which she returned.

Granny bustled past them. "I almost forgot." She disappeared into a room off the side of the vestibule. When she returned, Abigail blinked in surprise, for the older woman held in her arms the diaphanous white gown from the dress shop. "This is for you. I bought it this morning after Evan told me he was going to ask you to marry him today."

Through a blur of tears, Abigail gazed at Granny, the children, and then Evan. She hadn't felt so surrounded by love since she was a small child. "I . . . I don't know what to say. I love you all so much."

* * * * *

Two days later, an hour before sunset, Granny lowered the delicate gossamer dress over Abigail's shiny tresses. "Granny, it's so beautiful," the bride whispered as she gazed at her reflection in the wall mirror at the pastor's home. "Thank you so much."

"And you are more lovely in it than I imagined you would be," the older woman said as she fastened the tiny pearl buttons down the back of the gown.

When the wife of the only preacher in town heard of the pending nuptials, she insisted the bridal party dress for the wedding in the parsonage next to the white church. "It isn't often we get a full-blown wedding in these parts," the cheery little woman admitted.

Chip and Tyler contributed to the wedding by picking enough daisies from the field across from the chapel to form a wreath for Abigail's hair and a bouquet for her to carry.

At Granny's request, the local baker had stayed up all night baking carrot cake for the reception. "I can't get enough of that stuff," Granny admitted. "It's the cream cheese frosting."

As the sun sank behind the outcropping of hills to the west, Abigail watched the candles inside the sanctuary blink as she waited on the parsonage porch.

Strains of Beethoven's "Ode to Joy" wheezed from the pump organ inside the crowded sanctuary. There was standing room only inside the chapel. Every member of the Lassiter company had come to see the story lady's wedding.

Hawk Lassiter insisted on giving the bride away. He took her hand as she descended the parsonage steps. At the base of the steps, he transferred her gloved hand to the crook of his arm. "You are very beautiful, Abigail," he said. "Maybe I shouldn't have had such a faint heart."

She smiled. "Thank you." She knew he was teasing. From all reports, he and his child bride would be married upon arriving at Fort Vancouver.

They crossed the lawn in silence, each lost in his or her thoughts. At the foot of the chapel steps, their eyes met. Visions of what might have been flitted through Abigail's mind, but were quickly replaced by the strong, smiling face of the man waiting for her inside the chapel.

Taking a deep breath to steady her nerves, she climbed the steps and entered the vestibule. As the sanctuary doors swung open, she saw the silhouette of her husband-to-be, holding out his hand, bidding her to come to him.

The preacher told how Isaac went out to meet Rachel, his beloved. As the preacher spoke, Evan strode toward Abigail, meeting her halfway up the aisle. Eagerly, she slipped her hand from Mr. Lassiter's arm and placed it in Evan's outstretched hand. Together they glided to the front of the sanctuary to recite their wedding vows.

She was reeling from Evan's kiss to seal their marriage vows when she made the connection between Reverend Pierce's steel-gray morning coat and the man she'd encountered on Main Street two days previous. They were one and the same.

A cheer went up from the audience when the preacher declared them to be husband and wife. Chip, his father's best man, whistled through his teeth. Granny, Abigail's matron-of-honor, wept. Amy, the flower girl, and Tyler, the Bible holder, screeched with delight.

Above the excited din of the crowd, the minister shouted, "I have the distinct honor of being the first to introduce you to Mr. and Mrs. Evan Chambers. May God bless this union."

A reception followed on the church lawn with enough apple cider and carrot cake for everyone, courtesy of Granny Parker. Long before the partiers returned to their wagons, Evan and Abigail slipped away to a waiting buggy that took them to a one-room log cabin along the river, compliments of Hawk Lassiter.

"Do you remember when I told that couple we were married?" Evan asked her as the two-passenger buggy bounced over the rutted roadway.

The bride blushed and nodded. "I thought I'd die of embarrassment right there in front of them."

"I shouldn't have done that. I'm sorry for embarrassing you, my love. At the time, I thought it was funny."

Abigail giggled into her nosegay of flowers. "It was quite shocking," she admitted. The sound of her childlike laughter amazed her. She felt heady, like a giddy girl of sixteen.

"Do you forgive me?" he asked.

She placed her gloved hand on his jacketed forearm and cast him a dreamy look. "Of course I forgive you." She giggled again. "You didn't know you were a prophet, did you?"

"Hardly a prophet, more like a tease." He placed a tender kiss on her forehead. "Do you think you can abide my teasing for the next fifty years?"

"Fifty years? Is that all? What happens after that? Do you turn into a sober-faced judge?" She drew her mouth down into a puckered frown.

A smirk spread across his face. "Absolutely."

Abigail pressed her hand against her chest in mock horror. "No! Never that sober!"

Evan laughed as he reined in the horses. As he helped her from the carriage, the evening breeze ruffled her gown. The moon lit the pathway to the cabin door. The light from a lantern shone through the cabin window. Her gown, the forest, the cabin, the water slapping the shores of the river, and the man at her side were all exactly like her dream. This time it wasn't a dream; it was reality.

Like young sweethearts on their first date, they strolled hand in hand to the cabin door where he turned to face her. "I love you, Abby Chambers," he whispered, kissing her eager lips. Gently, his lips brushed against hers as he quoted, " 'Thou hast ravished my heart, my sister, my spouse. . . . How fair is thy love . . . how much better is thy love than wine. . . . Thy lips, O my spouse, drop as the honeycomb.' "

Abigail's heart leaped to her throat at the familiar words coming from her husband's lips. They were as new as their vows to love one another till death did them part, yet as old as the king who first spoke them to his love.

With tenderness, Evan swept his bride into his arms, nudged the cabin door open, and carried her across the threshold.

* * * * *

The next morning, the newlyweds returned to town, loaded their three children and their belongings onto a raft, said Goodbye to Granny and the other friends they'd made, then set off down the Columbia River toward Portland and the glorious Willamette Valley.

As the river raft pilot maneuvered the raft through the treacherous waters of the Columbia Gorge, the wind whipped Abigail's long braid about her shoulders. Water splashed her feet. A terrified Amy clung to her waist.

The raft bounced and shifted with the unpredictable current of the river. Lashed to the same pole in the center of the raft, Chip, Tyler, and Evan clung to one another. On seeing the fear in the two boys' eyes, Abigail threw back her head and laughed with abandon.

"Isn't this marvelous?" she called over the roar of the river.

Pale and decidedly uncomfortable, Evan stared at his new bride as if she'd lost her mind. "Aren't you frightened?" he shouted above the roar of the raging river.

She shook her head enthusiastically. "Not any more." Whatever fears and doubts she might have had regarding her future with the man she loved were gone. God had filled her with divine peace. Whatever troubles she and Evan would face in the future, they would do so together. She leaned back against her husband's chest. She reveled in the warmth and the thunder of his beating heart.

"Why should I be afraid of a few waves?" she cried. "I love it, every minute of it." Kissing his whitened knuckles that grasped the raft's center pole, Abigail refused to look back, turning her face decidedly toward the white water before them and their future lives together on the banks of the majestic Willamette River.

ANNIE'S TRUST

KAY D. RIZZO

Coming to an ABC near you in February 2011

It's an unimaginable dream come true! Annie, Serenity Pownell Cunard's friend and companion since childhood, is getting married! Annie loves Ned with all her heart, but will he allow her the freedom she enjoyed with the Pownell family? Ned has worked so hard to give Annie her own home next to Serenity, but he has questions and fears about their future together as well.

Trouble begins brewing right away as the Cranston gang interrupts Annie and Ned's wedding celebration. Although Annie and Ned argue over Ned's involvement in the Underground Railroad, she agrees to support him however she can. But, as troubles continue, Annie sinks into a deep depression.

Join Annie and Ned, and Serenity and Caleb, as they discover the importance of communication and trust, and learn deeper lessons of faith in God, and in His protection. You won't want to miss this next adventure in The Serenity Inn series.

More books in The Serenity Inn series

Serenity's Desire,
BOOK 1
Paperback, 224 pages
ISBN 13: 978-0-8163-2388-3
ISBN 10: 0-8163-2388-7

Serenity's Quest,
BOOK 2
Paperback, 224 pages
ISBN 13: 978-0-8163-2389-0
ISBN 10: 0-8163-2389-5

Josephine's Fortune,
BOOK 3
Paperback, 224 pages
ISBN 13: 978-0-8163-2421-7
ISBN 10: 0-8163-2421-2

Lilia's Haven,
BOOK 4
Paperback, 224 pages
ISBN 13: 978-0-8163-2423-1
ISBN 10: 0-8163-2423-9

Pacific Press®
Publishing Association

"Where the Word Is Life"

Three ways to order:

1 Local	Adventist Book Center®
2 Call	1-800-765-6955
3 Shop	AdventistBookCenter.com